Across the Way

Amy K. McClung

For information, contact the publisher, Hot Tree Publishing.

www.hottreepublishing.com

Editing: Hot Tree Editing

Cover Designer: Claire Smith

Format Design: RMGraphX

ISBN-10: 1-925448-30-4

ISBN-13: 978-1-925448-30-6

10 9 8 7 6 5 4 3 2 1

DEDICATION

This book is dedicated to the person who inspires every romance I write, my best friend, the love of my life, my husband, Daniel. Without him, I may never have begun this journey into writing.

PROLOGUE

MARIE

"Holy mother shit son of a fucking asshole!" I screamed at Satan's head as it appeared between my legs. No, I didn't suffer from Tourette's syndrome. I suffered from labor pains. Satan was how I referred to my gynecologist as she cheered me on with a smile while I tried to push a watermelon out of my vagina.

When my contractions began five hours ago, my mother drove me to the hospital. As we walked into the emergency room, I was able to take some of the pain away by easing myself into a wheelchair. With my feet placed strategically on the footrests, my mother quickly wheeled me to the registration desk.

"My daughter is in labor. Her contractions are about three minutes apart now. Can you please page her doctor? Dr. Grainger." The girl at the desk immediately picked up her phone and then typed something into the computer to dial the doctor directly. When there was no answer, she paged her overhead.

A few moments later, they wheeled me into the room and lifted me up onto the bed. Instantly, I grabbed my mother's hand and screamed out once more as the contraction hit.

"Where is he?" I asked in a panic.

"He'll be here soon, Marie. I checked on his flight a few minutes ago, and it is still showing on time. He should be landing any minute now."

"I need him here! He's the reason I'm in pain right now. He should experience this!" How was it that men got to do the fun part of making a baby, but didn't have to go through any of the pain and suffering?

My mother chuckled.

"Yes, he should. He will, don't worry. Just breathe."

I wanted to smack this woman for trying to calm me in my time of pain. On the other hand, I wanted to hug her for having gone through this agony with me twenty-eight years ago. Once I finally dilated to ten centimeters, the doctor asked me to push, but I wasn't ready.

"Wait, I can't. Not until he's here!"

"Who are we waiting on?" the doctor asked impatiently.

"The father. He'll be here soon," my mother promised Satan, squeezing my hand as though she thought it would help. Truthfully, I wanted to be knocked out instead of knocked up right now. Couldn't they put me in a nice slumber while the alien creature exploded from my nether regions? I knew it was the miracle of birth and all that hogwash, but I was good with not remembering the moment.

"Well, we can't wait for him. This baby is coming now. So give me a good push."

"Augh," I screamed with each push. More cursing spewed from my lips. I couldn't believe how far I'd come in the last few years. Three years ago, my only goal in life had been to take a trip around the United States. I'd never even had a serious boyfriend. My travel dreams came to life, and along the way, I found my dream of a family. I was married to the love of my life, and we were having our first child. My husband wanted four, but we'd negotiate that once I got over the pain of this one ripping me apart. It was hard to believe all of this began with a bucket list dream.

Three years earlier...

1

MARIE

Jayce popped into the local performance theater in town and requested to speak with the manager. I'd seen him pull this act before, so I held back and let him finish. The clerk asked him to stand to the side while he waited. He tapped his fingers methodically against the counter and the clerk looked nervous at the scene that might ensue. When I appeared, Jayce smiled as I gave him an expression that said he was abusing his power again.

"You can't come in here demanding to see a manager each time you need to talk to me."

"You work too much, Mo. You need to have fun. Your twenty-fifth birthday is next week, and I have a whole day of excitement planned for you. You did request the day off, right?" Placing his elbows on the counter, he rested his hands in his palms and gazed up at me as he batted his eyes. His goofball ways and adorable grin always made me putty in his hands.

"Jay, you know my plans. I need the money. Taking a day off will set me back on my goal, and I'm already behind by four years. Besides, birthdays aren't exciting after the twenty-first." The statement wasn't completely true because Jayce had always made every birthday special for me, even if my age didn't grant me any new abilities.

Jayce feigned offense at my response. "Are you kidding? At twenty-five, you can officially rent a car without the extra documentation and fees." He wiggled his eyebrows, and I laughed at how ridiculous he looked.

"How could I not realize the excitement of rental car freedom," I commented sarcastically.

"One day, Mo. Please, for me." He batted his eyelids while down on one knee ready to beg. In all the years I'd known him, he'd been consistent in making it almost impossible to say no to him.

"I'm sorry, Jayce. I can't." Even though I knew he wouldn't give up, I had to assert myself on this one.

Jayce released a deep sigh of frustration. "How much money do you make in one day between your management job here and bartending at night?"

My eyes rolled upward as I mentally calculated the amount. "Two hundred dollars at least, depending on the tips."

"Sold. I'll pay you two hundred dollars to spend your birthday doing fun stuff. What do you say?"

It was a thrilling offer, the chance of being off for a night when I hadn't had a day off work since graduating two years ago. "It's probably not possible anyway with such short notice, Jayce. They may not be able to find anyone to cover me.

Another sigh of exasperation and Jayce grabbed my hands in his. "You never know unless you ask. Just give it a chance. I can up the amount to three hundred, and then you'll even make a little overtime for the night." He wiggled his eyebrows at me again, and this time it worked like a charm.

"You win. I'll schedule myself off that day."

Jayce let out a loud whoop, and it echoed through the lobby of the theater. Laughing, I quickly responded to his next motion of thrusting his hand in the air for a high five. "Now, I have to get back to work. Go home and stop berating my employees with your inane requests."

Once Jayce left the building, Carina, the clerk, leaned over and said, "He's cute. I didn't even know you had a boyfriend. You've been holding out on me."

"Not a boyfriend. He's my best friend, practically my long lost twin. If you're interested, he's single too. I can hook you up."

Carina's grin widened. "Yes, please."

It wasn't a new concept for me to set Jayce up. He never turned down a beautiful woman, but he hadn't met one he connected with completely. Long-term relationships were not out of the question for him; he just hadn't met the right girl. Relationships were a topic we brought up often. By no means was he lacking in the looks or the brains department. At a little over six foot with thick, wavy black hair, he was the epitome of tall, dark, and handsome. With his crystal blue eyes and sweet southern charm, he could melt a female's heart in seconds. He legitimately was a straight A student and jock. Enrolled in a private university studying to be an architect, he would've graduated by this point if he hadn't spent his first three years pursuing a medical degree only to find out blood made him queasy.

Chattanooga, Tennessee was my hometown, but I might as well have grown up on a farm in the middle of nowhere. Family vacations consisted of trips to Nashville every few months to see my dad who lived there still hoping to get his music career started. He'd practically bankrupted my family in the process, forcing my mother to take on a corporate position in Chattanooga overseeing one of the popular tourist attractions. Jobs in Nashville weren't as easy to come by, and the offer in Chattanooga gave them a chance to do more than get by. Many days I resented him because it felt as if he cared more about being famous than being with his family.

Many girls cherish their fathers and hope to find someone like them one day to marry. Not me. I loved my dad, of course, but I had different desires for my future. Before turning thirty, I had one dream to accomplish, to see all of the United States and Canada. If I couldn't raise enough money, I had to see all fifty states at least. Raising the money for my trip had been tough, but the prospect of leaving Jayce behind was what weighed on my mind the most.

Jayce and I met in high school, in drama club to be exact. We had never spoken until we received the leads in the school play. We began meeting to rehearse lines together and from there became good friends. We were like twins separated at birth with everything we had in common: the same taste in books, movies, and music, as well as the same luck in relationships.

Jayce's parents divorced when he graduated eighth grade, and he moved to Tennessee with his dad to start his freshman year of high school. My parents separated the same year when Dad decided to live in Nashville permanently. They hadn't officially divorced, nor had they been seeing other people, but they felt like a divorced couple most days. Rarely speaking except for holidays and the occasional visits, they swore they still loved each other and wanted to stay true. It wasn't a life I dreamed of for myself. It was probably one of the reasons my relationships had been so screwed-up. I never imagined marriage or children; all I wanted was to experience different parts of this country. Canada made the list in order to say I'd left the country at least once. Traveling overseas alone was too scary of a thought. The biggest deterrence to overseas travel was the cost and how much longer I'd have to work to achieve my goal. Hopefully one day, if I settled down, it could be a trip I took with my future husband.

After high school, I wanted to put college on hold. Working two jobs to save up, it would take several years to go on my trip, but it would be worth it. Money saved by age twenty-one, travel for two years, and then decide on what college I would attend was the ultimate goal. Jayce had fought me on the idea many times, but he always gave in and played the supportive friend in the end. Deep down I knew he worried I was throwing my life away by working so much.

After my twenty-first birthday, it became obvious I wasn't going to reach my goal, so I pushed it back to attend college.

Even during that time, I spent my evenings working and putting away money. Last year, I graduated with a degree in business administration and jumped right back into working extra jobs to achieve my travel dream. In a way, I'd given up the exciting life of a twenty-year-old, the age where you make mistakes and learn the most life lessons for later. Instead, I dove headfirst into the work world. Jayce suggested I alter my dream to the states I wanted to visit most. He wanted me to have a life again and not become a workaholic, but I refused to give up just yet. Now I would start traveling by age twenty-seven and be ready to settle down at age thirty with a career. Every piece of my life had been planned out, and though adjustments had been made, it was important to me not to stray from those plans.

JAYCE

As a rule, Marie and I never kept secrets from each other, but there was one thing Marie didn't know, which was that I put money away for her trip fund. Being the child of divorced parents had some perks. As long as I attended college, they both supported me financially, and I also worked part-time at an auto repair shop. Her travel plans seemed a little crazy to me, but I wanted her to be happy. My concern was she'd work herself to death and never reach her goal. It was one of the reasons I wanted to help her succeed, besides the fact that nothing was more important to me than her happiness most days. She'd been a constant in my life, and I worried a trip around the states would change the norm for us, though.

Marie kept a datebook with everything written down, which made it easier for me to keep tabs on how much she needed. Once my bank account completed the remainder, I planned to tell her about it. It would be a going away present. We'd keep in touch. At least I hoped. Each time I thought about Marie leaving, it made my chest hurt. She was the one I ran to with good news, bad news, pretty much anything and everything.

Marie worked too hard, but I admired her for it. Sacrificing her time, her youth, a chance at love, all so she could fulfill a childhood dream. Some might find it silly, but I found it inspirational. She would put in eight hours at the theater and then work four to five hours tending bar at the most popular hangout in town. Even after all those hours, she'd still have a smile on her face and pep in her step at the end of the day because she knew it was a step closer to her goal. Her work ethic prevented us from spending much time together, which is why I felt obligated to stoop to actions like I'd pulled at the theater. It wasn't the first time I'd done it. Occasionally I'd show up at the bar just to see her too. Some might consider me pushy, but Marie knew I had nothing but love for her.

I pulled up to the auto repair shop in my run-down Jeep Wrangler whose color could be best described as mud, mostly because I drove through a lot of it. At one time, it was a dark shade of green.

The shop boomed with business today. "Jayce, glad you

showed up today. You know if you don't start being on time I'll have to let you go."

Flippantly patting the shoulder of my scolding boss, Zeb, I replied, "Good luck finding someone to work with you more than a week."

Zeb snorted. "I should never have told you about how bad my turnover used to be. Where you been? Off seeing that hot lady again?"

"That hot lady is my best friend, and she is young enough to be your granddaughter, Zeb. Stop being a perv."

Zeb answered with only a gruff laugh typical of someone who'd chain smoked cigarettes for most of their life. He went back to working on the car in front of him, and I grabbed my punch card and clocked in for the day.

January eighteenth was Marie's twenty-fifth birthday, and I had arranged a full day of activities for us. Tradition planned the first part of the day, a breakfast with her parents and maternal grandparents. Her father's parents had passed away before she was born, but she'd always been close to her mother's parents. Being their only grandchild, they kept her spoiled. Marie and her mother, Caroline, both grew up without siblings. It seemed I filled the void of the big brother she always wished she had. Of course, I was only a few months older than she was, but it still counted in her eyes.

Marie's father, Dalton, drove in from Nashville to see

them today. By the look on Marie's face, it was apparent that the best present she'd received was to witness her mother's elated look when she saw her husband. The two embraced and shared a tender kiss before grasping hands and walking inside. Maybe they were happier than she'd thought. Many nights I sat and listened to her doubt their love for one another.

"Hi, Dad," Marie said as she wrapped her arms around his neck and kissed his cheek.

"Hi, baby girl, do you feel twenty-five?"

"Not really."

"Why not?"

"Well, I hoped to be closer to my traveling goal, but so far, I have enough money saved to see barely half the U.S., and that's if I sleep in my car the majority of the trip. Provided my car makes it. I think I might start my career sooner than expected. Maybe I could still do the trip as a retirement thing."

Her father gave her a sad smile as he brushed a strand of hair from her face. "Sweetheart, don't give up on what you want in life. I haven't."

His "chasing your dreams" speech didn't sit well with Marie. She wouldn't want to abandon her loved ones for a dream, which might never come true. Her father had been in Nashville long enough that if he were going to make it, he would have by now. He was getting too old to be the next big thing, in my opinion. I didn't voice that to Marie even though I knew she thought the same thing. If I backed up her fears, then she would lose all hope of having her family together again.

Once her grandparents arrived and after ordering their meals, I stood up.

"I'd like to say a few words about my best friend, Mo. She works too hard. She spends too little, and she has spent most of her young life wanting one thing while she works to obtain it. I couldn't be prouder of her than I am this very minute. To Marie, Happy Birthday, beautiful." Holding my drink high in the air brought an end to my toast. "Now that I've said that, let's open gifts before the food gets here. Oh, mine will be given to you later today, though." The grin on my face grew wide knowing how much Marie hated to wait for presents. Teasing her was one of my favorite things to do because she always made the cutest face. Eyes squinted, nose scrunched up, and her mouth fighting to hold back a grin.

She put her hand beside her lips and mouthed, "I'll get you for that one!" Throwing her a wink, I grinned mischievously. Marie's parents chipped in together to get her the very expensive camera she'd been eyeing for months. Admiring the way her face lit up, something stirred inside me. When she laughed, her green eyes danced, her left cheek dimpled, and sometimes she even gave an adorable snort at the end.

I shook the thoughts from my mind and came back to reality. Her grandparents normally gave her money, and judging by the flat card they handed her, this year was no exception. I had no doubt it would be added to her vacation fund immediately. When she opened the card, though, she choked back tears as she read the following note:

Our dearest Marie,

Your birth brightened our lives more than you can ever know. On this day, twenty-five years ago, we started a fund for you. Originally it was meant to be a college trust for you to attend the best ivy league school possible because we knew you'd become the most intelligent young woman we know today. Through the years, each pay increase allowed us to add even more to the total. On your fourteenth birthday, you informed us of your dream to travel the country, so we began to double the deposit. On the next page, you will see what your balance is today. For your twenty-fifth birthday, we want you to begin fulfilling your dreams by taking the trip you've worked so hard for. We love you, sweetheart.

P.s. Grandpa says to bring him a shot glass depicting your favorite part of each state you visit.

Marie already had tears in her eyes, but the next page had her gasping so hard she choked, which threw her into a coughing fit. Instincts kicked in and I jumped up to help her. Through a whispered, strangled sound, she said, "Look."

As I read over the paper, my eyes bugged out before I exclaimed, "Holy shit!"

After pinching herself several times to wake up from the

obvious dream, she finally ran over to her grandparents. "This is too much… I can't… your retirement."

Her grandmother shushed her. "This is not from our retirement, it's from before. You enjoy this dear. We've watched you work so many long hours that you need this."

"But, with this kind of money we could have stayed together with Dad."

Her father looked up. "We knew about the money, baby girl. Your mother and I wanted you to have it. They offered to help us out, but we turned them down. In a way, we feel like we are helping make this happen for you too."

Marie stuttered the best response she could. "There are… I can't… this is—"

I couldn't watch her fumble anymore. "I believe what she is trying to say is thank you."

JOURNAL ENTRY

My dream of traveling the United States and Canada is finally coming true! The journey to get here was rough, but worth every step. The first thing I bought in preparation for my adventure is this book to keep track of my thoughts. In this journal, I will document what I see, who I meet, and what I learn along the way about different parts of the country and about myself.

My grandparents' generosity overwhelmed me. Gratitude would never be enough to repay them for such a tremendous amount. Even the balance sheet made me nervous with the amount of dollars it reflected. Though my parents knew about the savings account, I still felt guilty knowing it could've helped them be together if my grandparents had given it to them instead. Still, I have to push the guilt away and appreciate the sacrifices my parents and grandparents made for my happiness.

After breakfast, Jayce helped me celebrate my birthday in style. At the end of the night, he surprised me with a request I couldn't deny. I wish he could join me on this journey, but he has dreams of his own to follow. Jayce seems a bit nervous about me leaving. He hasn't told me, but he's been acting a little different. We haven't been apart for more than a few days since we met in high school. He'll be all right. I have faith in him. I was more worried about how I'd survive without him being right down the street from me where I could see him whenever I wanted.

As the time gets closer to leave, I grow more nervous about saying good-bye. What if our friendship isn't the same when I return?

My next entry will be the day I leave.

♡Marie

2

MARIE

After breakfast, Jayce whisked me away for a day of fun. In the car, he handed me a check. "What's this?"

"It's your money for spending the day away from work. Remember, we discussed two hundred dollars."

"Um… you did see the piece of paper with the bank balance on it, right? I think you can hold onto this now." Folding the check, I slipped it into his jacket pocket.

"Good point. I had a birthday present for you, but there is something I need to tell you about first," Jayce offered. "I've been dishonest with you about why I took the auto repair job. My parents have been paying for my college and letting me stay with them because all of the money I've earned has gone into a bank account for you."

His admission floored me, and I was sure I misunderstood. "What?"

"I wanted to help you fulfill your dream more quickly. I've been saving, so that when my contribution could help complete your goal, then I would tell you. Now that you have the bank account, you don't need it. I have an idea for the money, though."

Unselfish would be the best word I could use to describe his gesture. *What do you say to someone who has sacrificed so much to make you happy?*

"Jayce, this… I don't know what to say." Speechless was not a normal thing for me when it came to Jayce especially. He had always looked out for me and been my rock, but this act of selflessness was beyond anything I'd received from anyone.

"Listen to my idea first, and then you can respond. I don't have enough saved to go with you, but I can meet you along the way at times. Let's make a date, right this minute. On the fifth day of every third month, I'll meet you in whatever town you're in for a few days."

Having Jayce set up a meeting date for us was the next best thing to him traveling with me. I would plan my itinerary so we could share the most anticipated destinations together. All I could say was, "I love it!"

Jayce sighed. "My plans for the rest of the day seem lame after your grandparents' gift. I wanted to be the one to make this day as memorable as possible, especially since we'll miss the next two, possibly three birthdays together."

Hand on his leg, I said, "I'll admit, it's hard to outdo a gift worth thousands of dollars, however, every one of my birthday memories in the last few years have involved you and not the gifts I received. So, tell me your plans."

"Screw my lame ass plans. Do you still have sick time at work?"

"Yeah, why?"

"New epic plans have been created in my head now. How about I take you to see your first state? It's about a five-hour drive but if we stay up all night, we can drive back tomorrow, and you can call in sick to work. Are you up for a little gambling?"

"Gambling?"

"Tunica, Mississippi. You can mark the state off as visited, plus we can gamble for the first time in our lives. The trip will be my treat."

"How can I call in sick to work? I already took the day off, and I'm going to be giving them my notice so I can leave on my trip. It seems extremely irresponsible."

Jayce laughed. "Exactly! You are twenty-five years old Marie, and you've never been irresponsible in your life. Live it up a little. Playing hooky from work is a must for every twentysomething! Hell, in your thirties and forties you should play hooky every now and then too, just for your sanity."

"If we go, I should be the one to pay considering my recent bank account growth."

Jayce shook his head and stated emphatically, "No way. I want to do this for you. I've been saving all this money for you. Let me use a little of it."

"Let's do it." How could I say no to such an offer? Jayce had the power to convince me to do just about anything and he knew it.

Jayce made a U-turn and drove to the interstate. I called down to the hotels in Tunica and booked a room at the high-rise casino using Jayce's credit card, one room with two beds to make it cheaper on Jayce. I was still reeling from the shock of knowing he had worked all this time to help me achieve my goal.

JAYCE

Bells, whistles, cheers, and curse words filled the casino as we checked in to our room. When the manager on duty discovered it was Marie's birthday, he upgraded us to a suite at no extra charge. The suite came with a king-sized bed, not a big deal for us. We'd shared a bed many times before with no awkwardness. A tub large enough to fit two or three people comfortably was in the bathroom, which was the size of a bedroom in a normal home. An image of Marie lying naked in the tub with her head resting against the wall swam through my mind. My heart rate increased as the visual became detailed, and my mind's eye drifted over her naked, wet body.

"What are you thinking about?" Marie asked, bringing me out of my erotic daydream.

Thinking on my feet, I said, "I can sleep on the couch if it makes you uncomfortable."

"It's a king-sized bed, Jayce. There's plenty of room for both of us." I wasn't sure what had put such erotic thoughts in my head about Marie. The idea of sharing a bed with her now felt awkward after seeing her naked in my mind. "Besides, I don't see us sleeping much."

The innocent phrase sent into my mind more dirty thoughts of us tangling in the sheets. I gulped loudly and stuttered, "Wh-what do you mean?"

Marie's head cocked to the side, eyebrow raised. She replied, "We're in a casino. I assume we'll spend most of the night gambling. What did you think I meant?"

"Nothing, just making sure we're on the same page. Let's get dressed."

On the way in, we had stopped to purchase dressier outfits for our night of gambling. The casinos weren't high-end like Vegas, but I wanted to do this night up right.

Marie picked out a simple black dress. She stepped from the bathroom in time to catch me halfway through the buttons on my black shirt. The last time she'd seen me shirtless, I'd been much scrawnier. Now my abs rivaled Channing Tatum's. The thought of him made me picture giving Marie a lap dance. Pink blush filled her cheeks as she looked away. If she could read my mind, she'd blush even more. Without making eye contact, she said, "You look sharp."

My eyes moved over her curves, taking in everything from the swell of her breasts peeking out at the top of the dress down to how sexy her calves looked in the heels she had chosen. Parts of my body were responding to her in ways they never had before.

"Wow. You clean up nice," I said, both charming and teasing her at the same time. It was nothing close to what I wanted to say about how I'd never noticed how sexy she was. I stepped forward, bent my elbow, and Marie wrapped her arm through mine and allowed me to lead her out of the room.

In the casino, the crowd had thickened. There were a few people dressed up, and most appeared to be locals who spent too much time and money gambling their lives away.

"I'll be right back." As I walked away, I noticed Marie reach into her purse to pull out a quarter and stop at the first machine she found. As I stood across the room getting change, I watched her excitement each time she put a quarter into the machine. Based on the little dance she would do by shaking her hips and waving her hands back and forth, it seemed she won a couple of times.

Bells and whistles drowned out my reappearance at her side. "For you," I stated, handing her a bucket weighed down by coins. "One hundred dollars in quarters, nickels, and pennies for each of us to use tonight, and it's my treat."

"This is too much, Jayce."

"Nonsense. Maybe we'll double it." Posture stiff with confidence, I stepped up to a machine, put a quarter in, pulled the bar, and won five dollars. Nudging Marie with my elbow, I winked and said, "Off to a good start already."

We came close to doubling our starting total the longer we stood there. Starting the night with two hundred dollars between us, we finished with three hundred fifty-six dollars.

Back in the hotel room, we collapsed on the bed together. Her naked calf grazed my thigh and I jumped up to hide the effect. An idea hit me to cover the awkwardness I felt.

"Hold on. There is something I want to do. Get up for a

minute." Marie stood to the side waiting for clarification. Taking the dollar bills from our bucket of winnings, I threw them in the air watching them float down covering the mattress. I flung myself onto the bed and rolled around in the money. At first, Marie stood by with her mouth agape at the strange moment, but when I stopped rolling around, she began to laugh.

"You act like it's a million dollars." Marie laughed harder with each word.

"You're only jealous I thought of it first." I gathered the money and handed it to her. "Your turn?" She shrugged, took the money in her arms and stood on the bed, then jumped up and down tossing bills in the air. Once she was out of money, she fell to the mattress, and I landed next to her, both of us laughing uncontrollably.

"Thanks for this tonight." Gazing at me, her smile reached her eyes, which had a twinkle to them. Seeing Marie happy was one of my favorite things to witness.

"Anytime you want to roll around in some dirty money, I'm your man."

"Not just for that," Marie clarified, "but for this trip. There's no one I'd rather go on my first out of town tour with than you."

"When do you plan on leaving and where is the first stop?" Part of me didn't want to know the answer. Putting a date on her departure would begin the countdown for her to leave me here by myself.

"To save money, I'm going to drive instead of fly for most of it. I thought I'd drive through Kentucky, Indiana, and up through Michigan. Then I'll make my way to Canada and drive from the east to the west coast and everywhere in between. My last stop will be Hawaii. I thought I'd end with a flight and cruise. Go out with a bang."

"Sounds amazing. That reminds me, I have a cousin who lives in Ontario. Her parents own a bed and breakfast up there. I'll give you her number, and you can stay there for one of your stops. I'm sure she'd be glad to show you around. Her name is Constance. We call her Connie. We haven't seen each other in years, but we were best friends as kids. Then her parents moved there, and we moved here. We keep in touch through e-mail, though." Constance had heard a lot about Marie over the years, so I knew she'd be delighted to finally meet the legend of my stories. The two had a lot in common. Constance never ventured out much either. For some reason, her parents kept her close to home.

"It would be amazing to know someone locally up there. Thanks, Jayce."

"So, where will we meet?" She hadn't even left yet, and already I missed her.

"I don't know. Once I get my itinerary worked out, we'll figure it out. I want to spend a minimum of four days in each place. Some states I'll stay a couple of weeks, so I can visit different cities. For instance, in South Carolina I want to visit Myrtle Beach to see the ocean. I'd also like to go to Charleston for the historical attractions."

"Do you think your car will make it to all these places?" I had serious doubts her eight-year-old hatchback would survive the trip around the country. For someone who had never traveled out of her own state, she'd put plenty of miles on her car between having multiple jobs, commuting for school, and going back and forth to Nashville to see her dad. I couldn't handle the thought of her being stranded in the middle of nowhere in that tin can.

"Before today, I would have said no. With my grandparents' money paying for my trip, I'm going to use the money I've saved to buy a brand new car. When we get home, do you want to help me shop for one?"

"Hell yeah!" I exclaimed excitedly and then grew serious again as another thought occurred to me. "We're going to need to get you a tire iron to put in the car. You're going to drive all over the country by yourself. It would make me feel better if you were protected. I'd rather get you a gun and teach you how to shoot, but so many issues exist with reciprocity laws between states, and you can't carry into Canada. Maybe we could take some self-defense courses together too."

"Self-defense courses sound great. I've always wanted to learn how to defend myself. I'll treat both of us to those." She grabbed the notepad and pen from beside the bed. First, we jotted down a timeline of everything she needed to do before the trip. Marie's safety was my first concern, which is why we made the self-defense classes and car shopping the very first items to check off. Next, we mapped out her trip and planned each of our meeting spots along the way. I knew once she left I'd spend my days counting down the time until I'd see her again. Each time I thought about it, I got a little pang of sadness in my chest.

JOURNAL ENTRY

Today I begin my journey. It's been four months since my birthday, and I am finally ready to get on the road. Jayce and I have spent a lot of time together during these last few months. He joined a self-defense class with me. We signed up for two, four-hour courses. The instructor placed us against each other, and I was able to flip Jayce both times. He swore he didn't go easy on me, but I find that hard to believe. As a last-minute gift for the road, he purchased a tire iron for me to keep in the car. It was small enough for me to slip it into a tote bag or a large purse if I had far to walk or felt uneasy.

For my new car, we chose an adorable cobalt blue sports utility vehicle. It's a hybrid, so it will be good on gas and still roomy enough to carry as much as possible. Jayce thoroughly enjoyed explaining all the gadgets in the car to me along with a tutorial on what to do if any of the warning lights came on. He tried to make me the car expert he is before I left, but there was no way I could learn or retain it all.

Last night, I stayed up until I cried myself to sleep. It seemed silly to be sobbing about being able to fulfill my dream, but mostly I was scared this trip would be a mistake. I hope I'm wrong, and it ends up being the best trip of my entire life.

I guess we'll just have to see.

∞Marie

3

MARIE

My dad came to send me off. Dad and Jayce loaded down the car while I listened to my mother ramble on about safety tips. The slamming shut of the hatchback saved me from the rest of the conversation. I silently sent up a "thank you" for the rescue.

"All set, sweetheart," my dad said. He wrapped his arms around me tightly, and I had to choke back the tears. My emotions had fluctuated between excitement and fear as I had gotten ready to leave everyone I loved behind. "You be careful out there. And just because you aren't going overseas doesn't mean I won't go all Liam Neeson if you don't call me to check in every day."

My dad's movie reference made me chuckle. "No worries, Dad. I can't promise every day, but I'll check in once a week."

He grunted, unsatisfied with my response. "Nope, at least

twice a week. If you can work in a face-to-face visit with Jayce every three months, you can promise me two quick phone calls a week to let me know you're safe."

With a sigh of defeat, I promised, "Fine. Twice a week."

Mom made me agree to the same terms, so I'd have to make sure to choose a night where I could conference them both to keep from repeating myself. When Jayce stepped up, the tears welled up in my eyes. The first fallen tear was met by a swipe of his thumb. "I'll miss you. I look forward to our first meeting in New York in July."

"Me too, Mo," Jayce said quietly. When he pulled me close for a hug, I wrapped my arms around him and breathed him in. He always smelled like apples and motor oil. The apple smell came from the air freshener in his car, and the motor oil smell was from work. It was a weird combination, but it was Jayce, so it was my favorite smell in the world. "I do expect a call every day. No arguments."

I whispered back, "Definitely." Clinging to him for longer than normal, I soaked in the moment as if I hoped he'd surprise me any minute now by saying he would take the trip with me. When nothing happened, I reluctantly let go and turned away.

Climbing into my car, I waved good-bye to my family for the next two years. When it was May in Tennessee, the weather could be anywhere from a comfortable seventy to the stifling eighties. Day one was a midrange temperature of seventy-five. About four hours from my hometown, I came to the Kentucky state line. When I saw the Welcome to Kentucky sign, I let out an excited squeal. I pulled over to the side of the road to snap a quick photo of the sign. Selfies at the state line would be the way to keep my pictures in order by state for the photo album later.

It would grow cooler the farther into Kentucky I drove. To manage my itinerary, I'd researched several cities in the state. My first stop was in Bowling Green to see the Corvette Museum. Cars weren't my thing, but Jayce asked me to go and allow him to live a little through my experience. It was a small favor to grant considering all he had done for me. Picking out the cars I knew Jayce would swoon over, I snapped a few selfies and bought a shot glass souvenir for Jayce and my grandfather.

An hour later, I still walked around the museum and found I was intrigued by the different body styles and the history of the cars. Bonding with cars made me miss Jayce. If he were here, he'd be telling me about the horsepower, the cylinders, and whatever other car stuff that would go completely over my head. Even if I had no clue what he was talking about most of the time, I still loved to watch his face light up as he talked about his favorite things.

Before getting back on the road, I stopped to grab a bite to eat at country restaurant. The hostess sat me at the table in front of the fireplace. After receiving my drink, I noticed an elderly man being seated at the table next to mine.

"Excuse me, sir," I called out.

Slowly he peered up from his menu. "Yes?"

"Would you care to join me for lunch? I'd rather not eat alone."

His wrinkled face appeared ten years younger as he smiled at the request. "I'd love to."

The waitress helped him change tables by grasping his elbow and escorting him over. After he had sat down, we placed our orders before getting to know each other.

"I haven't had dinner with a beautiful lady since before my wife died three years ago. We had a blissful marriage for fifty years. I'm probably old enough to be your great-great-grandfather."

"Grandfather would be as far as I'd go."

"Why is a sweet woman like you alone?" he asked. I watched as his hands shook unrolling the silverware.

"I'm taking the trip of my dreams. I'm traveling across the United States and Canada for the next year and a half or so. I've never had a real vacation, and I've worked really hard for this, so I'm taking time to enjoy it."

"A young lady like you should enjoy as much of life as possible," he said with a kind smile.

"It's a big step for me because I've become a bit of a workaholic lately. I grew up in Chattanooga, Tennessee and barely left the state until recently. Kentucky is my first stop on the trip."

"That's quite an accomplishment. My dad was in the Army. I've seen quite a bit of this country here. You're in for a treat." He grinned at me over the rim of his glasses. He reminded me of the little old man in the movie *Up*, although he seemed a bit happier than Carl Fredricksen did.

"Will you tell me about your wife?" Reading filled what little free time I had, so I loved a good story. I knew anyone who'd been married fifty years would have some great tales to share.

He gave a gruff chuckle and said, "First, I should tell you my name is Eckert, but most people call me Buddy."

"I'm Marie, Buddy. It's nice to make your acquaintance." I held my hand out to shake his. He lifted it to his face and gave the back of my hand a kiss. It was very old-fashioned and gentlemanly.

His crinkled face softened into a sweet smile as he began to tell his story. "My wife, Josie, was the love of my life. We met in the spring of 1947. I was eighteen, and she was sixteen. She was the best friend of my little sister, Catelyn. I'd enlisted in the Army and had been going through basic training when they met. When I came home, she had her over to spend the night. She walked into the room and stole my heart the very instant I laid eyes on her."

"Love at first sight?"

"Absolutely. Of course, the little bit of an age difference seemed much larger to our parents. They wouldn't allow us to date. So I stayed away from the house as much as possible to take my mind off her. We didn't see each other again until 1952."

"Was she with your sister when you saw her again?" I asked, truly interested in this man's love story.

"She was working in a bar. I walked in, and when her eyes met mine, my heart remembered her instantly. Unfortunately for me, she had a fiancé. Again I had to love her from afar and do my best to move on. Ten years later, I saw her again. She worked as a cashier at the local food market in my hometown. Her fiancé had left her for another woman. I asked her out to dinner that night. When she said yes, I was so excited I went and bought a ring. On our first date, I proposed and we were married two months later by a justice of the peace."

"That's quite an amazing story," I replied with genuine awe. The waitress interrupted with the food, so we took a few bites before I asked anything more. "Did you have children?"

"Seven of them, four boys and three girls," he replied proudly. "Now I have fifteen grandchildren and two great-grandchildren." He leaned forward reaching for his wallet in his back pocket. He flipped it open to show her a sleeve full of pictures. "I know most people keep their pictures in phones these days, but I like to keep mine close and don't want to worry about a battery charge keeping me from seeing them when I want."

Buddy kept me mesmerized with more stories of his children and how they acted growing up. The hard times they suffered when money was tight and the beautiful moments such as weddings and graduations. The last story he had broke my heart.

"Josie died three years ago on this day. We went to sleep one night, and she never woke up. I prayed that I'd go shortly after. I didn't want to live without my Josie. Then my first great-grandchild was born, and I knew I needed to stick around a few more years."

The waitress brought out separate bills, and I grabbed Buddy's before he could reach for it. "I'd like to pay for your meal. It's been a real pleasure having lunch with you today. It's the least I can do."

Buddy walked me up to the counter and bought a bag of Andes mints. After I paid, he took two and handed me the rest of the bag. "What's this?"

"Josie and I liked to bring our kids here to eat, and tradition was we'd buy a bag of these at the end of the meal as a treat. I'm a sucker for tradition."

It meant the world to me to be a part of such a special custom, no matter how simple it was. "Buddy, would you mind if I snap a photo of us to capture this moment?"

Grinning widely, he bowed his head politely and replied, "I'd be honored. What is it the kids call them these days? A snappy?"

"Close. It's called a selfie." Turning toward the camera and smiling with my head next to his, I snapped a photo. Wrapping my arm around his neck, I hugged him close and kissed his cheek for the second one. "Thanks again for lunch today, Buddy. You take care of yourself."

"You too, Marie. Be careful out there, young lady."

Getting in my car, I set the GPS destination to Louisville, Kentucky. I wanted to spend a few nights exploring the city, checking out a few local hotspots and museums. Louisville proved to be a pretty happening place. The Galt House Hotel had been highly recommended by my new best friend, Google. It had a bar located in a crosswalk-type section between the two towers of the hotel. For two nights, I mingled with other guests and tried crazy alcoholic drinks. One night, I tried a local pub around the corner from the hotel and decided to make note of it in my journal as having the best fish platter I'd ever tasted. Each stop along the way made me wish Jayce were there to share it with me.

On my last night in town, I ventured over to Fourth Street

Live! to do a little shopping and enjoy a concert taking place in the evening. The view from the street was like what one would expect Vegas to look like with the bright neon lights. A few drinks into the night, I got out on the dance floor. As I shook my hips and moved to the beat, guys would come up to dance. Luckily none of them pressured me for any after-dancing entertainment. I wasn't looking for love, or lust either, right now. After dancing with four different men, I decided I'd had enough. On the way back to the hotel, my phone rang.

"Hey, handsome."

"Hello, gorgeous. Are you living it up?" Jayce asked.

I chuckled thinking about my night. "A little. I just left a concert in Louisville. I danced a little, drank a little too much, and I'm on my way back to my hotel now."

"Are you walking alone?" he asked with concern.

"I'm fine, Jayce. The streets are pretty crowded around this area. You can keep me company until I get to my hotel. How are things with you?"

"Good. I miss my best friend, though. I don't like the idea of you walking strange streets alone. You need to be more careful." His overprotective nature was endearing.

"Trust me, I'm fine." The gold-lined revolving door of the hotel spun at a snail's pace in front of me as I stepped in and walked through to the other side. I pushed the up button on the elevator and stared at my reflection in the golden door. This hotel really had a thing for gold. "I'm back at the hotel, Jayce."

He sighed, relieved.

"Good. Where's your next destination?"

"Bed."

He chuckled softly. "I meant on your road trip."

Covering my mouth to stifle a laugh, I replied, "Oops, sorry. I'm driving into Indiana tomorrow. I plan on spending a few days there. My first stop will be the amusement park in Santa Claus."

"I'm jealous." He pouted and whined teasingly, but it seemed it wasn't completely untrue. He sounded sadder than usual, and I was sure he missed me as much as I missed him.

"You'll get to experience New York with me, and that's better than any amusement park, I'm sure." If I hadn't been able to do this trip, New York was on my short lists of states I had to experience in my life at some point. Broadway, Ground Zero, Rockefeller Center. I wanted to see it all.

"I can't wait. It's been so boring here since you left."

"Aww, I'm sorry, J. I miss you too. But I need to go. I'm exhausted and need to get out of these clothes and into a hot shower."

"Are you trying to seduce me by phone?" Jayce gave a low throaty growl, which was so sexy it threw off my balance for a moment.

I purred seductively into the phone, "That'll cost you $3.95 a minute. Are you up for it?" I had no idea what had come over me.

Jayce grew silent on his end of the line and stuttered as if my seductive teasing affected him. He laughed to ease the tension and said, "I'll take a rain check. Talk to you later. Be careful."

After hanging up, I couldn't help going over the

conversation in my head again. Jayce's deep throaty growl, even though he had been teasing, sent tingles all over my skin. Before I left, my fear had been that distance would affect our relationship negatively and we'd drift apart. Now I was wondering if the old adage was true, if absence really did make the heart grow fonder.

Clearing my mind of the awkward thoughts, I crossed the room. My room was on the sixteenth floor of the hotel offering a vast view of the scenery in the city. I stood at the window with a wide grin as I thought about how perfectly my stops had gone during this first state on my trip.

———————

I sat up in bed with a smile on my face and a spring in my step. For a moment, I got on my own nerves as I looked in the mirror and saw my over-the-top cheery smile. In the shower, I serenaded myself with a feisty rendition of "Dancing Queen." Steam filled the room like a fog machine on a concert stage. Using my back scrubber as a microphone, I put ABBA to shame, and at the end of the performance, I gave the empty room a naked bow as the imaginary crowd applauded. Giggling at the ridiculousness of my fantasy concert, I wiped away the steam from the mirror and finished getting ready for the day.

Santa Claus, Indiana, was about an hour from Louisville, Kentucky. I grabbed a breakfast sandwich from the hotel café, along with a piping hot cup of French roast coffee, and got on my way.

The amusement park, Holiday World, was pretty crowded, which is what I expected for the end of May. School had let out, and parents were enjoying a summer vacation with their children. Most people running through the gates were in large groups. This made me miss Jayce more than ever as the loneliness crept in. Across the way, I spotted a young woman about my age walking in alone. She was petite with short blue-and-pink highlighted blonde hair.

"Hi, are you here alone too?"

"Yeah, my girlfriend was supposed to meet me, but she had to work. I decided to come alone, but now I'm kind of regretting the decision."

"I know the feeling. My name is Marie." I extended my hand to her.

"Samantha, my friends call me Sami."

"Well, Sami, I'm on my own and would love some company. Would you like to spend the day with me?"

"I'd love to!" she exclaimed. "And, it just so happens we bought our tickets early, so here, you can have my girlfriend's that way it won't go to waste."

"Thanks! In that case, lunch is on me later."

The best place to start the day seemed to be the biggest roller coaster in the park. We were both excited that our good luck landed us in the front row where we had the most adrenaline-pumping view. Our screams were deafening as we sped down giant hills and raced sideways around curves. It was exhilarating.

After riding several more coasters, only slightly smaller or slower, we took a break to sit and have a cold soda. Sami's phone rang, and I eavesdropped on the one-sided conversation.

"Hey, baby," she answered, obviously speaking to her girlfriend. "I'm having fun, but I miss you. I met a girl named Marie. She's traveling by herself, so we're doing the buddy system on all the rides." Blushing, she dipped her head with a grin. "I'll do my best. Love you."

I twirled my straw around in the drink rhythmically while I waited for Sami's call to end.

"How long have you two been together?" I asked once she hung up.

"Two years. We met the first year of college. Neither of us had come out of the closet yet, but we both knew by high school that we liked girls instead of boys. I think she was going to propose today. She was incredibly disappointed about not being able to go, and this is where we had our first date."

"That is so sweet!" I felt a pang of envy in my chest at never having been in love or close to engaged. At times, I'd often wondered if I had been giving up something even better than a dream trip around the country. Considering the long hours I worked, I hadn't had much time to date. Not that I needed a man to make me happy or fulfill me, but at times I did long for a little passion.

"Do you have someone special in your life?" Perhaps the envious look on my face screamed loneliness because Sami seemed almost nervous about asking the question.

"No. I've been planning this trip for so many years that I've sort of put dating on hold until it's done. The only special guy in my life is my best friend, Jayce."

"Nothing more than friendship there?" Sami's eyebrows

lifted with curiosity.

"No, never. He's like a brother to me." I cringed a little at the words because it hadn't felt like talking to my brother last night when I was flirting or having naughty thoughts. But it was Jayce. He'd always be my best friend, and I'd never try to push for more because I couldn't stand to lose him. "He's the most important person in my life. If we ever even contemplated a relationship, I'd be terrified of it not working out."

"You never know until you try. Have you ever kissed him to see if those feelings are there?"

Anxiety stirred inside me, making the simple questions more like an intense interrogation. "I think we should go to the water parks next. It's getting hot out here. Are you up for it?"

Sami lifted her shirt to reveal a bikini top underneath. "Hell yes."

"What are you doing after this today?" I didn't make plans any further than jotting down a few things I wanted to visit in each state. I would jump at any chance not to spend this entire trip alone.

"Picking up Kat, my girlfriend. You could come with me and meet her if you want." Spending the day with people definitely sounded better than exploring things on my own.

"I'd love to. I was wondering if you could put some streaks in my hair." Since the trip was all about exploration, I was going to get myself a makeover too.

"You like this?" Sami grabbed a handful of her hair. "Kat did it. Her hair is crimson red with black streaks. You'll love it. She lives to do hair. It's good practice for her. She's in cosmetology school."

We spent another hour at the park before we decided we'd had enough fun. Sami gave me directions to her house and said to give her about an hour, enough time to pick up Kat. In the meantime, I took a moment to call my favorite guy.

"Hey, Jayce."

"Hey! I was just thinking about you. Where are you now?" Genuine excitement oozed from him at hearing my voice, and it made me all warm and happy inside.

"Holiday World in Indiana. I met a cool chick named Sami, who I hung out with all day. Now I'm going to her house where her girlfriend is going to give my hair a makeover."

"Ooh, sounds interesting. Just don't go Britney and try the bald thing. I think your head is too misshapen."

I snickered and clarified, "Funny. Nothing *that* drastic." I left out the specifics of the creative color of the highlights because I wanted to surprise him with a selfie later.

"I miss you, Mo. It's only been a few days, and I'm going nuts here." His voice was gloomy, and I could imagine him sitting there fidgeting with his nails, a nervous habit he had.

"I miss you too. It'll be time for our meeting in New York before you know it." Each time I talked to him, it made things both harder and easier. I loved hearing his voice and being able to talk to him, but it hurt not to see Jayce in person. Right then, I'd have given anything to hug him. After only a few days, I already felt homesick. Moments of loneliness kept me motivated to meet new people along the way, though.

Sami and Kat were opening their front door when I pulled

into the driveway. Sami turned around and waved me inside.

"Marie, this is Kat," she stated as I stepped over the threshold into what seemed like a different world. The living room décor was eclectic to put it mildly. The plush, deep-crimson velvet couch went well with the dark-as-night velvet curtains behind it. The table lamps had a dim light with multi-colored scarves tossed over the tops. It reminded me of a scene in a cheesy eighties movie I once watched. It was retro, and a little over-the-top, but still very cool and unique much like the residents themselves.

"You were right. I love her hair," I commented as I took in Kat's appearance. Besides the cool hair, she was drop-dead gorgeous. Her dark hair was the perfect contrast to her pale blue eyes and pale skin giving her a very exotic look. "So do you feel like giving me a makeover?"

"Hell yeah, I live for that stuff." Sami grinned at me when Kat repeated the comment she'd made earlier. "Thanks for keeping my girl company today. I hated that I missed it." Kat kissed Sami's cheek.

Kat grabbed my hand and pulled me toward the bedroom. She pointed to the bed for a seat and brought out a selection of hair dyes. "How drastic do you want to go? Your blonde hair gives us an easy pallet to work with."

A few hours later, aluminum foil filled my hair and a frozen margarita filled my hand. Pink and purple streaks were my final decision on the hair color. After the timer had gone off, Kat removed all the foil, washed out the excess dye, shampooed and put a special conditioner in my hair, and styled it, all before letting me see the end result.

"Wow," Sami and Kat gasped in unison.

"Let me see!" I bounced up and down in my chair excitedly. When they turned to show me the mirror, it was easy to see my complete satisfaction at the outcome. "Take a picture, so I can text my friend, please." Kat snapped the photo, and then the three of us pressed our faces together to get a group selfie to send as well.

Changing my hair was a drastic move for me. Although I'd always wanted to put colorful streaks in my hair, I'd never had the nerve to do it and always worried it would affect my job. As a bartender, I could look however I wanted for the most part, but managing the theater called for a more businesslike appearance. Staring at the photo now, I barely recognized the new me. Not only the hair color, but the spark of confidence I spotted in my eyes.

Me: The first pic is my new do. What do you think? The second is the new Mo with her friends Sami and Kat.

Jayce: Wow.

The three letters were enough to give me goose bumps. Leaving Jayce speechless was quite a feat. Texts from him were never less than a full paragraph. One reason I rarely sent him texts was that it was easier to let him say everything out loud. High on emotions, I couldn't stop grinning from ear to ear.

Sami and Kat convinced me to stay with them for the next few days, so they could show me around their favorite spots of the surrounding cities. I didn't want to intrude, and I hesitated momentarily to accept, but secretly I was happy to be invited to stay. I would miss these two when I left. I wished I could pack them up and take them with me.

They didn't choose the usual tourist spots to show me. Instead, we did activities the two enjoyed. We hiked through a state park on a wildlife watch. One day, we spent an afternoon in the park painting pictures of the scenery with a group of other amateur artists. The picnic basket and bottle of wine made the time even more interesting. With barely a drop of wine left, Sami pulled her tablet from her backpack and grabbed my phone. She quickly dialed up Jayce on her tablet and waved when he accepted her FaceTime request.

"Are you Sami or Kat?" Jayce asked, making my head twist to see where the voice originated. I snorted a giggle when I saw him on the screen. Poking my tongue out at him made him chuckle as well.

"I'm Sami. We've loved having your girl around. We're trying to convince her to move here with us."

"No can do, Sami. I'm pretty attached to my girl. There's no way I could stand for her to live that far away."

Sami's bottom lip poked forward in a pout, and I took the tablet away. Leaning in, I kissed the screen making Jayce shake his head. "Hi, Jayce-y. I miss you."

"How much has she had to drink?"

Sami held the bottle of wine up to show him. "At least half of this. She's a lightweight."

"Get her home safely for me, Sami. She's the only friend I've got."

Sami had to remind me of kissing the screen later because I had no recollection, but she brushed it off as a drunken act. I wasn't so sure it was the fault of the wine. Thoughts of kissing Jayce ran through my mind a lot lately. If it had happened with anyone else, I'd be more embarrassed by my actions. At least if it came up again, Jayce would probably believe the drunken excuse.

Saying good-bye to Sami and Kat was harder than I expected. The few days we spent together had bonded us. I made sure to get their phone numbers and e-mail addresses, to friend them on Facebook, and to get any other form of communication I could acquire. They promised to make a visit to Chattanooga sometime for me to show them around my hometown. Both girls were anxious to meet Jayce in person too after I'd talked about him nonstop.

While staying with the couple, I had dreams of Jayce that were of a different nature than ever before. Previously I would have dreams of us in silly situations where the most scandalous thing was showing up to school naked. Now my dreams still had us naked, but in a different manner.

The first dream I had was innocent and romantic with a simple kiss Jayce gave me on my lips. In the next dream, it was as if we went from first base straight home, skipping every base in between. Writhing bodies, tongues dancing, and a soundtrack of moans and gasps filled my night. Waking up in a sweat, I rolled over wishing I'd find Jayce next to me. When he hadn't been there, I'd wished I was more into toys as I lay there unsatisfied and wanting. In my defense, I was in a house with a couple that were very much in love. I needed someone to star in my romantic fantasies, and Jayce seemed to be on my mind the most.

4

MARIE

As I crossed the line into Michigan, my phone rang. I pressed the button on the steering wheel to activate the hands-free option.

"Jayce?" I couldn't see the caller I.D., but I took a guess since he was the person who called me the most.

"Nope. It's the other man in your life. The one you haven't called in over a week. I thought we agreed on twice a week? If I hadn't spoken with your mother, I'd be sending the police to look for you." My dad's tone of concern did not go unnoticed.

Releasing an audible sigh, I replied, "Sorry, Dad. I'm fine. I tried to call you one night, and no one answered. It was the same night I talked to Mom. She isn't happy with me either. I promise to do better."

"I hope so. How's the trip so far?"

"Amazing. Besides the scenery, the people have been

fantastic. I've already made a couple of lifelong friends." I'd only been gone a short time and already received an e-mail from both Sami and Kat.

"Well, I've always said you have never met a stranger, Marie, so that doesn't surprise me. If you were an introvert, you'd never have been able to make this trip alone. I'm proud of you. But if you don't start calling me more often, I will have to strap on my Liam Neeson persona and come after you."

"Yes, sir," I replied with a laugh.

Before he'd let me hang up, I had to promise to call him in three days. Traffic came to a standstill. Glancing ahead, I spotted the reason for the traffic jam as a pair of blue lights spun on the shoulder about half a mile forward. I rolled my eyes and groaned at the rubbernecking drivers until I was able to creep past the dreaded lights. Once I passed the attention-grabbing police officer, traffic took off as though in a race to catch up to where they should have been.

The interstate parts of the drive didn't appear much different than home. When approaching big cities, though, the real differences became clear. Occasionally I would stop to capture photos of the skylines of cities along the route.

The weather improved the farther north I drove. The Great Lakes became the next anticipated destination for me. Instead of stopping in some of the closer cities in the state, I drove straight to a small town called Ludington my friend Carina at work had suggested.

Carina's family owned a large home on a cliff overlooking Lake Michigan. She gave me the address to check out the view because the house was usually empty for the early part of the summer. When I pulled up, I had to double-check the address to make sure it was the right place. The slate gray house was practically a mansion compared to most other homes I'd seen. I parked in the curved driveway of the front yard and made my way around back to stand on the cliff and look out. To prove to Carina that I'd stopped, I snapped several pictures of the view and a selfie or two as well.

Putting my camera away, I took a moment to appreciate the surroundings. The view was breathtaking to put it mildly. A cool breeze ruffled my hair as I breathed in the enchanting scents on it. A staircase to the right led down to the beach below.

I climbed into the backseat of my car and changed into a swimsuit, putting a pair of capris and a loose T-shirt over the top. I placed my tennis shoes in a tote bag and slid into flip-flops. The rest of the bag included two towels, a few snacks, my Kindle, and a couple of bottles of water.

Once down on the sandy shore, I spread out a towel to place my things on and then walked to the edge of the water to stare out at the massive lake. The water was as clearer than any lake I was used to. Far down to the left side of the shore was a lighthouse. Before leaving to find a place to stay for the night, I wanted to walk down to see it up close.

In the meantime, I needed a few moments to relax and unwind. Slipping off my shoes, T-shirt, and capris, I lay flat on the towel and pulled the sunglasses from atop my head down over my eyes. I sighed in exhilaration as I soaked in the afternoon sun.

My moment of relaxation was disturbed by a male voice shouting, "Heads-up!"

I sat up in time to be hit on the side of the head by something. The voice was closer as he knelt down in the sand before asking, "Are you all right?"

My glasses had been knocked crooked by the flying object I'd since discovered was a Frisbee. "I think I am."

The stranger chuckled a little and remarked, "You know, most people duck when they hear heads-up. I didn't expect you to literally bring your head up."

I rubbed my forehead, which throbbed a little from the impact. "Which makes you think about how stupid a warning like that is, don't you agree?"

He chortled a bit more. "Touché. I apologize. My buddy wasn't paying attention where he was aiming." The buddy in question waved from across the way and cupped his hands in front of his mouth to yell out his apology.

"No harm, no foul."

"Would you like to join us?" the handsome stranger asked politely.

"Um… well…" I hesitated as I glanced over at the friend waiting patiently.

"How rude of me, I should introduce myself. I'm Brady and my friend over there is Manny." Taking a moment to size Brady up, I was tongue-tied. He wore a sleeveless shirt and his sun-kissed biceps flexed as he extended his hand in greeting. His blond hair was thick, and his bangs swept over his forehead. When he tossed his head back to move them aside, he gave me a glimpse of soft green eyes.

"Marie," I replied, grasping his firm hand. I peered over at Manny noticing his long black hair tied back with a rubber band. "Manny?" Caramel-colored skin wrapped over bulging muscles, his kind eyes were a deep chocolate brown, lips a pale pink framing gleaming white teeth. If all of the men in this state looked like this, I might just have to move to Michigan.

"His dad was a big MOTU fan." Brady paused and then clarified, "That's nerd-speak for Masters of the Universe. His favorite character was named Man-e-faces. He's lucky his dad didn't add the faces part. I suppose it's also better than being named He-Man or Skeletor."

"It could've been even worse if he'd been a Transformers fanatic. He might have been named Optimus Prime or Megatron," I teased. I had been a bit of a tomboy when I was younger and loved to watch all the cartoons geared toward boys.

A wide grin spread across his face, and he placed his hand over his heart. "A girl who knows her eighties cartoons. Be still my heart."

I laughed at his adorable expression and stood up to get dressed. "Let me slip on some clothes, and I'll join you guys."

"You look great the way you are," Brady flirted, making my stomach pull with a tingly sensation as his eyes drifted over my half-naked body.

"Thanks. You're sweet." I smiled and felt the blush as it crept up my cheeks. Slipping on my capri pants and flip-flops, I left the T-shirt behind. It didn't hurt to show off the girls a bit, and my bikini top was too cute to cover. As Brady ran ahead, I quickly adjusted my top to make sure not too much, or too little, of the "ladies" was exposed.

We ran back and forth chasing the Frisbee for the next hour until we were all short on energy.

"Grab a bite to eat with us?" Brady offered.

"Actually, man, I have to get going. It was nice to meet you, Marie." I watched as Manny and Brady exchanged a look, and it gave my ego a little boost.

"You too, Manny."

When he left, I turned back to Brady and said, "Smooth move. Is he always your wingman?"

"Was it that obvious?" His mischievous grin displayed sparkling white teeth and adorable dimples.

"Not at first. I hope you don't reel in every girl by giving her a concussion first, though." I peered up at him through my eyelashes trying to hold back a smile as I teased.

Brady gently slid his fingers across my forehead and then through my hair sending shivers across my skin.

"You have a bit of a mark there too. I at least owe you dinner." His touch comforted me, drawing me into his web of flirtation.

"I probably need to tell you that I'm not from around here."

Brady's lips turned up in a grin revealing those panty-dropping dimples again. "I noticed the slight southern twang in your voice, and I'd remember someone as beautiful as you around town. Where are you from?"

"Chattanooga, Tennessee. I'm traveling the country."

Brady's expression dropped to disappointment.

"Damn. So how long are you here then?"

"A few days. A week at most. I haven't decided."

He leaned forward and spoke softly, "Will you have dinner with me tonight?" He stood so close, his breath kissed my forehead.

"Wow, you don't waste any time."

Brady shifted his weight to pull back a little. I missed the closeness immediately.

"You didn't give me much choice. I have a few days, possibly a week, to get to know this beautiful southern belle in front of me. I'm not passing up the chance."

Before responding, I took a moment to let my blood sugar drop from the sweetness overload he was dishing out.

"I'd love to."

"On second thought, I phrased that wrong. I want more than dinner." Eyebrow raised, lips turned up in a crooked smile, he said, "I want you to spend the rest of the day with me, maybe all night."

"Um…" I stuttered out the nervous sound as I contemplated the innuendo beneath his request. Heat crept up my cheeks and between my thighs at the idea.

"Yep, I phrased that wrong, too. By all night, I'm not making assumptions. I meant I'd like to get to know you, by talking."

My phone rang, and I glanced down to see Jayce's face pushed up against the screen making a funny expression. When I first got the phone, I'd asked him to let me take a photo for my contacts, and he'd responded in that way. For the first time since we'd met, I ignored his call. I'd never chosen anything over talking to Jayce. A twinge of guilt weighed on my conscience.

"That's not a boyfriend, is it?" Brady asked curiously.

"My best friend. I'll call him later tonight."

Brady gallantly carried my tote bag up the hill to the car after I packed everything up. Manny had driven them, so he had no way to get home. Another smooth move he'd used to spend more time with me. Being desired was the ultimate compliment in my opinion. Brady was still a stranger, and I wasn't crazy enough to trust him completely. With utmost discretion, I moved the tire iron from the tote bag to the bottom of my purse just in case. It would take dire circumstances for me to use it, but the way the world was today, you never knew when you'd have to defend yourself.

After loading the car, he reached down to grasp my hand as we walked the concrete bridge out to the lighthouse. My hand felt tiny in comparison to his, and his thumb rhythmically rubbed circles against my skin as we walked. When we reached the end, we posed for a self-portrait when an older gentleman offered to snap a picture of the two of us together.

In turn, he asked if we'd snap a picture of him with his twin daughters. The girls must have been around six or seven years old, and they posed as though they were supermodels. One had her head tossed back as the wind blew her hair, and her hips were cocked forward with one shoulder leaning in toward the camera. Brady whistled and said, "Sashay, Shante!" snapping his fingers in the air at the same time. The little girl blushed and giggled.

Brady entertained the girls for a few minutes, and I watched in complete awe. His contagious laughter infected everyone around as they goofed off making different faces for the camera. Afterward, we waved good-bye to the family and turned back toward the town. I linked my arm through his.

"You're great with kids."

"My parents divorced when I was ten, and my dad remarried a few years later, shortly after I turned sixteen. He and his wife had a set of twins, so I've had a lot of experience with little ones. It seemed whenever I went to their house for the weekend, I was their live-in babysitter."

"Your dad didn't spend time with you?" I knew how it felt to have an absentee parent. Even if my dad didn't live with us, though, I'd always known he loved me because we talked on the phone all the time.

Brady sighed. "Not really. You know that whole "Cat's in the Cradle" song about the dad who values work more than his son?"

I remember the song well. As a kid, I felt it was about me with my dad being away for work. As I got older, I began to understand it more fully, and he'd never abandoned me entirely either.

"That's my dad. Only, I don't plan to be the son in the song. My job pays the bills and keeps me happy, but it's not my life. I'm doing online classes to better myself, but I'd never let a job come before family. He's had two miserable marriages and three kids he doesn't want. I'm never going to be like him." Brady took a deep breath and stopped. "I'm sorry, I got too deep there."

"You can never go too deep with me." I clamped my mouth shut after my words had spilled out.

The blush on Brady's face and the way he stuttered his next question of, "Would you like some ice cream?" opened my eyes to the faux pas.

The abrupt subject change was highly appreciated.

"I'd love some." I considered apologizing for my earlier wording but decided to let the ice cream be my saving grace.

The homemade ice cream shop was a short three-block walk. I was enjoying his company so much I wouldn't have minded if we kept going. Brady ordered strawberry, and I ordered chocolate chip; both of us requested two scoops in a fresh waffle cone. My mouth watered in anticipation.

Brady's tongue lapped out at the sweet cream concoction, and my cheeks warmed as a blush crept across my skin. Images of the naughtier ways he could utilize his tongue invaded my mind, and I bit my lip to keep from moaning. His eyes were closed as he enjoyed the snack, and after a moment, he paused and opened them suddenly.

"Are you watching me eat?"

"Creepy?" I remarked.

"A little." He winked good-naturedly. "If you don't taste yours soon, you're going to be wearing it." His tongue flicked out once more against the top of the cone, and I was ready to come undone.

Peering down at my cone, I knew he was right. The ice cream was liquefying quickly. The first taste was creamy, and each chocolate chip was decadence. It was the best ice cream ever, and I thought perhaps the company helped. Then it was Brady's turn to watch me eat. Seduction had never been my forte. To avoid looking like an idiot trying to be sexy, I went with eating in my normal fashion. The first big bite left a dribbling mess running down my chin. Brady reached out with a napkin to clean my face.

"You're cute when you eat ice cream. Most girls try to be all proper and take small licks. You went in headfirst like a starving puppy." Brady gave a hearty laugh when I reacted to his comment.

"You aren't as smooth without your wingman," I pointed out.

"Ouch." Brady grabbed his chest feigning offense at my sarcastic remark. "Forgive me, beautiful. I meant it as a compliment, honestly. It shows you're comfortable with me."

"Calling me beautiful gained you a few extra points to make up for it." I bit my lip to hide the giant goofy grin that wanted to occupy my face. I was enjoying my time with this man but still trying to play it semi-cool. It felt odd to feel so comfortable with another man especially with the nature of my thoughts about Jayce lately. Perhaps it was better to explore this growing attraction rather than screw up a beautiful friendship with Jayce.

BRADY

The afternoon had flown by, and the sun was setting. Marie's skin, covered only by a swimsuit top and thin capri pants, pebbled with goose bumps as the temperature dropped. We walked back to her car to grab a jacket. Though I had other ideas for keeping her warm, I was a gentleman first and foremost and wouldn't rush this nice thing we had going.

"When you leave Michigan, where is your next stop?" While she slipped into the backseat, I leaned against the driver side door.

"I'm going to Canada for a couple of weeks."

"Sounds great," I responded, and I meant it. I'd have loved to travel the country, especially with a beautiful woman like her beside me. "If I didn't have to work for a living, you know, to pay for stuff, I'd ask to go with you. I'm envious of how much you'll see."

"If it weren't for my grandparents supporting me through this trip, I wouldn't be able to afford not to work either. I was working two full-time jobs. What do you do for a living?"

Not having known any of my grandparents, I coveted Marie's family life.

"I'm a computer engineer. I work mostly out of my home, but occasionally I travel for work too. When you aren't traveling the country, what are you doing?"

"I was a manager at a theater in my hometown during the day and a bartender in the evenings. When I get home, I'm going to find a long-term career in my field, business administration."

As she spoke, my gaze dropped to her lips. Plump, pink lips that appeared to be soft as silk. I wondered how they tasted. A light sheen of lip gloss gave them a glimmer. Looking back up at her eyes, I saw a passion that matched mine. Shuffling her feet nervously, I watched as she bit the side of her lip and peered up at me.

Pulling her against my body, I wrapped my arms around her small waist. She barely caught her breath before I leaned forward and captured her lips with mine. Strawberry flavor filled my mouth, answering my question of what her lips would taste like. Her tongue teased its way into my mouth, and she ran her hands over the taut muscles of my back telling me she didn't want this moment to end.

"Come back to my place?" As I pulled away from the kiss, the invite spilled from my lips before much thought could be given. "Strictly to talk, I promise. No pressure for anything more." My lips spoke the words, but my actions told her I wanted more as I planted small kisses along her jaw and neck.

My brain tried to warn me I was moving too fast with this woman. I'd never been the player or the one-night-stand kind of guy. Knowing I only had a short time to get to know her made it hard to stay grounded.

Reality set in and I backed away from her ready to remove the offer when she said, "I'd love to." Apparently my kissing skills were quite convincing.

A cottage with two bedrooms and one bath was the place I called home. Taking her on a quick tour, I ended by saying, "Make yourself comfortable on the couch. Would you like a beer?"

"That sounds good, thanks." Her phone rang and she ignored it after looking at the screen. As I walked toward her, I caught a glimpse of the screen and saw the same guy's picture on it. She'd said he was a best friend, but it seemed odd she didn't want to talk to him around me.

"How long have you two been friends?" I asked instead of

ignoring the elephant in the room.

"Since high school. Tell me about you instead. How long have you and Manny been friends?" The abrupt subject change didn't ease my mind any. Not being the type to hone in on another guy's girl, I decided small talk was the best route to go for.

"Since high school as well," I replied.

"Has he always been your wingman?" Bringing the bottle up to her lips, she held back her smile long enough to take a drink.

"We share the title. I don't do it too often, and that isn't a line. I saw your face as you stared out at the lake like someone seeing one of the seven wonders of the world. I told Manny I'd never seen someone so enchanted over such a simple thing. At least it seems simple to someone like me who grew up around the Great Lakes." Brushing her hair off her shoulder, I kissed her reddening skin. "Your skin is pretty warm. You may be sunburned in the morning."

"You can let me know." She sat her beer down before leaning forward to kiss me. So much for taking it slow. I'd have to take her word on the friends only comment. The few sips of alcohol seemed to make her more brazen. My jeans strained with arousal as her sudden move took me by surprise. When I'd met this woman earlier today, I'd never imagined her being so forward. It was beyond sexy.

Straddling my waist without breaking the kiss, her tongue parted my lips. My hands slid up her back, underneath her shirt, soaking in the warmth of her soft skin. I wanted more of her.

She removed her shirt to allow full access. As my gaze found her bikini top, I licked my lips before brushing them across the swell of her breasts. Cupping her breasts with my hands, my thumbs grazed across the fabric, teasing her taut nipples. With one hand, she reached back and pulled the string on the top, letting it fall forward exposing herself to me.

Damn this woman was hot. Desire spiked in me as my thumbs swept over her pebbled nipples, making her moan. She gasped when my lips kissed her bare skin, and I thought my jeans would burst open if I didn't remove them soon.

Lifting her off me, I stood up, and removed my shirt. Jeans and boxer briefs fell to the floor in a pile. Quickly, Marie stripped the rest of her clothes as she drank in the sight of me. The desire in her eyes as she gazed over my body made me ache to be inside her. Ripping open a condom, I slipped it on, never taking my eyes off her. Hovering above her, my hands went to work on making sure she was ready for me. As her body bucked beneath me, I couldn't wait anymore. I slipped inside her and groaned as her body gripped me.

MARIE

Being with Brady was like nothing I'd ever experienced. I'd only been with two men before and had known both for several weeks before it happened. My nature wasn't to sleep with someone I barely knew. Something about Brady created confidence in me. Trying new things on this journey was expected, but I'd never imagined those new things would garner an X rating. After coming together on the couch, Brady carried me to his bedroom for the next round. If I'd thought his hands had been talented, they were no match for his tongue.

The following morning, I woke to Brady grinning down at me. It was a beautiful sight to see first thing.

"Good morning, gorgeous. You do have a slight sunburn."

The events of the previous night came rushing back to me, coloring my cheeks with embarrassment. "Hi."

He leaned over to bite my earlobe and said, "Ready for another go?"

Releasing a barely audible, "Oh yeah," was all I could manage with the heat pooling between my legs. Brady put on a condom before thrusting inside me once more.

After at least two more sessions, we collapsed on the bed exhausted.

"Are you hungry?" he asked.

"Famished." My stomach growled to reiterate how hungry I was. We'd skipped dinner the night before, so it had been almost twenty-four hours since I'd eaten anything other than an ice cream.

"Stay here, just as you are, and I'll bring breakfast to you." The words, *just as you are*, were said in such a seductive tone, they made my legs quiver.

Breakfast in bed wasn't something I planned to turn down. A twinge of guilt again attacked my conscience when I grabbed my phone off the dresser. There were several missed calls and texts. When I dialed Jayce up, he answered on the first ring intensifying my guilty conscience.

"Woman, I am coming to meet you and follow you everywhere you go. You had me worried to death. What happened to you yesterday?"

"I spent most of the day touring the city, and my phone was on silent." It wasn't a complete lie. Both facts were true, but the silence of my phone didn't keep me from knowing when he called.

"Do you like your bacon chewy or crispy?" Brady called out from the kitchen. Tensing up, I waited for the inquiry to follow.

"Who was that?" Jayce inquired.

Covering the phone, I said, "The crispier, the better." Releasing a defeated breath, I returned to my phone call. "His name is Brady. I spent the day with him yesterday."

Jayce reacted much angrier than I expected. "What the hell? You mean you spent the *night* with him. That's not like you, Marie." It almost sounded as if he were jealous, although it was unlikely.

"I know but it's something new and exciting. I thought you'd be happy for me."

"Happy? That you've decided to start sleeping around with every guy you meet?" The moment the words were out, I could tell he wanted to take them back. He knew I wasn't that type of girl, and I could hear the hurt in his voice as he apologized. "I'm sorry, Mo. I didn't mean that."

"It's fine. Look, I'm having a fun time right now. Brady is very sweet, and he's cooking me breakfast. Then he's going to show me around town for the next few days. I want to get to know him better, and I want to spend as much time with him as I can. So, I'll call you when I'm leaving Michigan." The way Jayce had reacted hurt so much that I wanted to get off the phone as quickly as possible and have a few days away from him to think things over.

"Mo, please don't be mad at me." In my mind, I knew his forehead was creased, and his lips were in the saddest pout ever seen. I'd never been able to stay mad at Jayce for long when that look appeared on his face. Even the memory of it caused the guilt to eat away at me.

"I'm not, I promise. I'll text you every day, but I'll call you next week."

"Be safe, Mo. Tell Brady he better treat you right, or I'll hunt him down."

Brady walked into the room as I hung up. "Jayce?"

"Yeah, he was a little upset with me, but he'll get over it."

He nodded and left the room for only a moment before returning with a tray full of food. Scrambled eggs, bacon, toast, and strawberries filled my plate. My stomach gave another growl just before I took my first bite. Brady sat quietly, picking at his food. He barely finished more than a few bites by the time half my food was gone. Noticing his lack of appetite, I set my fork down and wiped my face with a napkin.

"What's wrong?"

"I like you, Marie. I think if we give this a little time, we could have something special." His words sounded promising, although his face displayed disappointment.

"Why do you make it sound like a bad thing?"

"It is if you're already in love with someone else."

"Jayce? We're just friends."

"How'd you know I meant Jayce?" he asked in a matter-of-fact tone.

"He's the only guy I've mentioned," I replied defensively. We were headed down a road I wasn't ready to travel, so I grabbed each of our plates and set them on the nightstand. Sitting forward on my knees, I cupped his face and leaned in to kiss him. His body responded to mine, pulling me closer. A firm grip on my ass lifted me up until I straddled his waist.

"I like you too, Brady. Now, what are your plans for me today?" He wiggled his eyebrows suggestively making me giggle. "Besides that."

"Damn. Can't blame a guy for trying. Have you ever been kayaking?"

"No, but it sounds like fun."

"Then it's settled. We'll go kayaking. And I get to see you in that sexy swimsuit again." Nipping at my neck, he grabbed me close once more. If we kept that up much longer, we might have stuck with his first plans.

The thought of seeing Brady in a kayak with no shirt on and possibly soaking wet at some point was a pleasing image in my head. The point of this trip was to experience things I'd missed out on in life, and Brady was uncharted territory.

JOURNAL ENTRY

So now Michigan is my favorite spot. Each time I meet someone, it gets better. I'm not sure it can get any better than Brady. In the past week, we've walked the shores of a great lake. We've been to the lighthouse, gotten homemade ice cream, taken a hike in the state park, and I've spent every night at his home.

We've ended each amazing day by consummating a room in his house. Things are moving faster than I'm used to. We've only known each other a week, but it's feels like much longer. Our attraction to each other is so intense, and in a few short hours, I'll be leaving him. I didn't sleep last night. As much as I wanted to enjoy being wrapped in his arms, I felt suffocated with the thought of moving on. He's begged me to stay longer, but I have to stay on track.

We've promised to try to keep in touch, but I don't know if he'll wait for me, or if I'll be able to wait for him either. He's someone I will carry with me in my fondest memory, but distance may keep us from being anything more than a wonderful week of euphoria. I'm going to curl up under him one more time this morning before I get on the road again. It's been nice having someone to wake up with each morning. Our connection has grown strong in such a short time that it's as scary as it is exciting.

I hope I have the strength to leave.

∞ *Marie*

5

MARIE

As my weight hit the mattress, Brady rolled over to lay his arm across my stomach. Teardrops fell from my eyes at the thought of losing the touch of his skin against mine. Fingers splayed across my stomach, moving inside my shirt, slowly grazing a trail of heat up my skin. His scent, his touch, seduced me, making me want more. A strong hand cupped my breast, and I moaned as his lips caressed my neck.

Our last time together was slower and more intense as we took time to cherish every caress and every tremor of our release. Afterward, we lay together in silence. Neither of us wanted to talk about the inevitable good-bye rapidly approaching. Kissing my forehead, he combed fingers through my hair.

"Stay a few more days?" he whispered with desperation.

"I can't," my voice choked out. His thumb caught the tear

escaping my eye, and he wiped it away. "You could always quit your job and come with me?" I suggested only half kidding.

"If anyone could convince me to, it's you." His nose nuzzled my cheek.

"So you'll think about it?" I teased, knowing he couldn't drop everything.

"Sweetheart, I wish I could. You know I do."

Brady got in the shower while I packed. Tossing everything in the car, I ran back inside to find a pad of paper. I jotted a quick note telling him I couldn't bear to say good-bye and would call him later, ending with a plea for forgiveness. As I started out the door, he cleared his throat behind me. Standing there with only a towel around his waist, I shivered as my eyes raked over his body.

"You were going to leave me a note?" Brady asked with an inflection of hurt.

"I'm a coward."

He closed the space between us, and I cradled my head against his still wet chest. The water from his hair dripped onto my head as he held me. Stepping out of his embrace, I walked toward the door.

"I'll call you tonight."

"Good, I want to know you're safe. I put something in your bag while you were in the shower earlier," Brady said.

"Your T-shirt?" I inquired with a glint of hope in my voice. He nodded affirmatively. Every night, I'd slept in his T-shirt from Hard Rock Las Vegas where he'd spent his twenty-first birthday. "Are you sure?"

"I like the thought of you sleeping in it. Makes me feel closer to you."

Tears threatened to fall that would give Niagara Falls a run for its money. I was sure it couldn't get any more heartbreaking than this moment.

"Thank you for everything." Before Brady could respond, I ran out the door without looking back. Eyes straight ahead, I drove off, trying ineffectively to ignore him in the rearview as he stood at the door watching me go.

For the first hour of my drive, I cried until my head hurt. Three hours later, I pulled over to take a break and stretch my legs.

When I picked up my phone to call Jayce, I saw a text from Brady. It was sent a few minutes after I left him, and it simply read:

Brady: I could easily fall in love with you.

I typed a quick message in response.

Me: It wouldn't be hard for me either. I miss you already.

Jayce picked up on the second ring. "Hey, gorgeous! On your way to beautiful Canada?"

"Yeah." The word dripped with sorrow.

Jayce's voice dropped to a less than excited tone. "Was it that difficult to leave him this morning?"

"You have no idea, Jayce. I miss you. And we still have another month until New York." Loneliness had crept into my life like an unwanted houseguest. Being sad about leaving Brady intensified the feelings of emptiness I'd had since leaving home.

"Don't cry, Mo. I spoke to Constance yesterday. She's excited to meet you." I dabbed my face with a tissue from my purse.

"I'm excited too. I only wish you were here with me."

"I love you, baby girl." Jayce always called me baby girl to cheer me up. He'd mimic Shemar Moore each time, which always made me smile.

"I love you too, Jayce."

So many emotions fought inside me throughout the day. The people at customs must have taken pity on my pathetic looking self because I went through easier than I imagined. Then again, I'd probably watched too many movies and expected a crazy event to happen. Homesickness encompassed me, and I began to think I wouldn't be able to fulfill my dreams alone. My mind bounced between Brady and Jayce. My heart missed them both.

The road seemed lonelier than ever as I drove farther into the new country. Per the navigation system, I was merely an hour away from the bed and breakfast. The phone rang, I pushed the hands-free answer button, and my chest tightened when the deep voice spoke.

"Hey, sweetheart." The despair in Brady's voice made mine crack with emotions.

"It's good to hear your voice." He gave a light chuckle.

"Yours too, beautiful. This house feels empty without you. Have you made it to your next destination yet?"

"I'll be there shortly. Give me a few days to get acquainted with Constance, and I'll Skype with you one day if you want."

"Oh, I want. I miss your gorgeous face. At least we took

lots of pictures. If anyone walks in this house, they might try to send me to the looney bin. I have your picture up as my screen saver. It runs through all of the ones we took." Together, we'd captured as many moments shared as possible, which accumulated to around a hundred photos. The one of us taken at the ice-cream parlor on the last day was my favorite. Brady had taken a selfie of us sharing an ice-cream cone and just before he snapped it, I'd shoved it forward to smear his face and he was in the middle of a laugh.

"That's almost as creepy as you watching me sleep." I laughed.

"But not quite as creepy as you watching me eat ice cream." Brady echoed my laughter, and we were in a comfortable place again. "I'll let you off the phone. Text me when you get there, so I know you made it safely."

"I will. I'll talk to you soon."

I spotted the red brick building that the GPS warned was less than half a mile away. A large plantation house that you would expect to see in many of the southern states, trails of flowers, and a wraparound front porch gave it a stunning setting. Abandoning my bags in the car, I walked up to knock on the front door.

A young woman with an auburn-colored pixie haircut opened the door and gave a welcoming smile.

"Can I help you?"

"My name's Marie. I'm looking for Constance?"

The young woman's smile grew larger and more genuine.

"I should've known it was you. Jayce described you to a tee!" She threw her arms around my shoulders, hugging me close, and then she backed away and blushed. "Sorry, I'm Constance… or you can call me Connie."

Instantly, I felt a connection to Constance, much like the one for Jayce when we'd first met. Constance led the way upstairs, second door on the left, and gave me a moment to get acquainted with my surroundings. My home for the next few weeks was quaint and felt very homey in comparison to the hotel rooms I'd been staying in. For an even homier feel, I completely unpacked my bags, filling the closet and drawers. The last thing I pulled out was Brady's shirt. Inside of it was a note.

MARIE,

THE PAST WEEK WITH YOU HAS BEEN THE BEST WEEK OF MY LIFE. MY FAVORITE MOMENTS WERE WAKING UP TO SEE YOUR PORCELAIN SKIN AGAINST THE DARK SILK SHEETS ON MY BED. WHEN YOU SLEEP, YOU LOOK LIKE A CARTOON CHARACTER BECAUSE YOUR BREATHS BLOW YOUR HAIR FORWARD, AND THE ONLY PIECE YOU'RE MISSING IS THE "MEE MEE MEE" SOUND. THAT MAY NOT SOUND TOO CUTE TO YOU, BUT I FIND IT ADORABLE AND YOUR MOST UNFORGETTABLE TRAIT. NOW LOOK IN THE MIRROR AT YOUR LEFT SHOULDER BLADE, AND DON'T WORRY, IT'S NOT PERMANENT. AFTER YOU LOOK, TURN THIS LETTER OVER.

I MISS YOU ALREADY, AND YOU'RE IN THE SHOWER AS I WRITE THIS, SO I KNOW WHEN YOU LEAVE IT WILL BE EVEN WORSE.

YOURS,

BRADY

My room had a private bathroom attached so I removed my shirt and went to use the mirror. Twisting my body to view the back of my shoulder, I saw a red heart drawn there with *Brady's* written across it. With the letter still in hand, I turned it over to see the last part.

YOU HAVE MY HEART.

Never would I get a man's name tattooed on my body, but part of me was sad this sweet gesture would fade away. Constance was just in the next room so I ran to grab her so she could take a picture. When I explained it all to her, Constance bit her lip, and her eyes fell into puppy dog mode when she cooed over how romantic it was.

"You have to tell me all about this man. He sounds very swoon worthy."

"He kind of is," I stated dreamily. "Right now, I need a shower to clean the road off of me. After that, I'd love to spend some time with you."

Constance grabbed a set of fresh towels for my bathroom. She left them on the sink for me after showing me how to run the shower. Hot water rained down over my body, soothing my aching muscles from the long drive. Images of the last shower with Brady invaded my mind sending warm tingles coursing over my body.

Drying off with the soft fluffy towel felt so wonderful against my skin, I folded it over my chest and walked around the room in it while organizing a few more things. I took the collection of shot glasses for my grandfather and put them in a drawer to prevent accidentally breaking any. After everything was stored away, I slipped into a pair of lounging pants and a

T-shirt I'd bought in Michigan that read Ludington Unsalted.

Before going downstairs, I took a moment to explore the upstairs. Each room had been rented out on the expansive second floor of this house. Every door contained a chalkboard sign for you to write a message of your own on, whether it was your name or just a greeting or even "do not disturb."

Glancing back at my door, I noticed the chalkboard read *Welcome to the Family*, and it made me smile. As I padded my bare feet across the hardwood floor to the top of the stairwell, I had to squelch the urge to slide down the banister out of respect for my hosts. Jayce would have done it in a minute, and the thought made me giggle.

At the bottom of the stairs, I could turn right to go to the dining room or left to the living room. Constance sat in the room to the left making my choice easy.

"Mind if I join you?"

Constance set her book down and pulled her knees beneath her to free up part of the couch.

"Please do. I made some tea if you want some," she said pointing to teapot on the coffee table in front of her. The orange scent of the tea wafted into my nose as I poured myself a cup, a teaspoon of honey stirred in for a little sweetness. Crossing my legs underneath me, I curled up on the couch next to Constance.

"Did you get all settled in?"

"Yes. This place is amazing. I'd never leave if I lived here." Releasing a slow puff of air, I blew on my tea to cool it down.

Constance gave a smile, but it didn't reach her eyes.

"Most days, I'm content here. I'd like a chance to do what

you're doing, though. I've never been anywhere. I envy your quest."

"It's lonelier than I imagined it would be. I miss my family and friends, especially Jayce. We've never been apart for this long before." The warm liquid coated my throat as I breathed in the steam from my cup.

"Jayce is one of my favorite cousins. I can completely understand how you could miss him. I've tried to get him to visit, but it hasn't worked out. Has he told you any stories from our childhood?"

The prospect of hearing about Jayce's younger days had me giddy.

"A little, but I'd love to hear another perspective. I'm willing to bet there are some good embarrassing stories he's left out."

Constance laughed at my eagerness.

"Did he tell you that we played Barbies together?"

Tea spewed forth from my mouth in surprise.

"No! I mean, he's never been mister macho, thinking guys can't do girl stuff, but Barbies are a whole other matter."

"He'd come over to my house, and I'd offer to play video games with him, but he always wanted to play with my Barbies instead. My parents acted as judges, and we'd have beauty pageants for them: evening gown, talent contest, the whole shebang." Our laughter filled the room until a text came through on Constance's phone. After glancing at it, she jumped up excitedly.

"I lost track of time! I have a surprise for you!"

She ran up the stairs and returned a few moments later

with a laptop. Setting it on the coffee table, she began typing away. I watched patiently, assuming an explanation would follow. Constance turned the laptop, and Jayce's face was on the screen.

"Hello, sunshine," he exclaimed.

Sliding to the floor and getting eye level with the screen, I reached out to touch him as though he were tangible.

"I've missed that face."

Constance waved at Jayce.

"Sorry. I almost forgot, cuz. I'll let you two talk for a while." I mouthed a thank-you to Constance before she left the room.

"Are you and Connie getting to know each other?" Jayce asked.

"Yep. In fact, we're thinking of having a Barbie beauty pageant later." The smirk on my face couldn't be helped as I used my newfound information against him.

Jayce's eyes bulged, and he yelled out, "Constance!" loud enough that a cackle of laughter resounded from the other room. I snorted and Jayce rolled his eyes on the screen.

"I think I need to pay your mother a visit and get some embarrassing stories in reprisal," he taunted. After more shameless teasing, the conversation took a more serious direction. "Have you spoken to Brady?" When he posed the question, he almost seemed afraid of the answer. His eyes were averted from the screen, and his lips formed a thin line.

"He called earlier. I asked him to give me a few days because I want to visit with Connie." The part I left out was that I needed a little distance from him because the intense emotions I had from our short time together sort of frightened me.

The familiar look of anxiety came over his face as he asked, "Do you love him?"

The question I hoped he wouldn't ask lingered in the air. It was one I'd been questioning since I left Michigan.

"I care about him, but we've only known each other for a little more than a week. I don't feel like that's enough time to know."

Jayce appeared to deflate a bit in relief at my answer. It was a strange reaction; one I wasn't expecting. Before I could dwell too much on it, he changed the subject again. "I got a promotion at work."

"Really? I thought you'd quit since you were only using it to save money for me."

"I was, but I like it. Zeb promoted me to manager. It came with a nice pay raise." Jayce went on to tell me how Zeb's previous manager had been his brother-in-law. When his sister walked in on her husband sleeping with a female customer, she'd kicked him to the curb and so had Zeb.

Constance returned to the living room and saw we were still talking, so she turned to leave.

"Wait, Connie. Come back. Jayce, can I call you another night this week? I want to talk to Connie a bit."

"Sure, Mo. Thanks for helping us out, Connie. I'll talk to you both later."

Constance closed her laptop and poured another cup of tea for us.

"I had no clue about you and Jayce. I thought you guys

were only friends."

My forehead creased with confusion, and I tried to think back to what we could have said that made her make the assumption. "We are nothing more than friends."

"I don't know you that well, Marie, but I've seen enough lovestruck people to know that expression on your face when you saw him. You're in love with him."

Shifting uncomfortably in my seat I affirmed, "I love Jayce, but it's a best friend love."

Constance stared down at her teacup and scoffed. "Why are we sitting here sipping tea like a couple of old women? How about a margarita?"

"Now you're talking." Alcohol would help me forget the conflicting emotions I was having between Brady and Jayce for a bit. I'd never had trouble talking with Jayce about men until Brady came along. Now the subject had us both uncomfortable. It didn't make sense, and it hurt my head to think about it too much.

In the kitchen, we blended lime margarita mix with double shots of tequila in each. Lining the rims of the cups with salt, we clanked our glasses together and downed the first drink. Grabbing the blender, we carried it into the living room to finish it off as we talked.

"You and Jayce have been friends all these years, and it's never turned into anything romantic? Haven't you ever even been curious?" Constance sipped on her drink as her eyes danced with curiosity.

"Not in reality."

"What the heck does that mean?" Constance asked, her

face scrunched in confusion.

"Lately… well, first if you repeat what I'm about to tell you, I may never forgive you." Constance made an X over her heart with one finger and then closed an imaginary zipper over her lips. "Lately, I've been having sexual dreams about him."

Margarita sprayed from her lips in surprise.

"Somehow I didn't expect that to be your answer. Does sex with Brady match up to the dreams with Jayce? Forget I asked that. It's none of my business."

"Just between us girls, Brady is amazing in every way. There's something about those dreams though. I guess it's the fantasy aspect. Reality, even with Jayce, probably wouldn't live up to the hype."

"Do you think you were lonely or truly having feelings for Jayce? I mean, did the dreams stop after you and Brady met?" Constance really loved the girl talk and was asking for more information than I felt comfortable giving, mostly because I didn't know the answers to a lot of these questions.

"I'm not sure what the dreams mean. I had one after I met Brady too. You're the only person I've told about them. I could never admit it to Jayce and telling Brady would hurt his pride and his feelings… Enough about that. I want to know more about Jayce as a child. I need things to use against him."

Constance filled me in on a few more embarrassing stories of Jayce as a child, and I hoped I wouldn't drink so much that I'd forget to use them against him later. It was easy to see that neither of us were big drinkers because, after two full glasses, we were both giggling uncontrollably.

The next two hours, we drank margaritas until Constance's parents woke up due to our piercing laughter. It wasn't the best first impression for me to give, but it seemed to be worse for Constance. Her mother was outraged and politely, yet sternly, asked me to go upstairs. Eavesdropping accidentally as I made my way upstairs, I heard Constance defend her age saying she was an adult and could do what she wanted.

Constance's mother seemed as much distraught as she was disappointed, although I wasn't sure why. Too drunk to reason with anyone at that moment, I crawled into bed to pass out.

Breakfast hours were from six until ten. Around nine thirty, I stumbled out of bed and grabbed a robe to cover my half-dressed state. My hair had a mind of its own as it stood up in different directions, but I didn't care. The desperate need for a strong cup of java motivated me to make an appearance downstairs. Trying to do two things at once, fixing my hair and walking, proved impossible as I tripped on the last step and fell into the arms of another guest. "I'm sorry, sir."

With a creepy grin, he replied.

"You can fall for me anytime."

The cheesy line made my eyes roll until they saw brain, and I shuddered as I walked away from him. Constance was serving breakfast to a few patrons, so her mother walked over to the table.

"Hi, Marie. I'm sorry our introduction last night wasn't a happier one. I'm Constance's mom, Ruth."

"No apology necessary." If anyone should apologize, I felt it should be me because I caused a disagreement with her daughter.

Ruth flipped open a notebook and grabbed a pen from behind her ear.

"How do you like your eggs, dear, and do you prefer bacon or sausage?"

The margaritas from last night attempted retaliation as my stomach grumbled. "Scrambled eggs and dry toast would be good this morning."

Ruth snickered.

"Hangover special on the way."

JOURNAL ENTRY

For the fourth night in a row, Constance and I sat up talking about everything in our lives. After the margarita fiasco the first night, we've stuck with hot tea and cocoa as our nightly drink of choice. Most nights, we've fallen asleep on the living room couch, too tired to walk up to our rooms. Even though we've talked about everything, I still sense Connie is hiding something from me.

We skyped with Jayce one night and surprised him by having a Barbie pageant ready for his judging. He turned red with embarrassment at first but then got into it, and Connie's girl ended up the winner. They still have a huge toy room filled with things for visiting kids, and we both have enjoyed playing in there after everyone goes to sleep. I never had slumber parties as a kid, but Connie has helped me be childlike again. We even built a fort and slept inside it one night.

Her parents have refused to let me pay for my room, so I'm repaying their kindness by working for them during my stay. They've tried to refuse the help as well, but I haven't backed down. My first week has passed, and I feel like family surrounds me. I haven't spoken to Brady since I got here. This afternoon, Connie has somewhere to go with Ruth, so I'm going to try to Skype with him at that time.

I hope he's happy to hear from me.

∞Marie

6

BRADY

When Marie texted me about skyping, I jumped at the chance to see her beautiful face. Waiting patiently for the sound of her arrival, I fidgeted with my hair a moment. As she appeared on screen, I noticed she wore my Hard Rock Cafe T-shirt and a pair of cut-off shorts. I hardened instantly at the sight of her.

We both began waving excitedly and then erupted in laughter.

"We're dorks," Marie admitted with a snort.

"Yep. You're the sexiest dork I've ever seen, though," I flirted.

"You're pretty sexy yourself."

"Did you find the note I left on the shirt?" I'd been anxious to know if she thought it was a sweet gesture or somewhat stalker-like. Obviously I hoped for sweet.

Tugging the shirt off her shoulder to show me the now faded heart, she acknowledged, "I love it. I only wish it would stay around longer. I had Connie take a picture of it for me. When did you draw that?"

"Our last night. You were asleep, and the body paints were still by the bed from when we used them together. It gave me the idea, so I used a Sharpie so it would linger a little." As I recalled the memory, my voice lowered with the desire washing over me. Painting Marie's body had been one of our most sensual moments. At first, she'd giggled as it tickled her, but before long the passion had won over, eliciting moans of pleasure instead.

Thoughts swept me away into fantasy until I groaned in frustration.

"This is torture! I love seeing your face, but I want to touch you, hold you in my arms." She sucked her lips between her teeth, and I growled. "You bite your lip when you get excited." Lip biting was the first sign I knew she was feeling frisky. Nights when we'd be taking walks on the beach or sitting in the sand talking, she'd bite her lip as her mind started to wander with naughty thoughts.

"I must be biting it hard now. Every time I take a shower, I can feel you in there with me. Your shirt against my body makes it…" she stopped talking when my eyes closed, and I groaned again.

"How comfortable are you with me?" I asked a moment later as an idea popped into my mind.

"Considering I did several things with you I've never done

before, sexual and nonsexual, I'd say pretty comfortable. Why?"

"Have you ever had phone or cybersex?"

"No," she admitted with a hard swallow.

"Me neither. So let's experience another first together. Strip for me." Pausing momentarily, she appeared uneasy. We'd seen each other naked too many times for her to be self-conscious now. Making the first move, I stood up and removed my shirt. "Your turn."

Grinning mischievously, I saw the light in her eyes as she realized she couldn't resist me now. I watched as she ran over to the door and locked it before turning on a little background music. The first thing she removed was the T-shirt, leaving her bra exposed. Turning her back to the screen, she reached her arms around and unclasped the bra, peering over her shoulder as she tossed it away. Turning back to face me, her arms crossed over her naked breasts.

"You're such a tease," I grunted. Seeing her standing there in all her glory made me miss her even more. Not only did I miss the feel of her skin against mine, the soft graze of her nails against my back as I moved inside her, the gentle kisses she peppered over my chest, her scent, but I missed her warmth and her laughter as we lay naked in bed talking afterwards.

Her shorts fell to the floor next. In only a pair of lace panties and still covering her chest, she nodded toward me. As I removed my pants, there was no doubt, even through my boxers, I'd been happy to see her.

MARIE

Channeling my inner stripper, I moved my body as sensually as I could, hoping I looked like Demi Moore in *Striptease* rather than Elaine from *Seinfeld*. Twisting around, I trailed my fingers down my side before turning to reveal my breasts. Brady licked his lips and removed his boxer briefs.

As the heat in the room increased, there was a knock on my door. A squeaked, "Just a minute!" flew from my mouth in a panic. I gathered my clothes and whispered to Brady, "Put some clothes on in case they see the screen. I'll be right back." A quick kiss blown across my palm toward the screen, and then I opened the door to see Constance looking upset. "What's wrong?"

"Can we talk?"

"Sure. Give me a minute. Brady's on Skype. I'll tell him good night and meet you in your room?" Admittedly it was terrible timing, but Constance seemed so upset it would've been selfish for me to turn her away to have a moment of passion.

"Thanks, Mo."

Brady was still shirtless when I returned.

"You have to go?" he asked with disappointment.

"Connie's upset about something. We can try this again another time. I'm sorry. Can I call you tomorrow?"

"Please do. Sweet dreams, sweetheart."

Closing the laptop, I sat on the bed for a moment to cool myself down from the heated conversation we abruptly ended. With a quick glance in the mirror, I checked myself over for flushed cheeks or crooked clothing to avoid any embarrassing conversation about what she'd interrupted and headed down the hallway.

Constance sat on the floor of her room, with her back against the bed, staring at the wall. I gave a gentle knock before entering.

Constance looked up and requested, "Please close the door."

Squatting down beside her, I bumped her shoulder with mine. "This sounds serious."

"Did you mean it when you said that your trip had been too lonely?" Flashing big doe eyes at me with a sparkle of hope in them, I was taken aback by her question.

"I did. I've met a lot of pretty cool people along the way, but the in-between times can be pretty depressing. Why?"

"I've never been anywhere. I wondered if you would let me finish your excursion with you." Personally, I loved the idea, and my face displayed that joy, but I also knew it was somewhat sudden. Constance added, "I'll pay my way of course."

"To be honest, you'd only have to pay for your food. Everything else I would have paid for regardless. It's not like we can't share hotel rooms. I'd love you to go. Can I ask what brought this up?" I hoped the argument with her mother hadn't made her want to run away or anything so drastic.

"I haven't been completely honest with you. The other night, when my mother flipped out about me drinking, it's because I'm not supposed to have alcohol. When I was born, I was ten weeks premature. It was touch and go, and I spent the first three months of my life in the hospital. During that time, they discovered a heart defect. They told my parents it was too extensive, and I wouldn't survive past the age of five at the oldest. Here I am, at age twenty-one, proving them wrong. After our night of drinking, my mother made me see the doctor today, and he said there had been no change. My parents are very overprotective. To make a long story short, I've already outlived my life expectancy by sixteen years, and I've gotten nothing to show for that accomplishment. That's why I want to travel with you. You've inspired me."

The information spilled out of Constance with such grace and speed I barely had time to register it all. Did that mean she was so fragile she could go any day now? A barrage of questions flooded my mind. Constance patiently sat by and left me to take it in.

After sitting there in silence, I finally found my voice again.

"I'd love to have you with me, as long as you tell me if it's ever too much for you." Another question came to mind. "Does Jayce know?"

"No one in the family knows. My parents didn't want people to baby me, which is a laugh because they baby me more than anyone. Don't get me wrong. They've let me lead a semi-normal life, but I haven't ever had a boyfriend. I'm now living vicariously through your love triangle."

Index finger pointed toward my chest, I questioned the last comment. "I have a love triangle?"

Constance rolled her eyes. "Jayce and Brady."

With an overdramatic sigh, I reiterated what I'd said before.

"I've told you Jayce and I are friends. And as far as Brady, I'm not sure you can call it love." An idea I had perked me up. "I have one condition."

Constance beamed. "Name it."

"No more mention of feelings for Jayce or a love triangle." Constance heaved a sigh and made an X over her heart with her index finger in response.

"When do we leave?" she asked. A companion was the one thing my dream trip had been missing. Ruth and Martin, Constance's parents, took the news easier than either of us expected. They had conditions of their own, which were reasonable considering the situation. I made a promise to watch over Constance for them and to do my best to keep her safe. I thanked them profusely for allowing their daughter to travel with me. In three days, we would leave for our next stop, Maine.

Constance stood in the middle of the room with clothes strewn all over the floor, bed, and chair when I went to check on her packing situation. I twirled around in a circle looking at all of the chaos.

"Did a tornado blow through here while I was napping?"

Constance whirled around, with frazzled hair and wide eyes, and said, "I hate all my clothes."

I exploded with laughter. "Is that what this is all about?"

Constance's eyes grew even wider.

"I've never been anywhere! I've never had much of a chance to date either."

Hand on my hip I cocked an eyebrow. "You help run a bed and breakfast. You meet people all the time."

Constance had a handful of clothes, and she tossed them in the air with frustration. "Single men do not frequent bed and breakfasts. Our clientele normally consists of happy couples or elderly women." She scrunched her face a moment and said, "Sorry, no offense."

"None was taken. I wouldn't have picked a B&B either if it weren't for Jayce, so I get what you're saying. So you plan on meeting a guy?"

"You did." She had a valid point. It hadn't been my intention to meet anyone when I planned this trip. I didn't want Constance to be discouraged if she never met anyone.

"True, but I was by myself. I didn't have a choice but to interact with people."

"I want to meet people, Mo. I need to make more friends. Will you please take me shopping, so I can find some new things?" Pouting lips, hands folded in prayer, she batted her big doe eyes at me, and I caved.

Shopping was my least favorite thing to do in the world. It was a necessity, never something I did voluntarily or for pleasure. Constance was in such a state I didn't have the heart to let her down.

"Let's go shopping."

Four hours later, we unloaded ten bags containing new clothes for both of us. New coats for the winter months, new bathing suits for the beaches, and we each bought a couple of fun dresses to wear out on the town. Shopping had never been enjoyable until I experienced it with Constance.

The room still sat in shambles with the littering of clothes everywhere. Ruth had refused to clean it up and told Constance she would need to collect the clothes herself and pack them up for charity if she no longer wanted them.

Before unpacking the new clothes, I helped Constance get rid of everything she had outgrown physically or fashionably. Three trash bags full of clothes were propped beside the door when we finished. The next step was to pack all the new clothes into her luggage. Luckily we were very similar in size and could get away with wearing the other's clothes if needed.

We were up until one in the morning getting everything together and making lists, so we didn't forget important items. The last time I'd looked at the clock, it had been one fifteen. I must have passed out shortly after.

Constance awoke first and in the best mood of her life. This trip was more than a vacation. It was a life experience she desperately needed. Sitting up next to the bed, my head was bent sideways. Constance gently lifted my head and slid a pillow under it before taking a shower.

The considerate gesture woke me up, and I groaned as my neck cracked and popped. Groggily I stood up, and my socked feet slid across the hardwood floor all the way back to my bedroom. The clock read six o'clock, and our plan was to leave at eight. A few quick taps and I set up an alarm for an hour later and fell face-first onto the mattress.

JOURNAL ENTRY

Constance joined me on my journey today. It makes me happy to have the company. The loneliness I've had since I left Brady has vanished. Our ride to Maine was long, but we survived it with music, trivia, and other select road games. When we crossed the state line, we found the first nice-looking hotel and checked in. We both fell into the bed exhausted. When I woke up, I had four missed calls from Jayce. I called him back and found out he's booked his flight for New York and needed to give me the information so we could pick him up at the airport. I'm nervous and excited to see him again.

If I hadn't known about Constance's heart condition, I wouldn't have thought she was any different than a normal twentysomething. She's full of life and energy. She's become the sister I never knew I wanted in life. I never hated being an only child, but now I knew what I was missing.

Today, we're going to explore Maine. Connie's favorite author is Stephen King, so she is exceptionally happy this was our first state to visit. We're going to explore as much as possible.

In two weeks, we leave for New York where I will finally see Jayce.

∞Marie

1

MARIE

"Get up! Get up, get up, *get up*!" Constance shouted jumping on the mattress next to where I *was* sleeping peacefully.

"You are overstaying your welcome on this trip very quickly," I mumbled groggily.

"It's almost eleven. We need to eat something, and then we have the Stephen King tour at two, so we need to go now! Get *up*!"

Grumbling curse words under my breath, I took the quickest shower possible, so we'd have time to eat. Constance had to have food with her medicine. Normally the first day in a state, I would rest from the long drive the day before. I'd wander around the hotel enjoying the pool, the gym, and any other amenities they offered. Constance, however, was a doer. She wanted to see and do everything. She didn't consider the fact that we had two full weeks, and that one day wouldn't make a difference. I had to empathize and remember this probably felt like the last wish to Constance, and she only wanted to enjoy it to the fullest.

Her wish wouldn't be denied, so I didn't argue when pulled from a wonderful sleep. The hot water of the shower helped me put on a happy face and begin to get excited about the day too.

Constance was on a steady high during the entire excursion. The tour included sites from different movies and even a pass by the star's residence. My knowledge of Stephen King came from a few books and movies but was nowhere near the extent of Constance's. She stayed in a permanent state of awe during the entire trip. When we stepped off the van at the end of the day, she was exhausted and a bit grouchy.

"What do you want to do tomorrow? Any ideas?" Her silence had me worried, so I tried to elicit conversation from her to make sure she wasn't homesick or worse, physically sick.

"I don't know," she grumbled.

"We could see the port or move to a new city to see what we can find. Do you want to look up some ideas on the laptop?"

"I don't know," Constance repeated.

We hadn't known each other long, but I knew something was off. She'd never been this quiet.

"Okay. We can call Jayce if you want—"

"I said I don't know!" Constance screeched. She collapsed to the floor in exhaustion and began to gasp for air.

In a panic, I fell to my knees beside her.

"What can I do, Connie?"

"Hospital," she croaked out through several strangled breaths.

That's all I needed to hear before I picked up the phone and immediately dialed 911. Explaining the situation to the operator was difficult since Constance was unable to speak much. All I could relay was what I saw with my own two eyes.

Paramedics were on their way. Trying to remain calm, I held Constance's hand and stayed next to her.

"Connie, I'm scared, is there something I can do to help you?"

Constance shook her head as she tried to take soothing breaths. When the paramedics arrived, they had a torrent of questions about her health condition. I tried to relay everything I knew, but felt like it wasn't enough. Following the ambulance, I dialed the person who could always calm me down.

"Hey, beautiful, what's up?" Jayce said cheerily.

Hyperventilating when I heard his voice caused him to panic because he knew I didn't freak out easily.

"Something's wrong with Connie," I cried out between sobs.

Jayce tried to stay calm. I could hear him taking a few deep breaths before speaking again.

"What happened, Marie?"

"Her excitement over today may have been too much, and it's my fault. She's like a sister to me, Jayce. I'm scared." Her parents might never forgive me if I let something happen to their daughter. Jayce didn't even know how serious this could be yet.

"Call me back as soon as you know what's wrong. If I need to fly out there today, I will. In the meantime, I'll call my aunt and uncle and let them know what's going on."

Relieved not to have to make another call, I replied, "Thank you. I know I should've called them first but—"

"No need to explain," Jayce interrupted. "It's better if I call them. They know me, and right now, you sound so panicked it would only scare them."

The registration desk was only a few feet from the emergency room entrance. "Constance MacNeil was brought in here by ambulance. She has a heart defect. Can you tell me how she is doing?"

"How are you related to her? I can only give information to the family."

Emotional truth was all I had in this moment. "I'm her sister."

"They're running some tests now. I'll have the doctor find you when they have more news. There's a waiting room down the hall to your left."

I called Jayce back to tell him what little information I had obtained. Honestly, I didn't know any more about Constance, and I didn't want him to worry.

In the waiting room, a television hung on the wall. It stayed on the same channel while continuous news footage with a ticker of information filled the bottom of the screen. My eyes were focused on the TV as if I was reading it intently, but my mind raced with worry for Constance.

Noises in the room caught my attention as I watched a family grieve over bad news being delivered by a doctor. The young couple held on to each other and their small child as the devastation rolled across their features and spilled from their eyes. A deep ache in my chest grew as I feared going through those emotions myself over Constance. I needed to keep my mind from going to the worst-case scenario.

Grabbing my phone out of my purse, I texted Brady without telling him what was going on. He didn't know Constance, so it would give me something different to talk about without worrying more.

Me: Are you busy?

Brady: Never too busy for you. How's the trip?

Me: We're in Maine right now, took a Stephen King tour today. Connie is sleeping so that's why I'm texting instead of calling

Brady: Is it nice having someone along with you?

Me: Definitely. She's practically like a sister to me already.

The distraction didn't work. My mind raced with thoughts more than ever as I pretended nothing was wrong.

Me: I need to go. I'll talk to you later?

Brady: Sounds good. Be safe, Marie.

The doctor came out an hour later and explained that Constance had suffered an episode due to overexcitement. In layman's terms, her heart had been overworked with the excitement of her activities, and she needed some rest. He informed me the best medicine would be two days of complete rest before trying to do anything strenuous. And even after, she needed to take breaks every few hours to sit and relax.

"She cannot miss a single dose of her medicine," he said.

"She's been taking it every day."

"She has three doses a day to take, and she missed a few doses this week which is what caused the episode."

Why hadn't I learned more about Constance's condition and medical needs before agreeing to let her come on this trip? The doctor gave me a rundown of all the details, so I could make sure this didn't happen again.

She agreed to the terms, and when we went back to the hotel, I left Constance to nap and went out to buy several games for us to play in the room. Upon my return, Constance was sitting up in the bed watching the weather channel.

"Are you worried about storms or something?"

"There's nothing else on to watch," Constance said before pointing the remote at the TV and turning it off. "I'm going to get a flight home tomorrow," she stated sullenly.

My mouth fell open in surprise at the revelation, and I dropped the shopping bags from my hands. "What? Why?"

"I doubt your dream trip included going to the hospital or visiting the states only to explore their different hotel rooms. You need the freedom to investigate, and I'm holding you back." Constance's eyes misted with tears threatening to spill over.

Taking a seat next to Constance on the bed, I reached up to place a hand on her shoulder.

"If I thought you were a burden, I'd let you know. The doctor said you needed to take breaks. We'll lie on the beach when there's one nearby. Or we'll visit different state parks and take in waterfalls or relax and have a picnic. Even in big cities like New York, we'll take a carriage ride through Central

Park, take in a Broadway show, visit the 9/11 memorial. We can do plenty of things that are relaxing as long as you take your medicine the way you're supposed to. Right now, I want you to put all your pills on the bed and give me the lowdown on when you take them and how many, etcetera. I'm going to make a schedule of medicinal dosages."

Constance's tears spilled forth, and she wrapped her arms around my neck.

"Thank you. I love you, Mo." She had picked up the nickname Jayce always used for me, which tugged at my heart strings and made me miss him more.

"I love you, too."

A FaceTime request from Brady interrupted our moment. Our attempt at cyber relations in Canada was the last time we'd spoken.

"Answer it," Constance urged. "I'm going to take a bubble bath."

She left the room, and I checked my face and hair in the mirror before answering. "Hey, Brady!"

"Hello, beautiful!" he responded happily. "I was afraid you weren't going to answer. How're things going with Constance?"

"Really well."

"That's great. I've been worried about you being alone all the time. Although, I wish I could be the one with you."

"How's Manny?"

Brady chuckled.

"Feeling withdrawals from his wingman days."

"You don't owe me anything, Brady. You should date.

You're an amazing guy who any girl would be lucky to find." Stringing him along was never my intention. I felt selfish for asking him to wait, especially when I couldn't promise if we'd ever even see each other again.

"There's only one girl I'm interested in at this moment. In case that wasn't clear, it's you." His smile was as genuine as his heart, one of the things I adored about him.

It was my turn to laugh softly.

"I picked that up. But, seriously Brady, if you meet someone else, don't hesitate to give it a chance."

"Is this your way of breaking up with me?" Brady inquired.

"It's my way of giving you the freedom to keep on living. Who knows if we'll ever see each other again." Constance's recent episode gave me a new outlook on life. I wanted Brady. I dreamed of him practically every night since we parted, but I wasn't sure if it was love or lust. It would be wrong to ask him to wait two years for me to finish the trip and decide if we could be together. "I'll be on the road for a good while. And since we live so many hundreds of miles apart, who knows what will happen?"

"Here's the deal. I want you, Marie. That's the truth, and if you decide you want me too, you know where to find me. I'm going to call you when I miss you, and I'm going to send you the occasional text to check in. If, and it's a big if, I meet someone new who sparks my interest in the way you do, then I will give them a chance. How does that sound?"

"I can agree to those terms." A twinge of jealousy tugged at my chest at the mere mention of him meeting someone else. Perhaps there was something more than I realized between us.

JOURNAL ENTRY

I'm writing this the evening before we leave for New York. Tomorrow we pick Jayce up at the airport, and I'm freaking out. Constance is asleep, and I don't think she has any clue how nervous I truly am.

For the last few weeks, we explored much of the New England coast and spent a lot of time doing outdoorsy things. Constance kept to her medicine schedule like clockwork. She's had no more episodes. Besides nerves about seeing Jayce, I'm scared the bustle of the Big Apple may be too much for her heart to handle.

I had to fill Jayce in on a few things we need to watch for when we're together. I made him promise we would take it as easy as possible on her. He called me last night to verify his flight information one last time, and the subject of Brady came up. I've noticed Jayce has started acting a bit jealous anytime we talk about him. His behavior makes me think he's falling for me, and I'm not sure what to do about it. My feelings for him are definitely evolving into something more than they were before, but I'm terrified of exploring them further.

Jayce and Brady are both amazing men. Any girl would be lucky to have either of them. Each deserves a woman who can give him her whole heart, which is something I don't know if I can do. Am I being completely selfish by holding on to Brady? Am I leading Jayce down a road I'm not ready to explore? I'm finally getting sleepy. I think the nerves are calming. I'm going to try to rest up for the big day tomorrow.

Here's hoping it feels like old times with no awkwardness.

Marie

8

JAYCE

Travelers, happy couples, and families reuniting filled the airport. It resembled an opening scene from a movie, and my shattered nerves seemed to make everything move in slow motion.

I was pulled from my theatrical daydream when I heard my name being called out. Marie stood there waving at me with an immense grin on her face. She took off running to me and jumped into my open arms wrapping herself around my neck and legs and waist. She practically tackled me, and I held her up trying to keep my balance as I laughed. The awkwardness I had feared was absent from the moment. She giggled next to my ear and climbed down.

Holding her face in my hands, I said, "You smell much better in person."

She smacked my chest playfully. "What does that mean?"

"It means that most days I talk to you from the auto shop and I smell grease and dirt around me. In person, you smell like…" Pausing to run my nose along her neck, I finished by saying, "Flowers." Goose bumps rose on her arms at my touch and whisper. It seemed I had an effect on her as much as she did me.

She pulled away before the awkward showed its face.

"Constance is waiting for us. Let's get your luggage."

We watched the luggage pour out onto the belt and waited until the unique lime-green hard case came out. I snatched it up as though it weighed nothing. When I sat it down, I noticed Marie try to lift it without success. My physical strength appeared to impress her, giving me a little ego boost.

"I think almost three months apart was too long. We should have made our meetings once a month."

"I agree," I said. "Maybe we can try to meet every other month at least." Constance got out to open the hatchback and to give me a warm embrace. "It's so good to see you, Connie."

My first request was to find a restaurant with pizza, a food New York was known to make well. I was a man and I loved to eat. Marie had always teased me about the amount I consumed in just a day.

Pizza had to be put on hold for a while, though. The first thing we had to do was find the hotel to park the car, and then we'd use cabs and subways for the duration of the visit. Marie had given me the task of booking the hotel for us, and I patted myself on the back when I spotted my choice.

The Hilton in Times Square seemed the perfect location. The valet took Marie's keys while a bellboy took the luggage to the registration desk. The room was on the thirty-first floor and had an amazing view of the city. None of us could wait to see the view. When nightfall came, it was with the beauty of the neon lights illuminating the surrounding skyscrapers.

"Holy crap, this is awesome," I exclaimed staring out the window. "The streets are packed with people! I've never seen this many buildings smushed together." Twisting around quickly, I saw both girls jump back startled. Admittedly, my excitement over this trip was hard to contain. "I have a surprise for you guys." In my suitcase on the bed, I found an envelope. "Tickets to the Lion King tomorrow night."

Marie gasped. "Are you serious? How did you manage to get those?"

"I have my ways." I winked. My ways came down to using some of the extra money I'd earned being a manager at the shop. It wasn't a cheap surprise, but I knew how much Marie loved the movie. She had told me before she'd wanted to see it on Broadway.

"Tonight we enjoy the nightlife in New York, and tomorrow we see a matinee show on Broadway."

Constance left us alone while she went to get ready for their night out on the town. Plopping my butt down on the bed, I patted the spot next to me for Marie. With my arm around her shoulder, I leaned over to kiss her cheek.

"How's she doing?" I whispered, referring to Constance now that we had a private moment.

"Good. She's good. This trip has been helpful for her, I think."

"It's been good for you too. You're different. You spent

the last few years working long hours and missing out on life. Now you've got pink and purple hair. You're enjoying life to the fullest. I couldn't be prouder of you."

Constance stepped from the bathroom in a black, strapless sundress. She slipped on some black sandals with red cherries on them and put her hair up in a messy bun. We stood with our mouths agape. She twirled around and held her hands out to the side.

"Does this look okay?"

"You look hot!" Marie gave a whistle after her exclamation. Constance laughed and clapped her hands.

"Your turn, Mo," she said.

Constance sat with me this time.

"So, cuz, it's been too long since we hung out. Thanks for not telling Marie about my condition before she came to see me. I covered for you and said no one else in the family knew. It wasn't a total lie because you only found out recently. It was a good idea you had for me to ask her about tagging along. It took my parents a while to agree to let me go, but they felt better once they spoke with the doctor."

"You didn't tell Marie it was my idea, did you?" Secrets weren't something we had in our friendship. However, when Marie brought up the idea of traveling, it scared me to imagine her doing the entire trip alone. Constance wasn't around to be protection for her but a companion instead. It hadn't been my original idea.

When I called Constance to ask her about showing Marie around, she went on and on about how awesome of a trip it would be and how much she would love to do anything other than sit around the B&B all day. Once the idea was out there, all she had to do was convince her parents and eventually convince Marie when the time was right.

"No. I didn't know how she'd feel about it." Constance glanced back at the bathroom as if worried Marie would overhear us.

"We'll keep it our secret. Did she talk to Brady a lot?" From the moment I'd arrived, I'd wanted to ask about Brady as nonchalantly as possible.

"Once or twice, and I think that's it. She and I were together most of the time. Why don't you tell her your feelings have changed, J?" Constance always could see right through me as a kid. I supposed that hadn't changed.

"I'm still working through them. She virtually told me she was in love with him." Unfortunately, we were on the phone and not FaceTime when she told me this heartbreaking news. Her voice sounded sincere, but I needed her facial expressions to tell me the truth.

"She lied."

"How do you know?" I asked unconvinced.

"She told me. Well, she didn't tell me she lied to you, but I asked her if she was in love with him. She said she barely knew him, and she cared about him but didn't see it turning into anything else."

"No offense, but maybe she didn't feel comfortable telling you she loved him. We've known each other a lot longer, and she tells me things she's never told anyone." In this case, I hoped Constance was right and I was wrong, but I still had my defenses up.

"Trust me. I've seen her talk to him. She cares about him, but her eyes don't light up the way they do when she speaks to you."

My chest swelled with confidence at this revelation. Maybe Marie's feelings were changing for me in the same direction mine were changing for her. Marie stepped out of the bathroom before I could question Constance further. My mouth fell open, and my body reacted to her allure. Her hair was pulled back into a ponytail exposing a long neck accentuated by her dress straps. The red dress tied around her neck and had a black belt in the middle with a flowing skirt and black lace over the top. Her feet were bare, and she had a pair of sandals dangling from each hand.

"Which pair goes best?"

Constance pointed to the pair in her left hand, black sandals with ties up the length of her calf. Marie sat in the chair across from me and began to strap up her shoes. My eyes glazed over as I felt a new admiration for her, taking in her silky smooth legs and beautifully pedicured feet. Thoughts of running my hands across her smooth skin, pushing her skirt upward as I massaged her thighs, tasting her, filled me.

"Does it not look good?" she asked, jerking me out of my daydream. No pun intended.

"No. I mean, yes. You look beautiful." Sexy as hell was what I wanted to say. I excused myself to the bathroom where I slipped on a black button-down and slacks. One accessory I sported couldn't go with me out into the world. Focusing on the mirror, I kept thinking about the grossest things I could until my pants stopped saluting.

The skyline of Times Square was lit up with neon. It wasn't like living in a big city in Tennessee. The neon lights encompassed everything. People crowded the streets, and the normal night sky that should have been full of stars was empty, a vast space of darkness, and the only dark spot visible.

With Constance and Marie on my arms, we walked the streets for about an hour before finding a nightclub to try out. The line was pretty long, but I slipped the bouncer a little green gift, and we went right in. The music inside was deafening, forcing us to use hand gestures to motion toward the bar. The girls wanted a couple of fruity concoctions while I stuck with a nice refreshing beer.

When a slow song came on, Constance shoved her elbow into my side and tipped her head toward Marie as a hint. Rubbing the pain in my side from her bony little arm, I took the hint brilliantly. Marie grinned widely when I stuck my hand out in invitation. We swayed to the music with my arms around her waist and her head on my shoulder. The aroma of her vanilla perfume sent waves of lust coursing through my body. My hand moved to the small of her back as I brought her closer.

"I missed you, Mo." My mouth was pressed to her ear, and I felt her shiver as I spoke.

Her reaction was quick as she stepped back from the contact of the dance, pointed to the bar, and patted her throat to demonstrate thirst. Either the thirst had hit her quickly or my moment of intimacy had freaked her out. Instead of dwelling on the matter, I followed her to the bar and ordered us drinks.

Constance seemed to be enjoying herself as I watched her bob her head to the music with a giant grin on her face. A hand against her lower back moved my attention as someone leaned in and spoke to her. A slightly inebriated college girl squeaked loudly in her ear. In the next moment, she planted a kiss on Constance's lips making my eyes widen in surprise. I leaned closer to hear what that was about.

"Sorry, I'm pledging a sorority and one thing I had to do tonight was kiss a girl. I wanted to choose the most beautiful girl in the room."

The gesture flattered Constance. I could see the blush fill her cheeks as her face lit up with a smile that made her eyes dance.

"Thanks. I never mind compliments." The girl waved and walked away. The young man sitting next to her leaned over and yelled, "That was the hottest thing I've seen all night." He reached forward. "I'm Clay. Can I buy you a drink?"

Tugging on Marie's arm, I pulled her over closer to Constance. I wanted to keep an eye on her with this guy laying down smooth lines.

"Sure. I'll have another of these," she answered, holding up the empty glass in case he couldn't hear. Clay motioned to the bartender who brought them two more drinks. I recognized Constance's pink drink as a Shirley Temple, a nonalcoholic cocktail of Sprite and cherry flavoring with a garnish of maraschinos.

Constance reached for her drink and noticed me for the

first time it seemed, by the surprise in her eyes.

Immediately she introduced us to Clay, who asked if we'd like to all grab a coffee at his favorite cafe on the way back to the hotel.

Some might call me overcautious, but I wasn't sure I wanted Constance anywhere near this guy, and I certainly wasn't sure I wanted him to know where we're staying. Before I could voice my concern, Constance turned him down. Clay didn't push. He seemed to be okay with her answer, which gave me a better feel for him. If he'd pressured her, I'd have grabbed her arm and walked as far away as possible.

Clay excused himself and the three of us talked it over. "Are you sure you don't want to meet him for coffee? We'll be there with you. It would be a nice chance to talk to someone in a better setting," Marie suggested.

"I'll have your back no matter what you decide, Connie." I'd never let anything happen to these two women under my watch.

Constance glanced back at Clay who sat alone at the other end of the bar, people watching the couples on the dance floor.

"I'll be back." We watched as Constance walked over to him and his face lit up as his head nodded. I waved the bartender over and closed the tab before grabbing Marie's hand to head out.

The diner reminded us a bit of the one on the show *Friends*. We scored seats in the middle of the room in a moment of good timing or pure luck. Ordering up a cappuccino for Marie, an espresso for me, coffee black no sugar for Clay, and herbal tea for Constance, we sat down and spent the evening talking.

Clay doted on Constance, and she might have had a permanent blush to her face. He found little ways to touch her hand while speaking or running his fingers across her arm. Little fidgets of her fingers and the biting of her bottom lip displayed how nervous she felt. In an effort to remove the attention from her momentarily, I brought up the play we'd be seeing the next day and asked if he'd like to meet for dinner afterward. Clay gave a resounding yes, and Constance couldn't contain her elation.

While the two of them talked, I leaned over to whisper in Marie's ear. "I love seeing her happy. You put that smile on her face." The proximity of my mouth against her ear sent shivers dancing across her skin.

"Clay had something to do with that." She stumbled over her words and pulled back a little. Noticing the movement, I placed my hand on hers.

"Am I making you uncomfortable?"

"Of course not. I've never been uncomfortable around you."

I smiled at her words, not quite believing them. "Dancing with you earlier was different, don't you think?" I pushed to restart the conversation we'd earlier avoided. Our intimate dance had her running for the hills. Her reaction was difficult to swallow.

"Different how?"

Sliding my fingers along the top of her hand, my breath quickened when she bit her lower lip.

Before we could continue, Constance asked, "Are we ready to go back to the hotel?" Eyes drifting down to our hands as they quickly pulled apart, she cringed and mouthed, "Sorry," at Marie, noticing she'd interrupted our moment.

JOURNAL ENTRY

Our first night in New York was amazing. Jayce made the experience even better by being there, I think. Constance met a guy, Clay. He seems like a real sweetheart, and he's put a smile on her face. She's never had a boyfriend before, so dating is new for her. Not that they've had an actual date, but just the prospect of eating dinner with a guy who shows an interest is all new territory. He walked us back to the hotel, and they stayed in the lobby talking for two hours after Jayce and I went to bed.

When she came in the room, she told me he'd given her a good night kiss. Constance and I shared a bed for the night, and she fell asleep before me. As I lay there, thinking about everything going on, I heard Jayce say my name. I answered him and waited for what he needed before realizing he was asleep. It warmed my heart to think he dreamed of me. I only wondered what kind of dream. Jayce has been different lately. Perhaps it's our time apart making things a little awkward.

Brady left me a voice mail to tell me he couldn't stop thinking about me and wanted to meet up when I made my way to Ohio. Tomorrow, I'll call him and set it up. I feel a bit guilty listening to his voice as I wonder about Jayce's thoughts on me. Brady and I have never made anything official, but it still feels like he is giving this relationship a better chance than I am some days. I don't want to be the girl torn between two men, but I can't help the things in my mind.

It's hard not to feel attracted to Jayce after everything he's done for me lately. He took a job to help me achieve my dream trip, and he's gotten me tickets to see my favorite Disney movie on stage. Each gesture makes me see him in a different light. I've been an independent woman for years without needing a man on my arm or anyone to take care of me. Suddenly, I feel like the only thing I think about is love.

For now, I'll say good night because I finally feel my high fading from the day, and the exhaustion is setting in.

♡Marie

9

MARIE

The Lion King show was spectacular, giving us plenty to talk about the rest of the evening. The day had taken a lot out of Constance, though, so she called and asked Clay if they could postpone dinner for a few hours. After the play, Constance went to take a nap while Jayce and I took a walk.

"I've been doing a lot of thinking lately, Mo." Jayce reached for my hand. "I've been thinking about you and me and this friendship. When you were home, we were like siblings, but when you left, something changed." Curious as to what he would say next, my feet stopped in their tracks. People were moving all around us in a rush to get to whatever important meeting they had.

As I stepped back away from the crowd, Jayce pinned me against the building. He leaned forward and pressed his lips to mine. Stunned at first, my hands fell to my sides. I stood motionless, unsure if I was ready to kiss him back. Giving in to the moment, the result was a fireworks-worthy kiss I felt all the way to the tip of my toes.

His hands cupped the back of my neck, fingers massaging my skin. I grabbed his waist, tugging him against me. The tip of his tongue grazed my bottom lip, causing a pull of wanting in my stomach. Brady was the closest person I'd ever come to being in love with, and even kissing him didn't compare to this kiss. But it was Jayce, my best friend, the most important person in my life. The anxiety of a failed relationship with Jayce was more than I could handle. I pushed him away as the reality of the situation sank in fully.

"What's wrong?" he asked, running his fingers through my hair.

"Everything. We can't kiss like that, Jayce. You're my—"

Jayce interrupted me. "Everything. At least I would have said you're my everything. I think we have something amazing, Mo." His eyes twinkled with joy.

"You *are* my everything because you're my best friend. I don't want to lose what we have." The mere thought of losing him made my stomach twist in pain.

"Why would we need to lose it? What if we could make it even better? That kiss felt—"

"It doesn't matter how it felt. What if we can't make it work? I don't want to lose you," I said before Jayce could finish.

"You wouldn't lose me. No matter what happens, we will always be friends because I love you, Mo. But if you're not ready to explore this, I'll back off. Promise me you'll give it some thought at least?"

All I'd been doing lately was thinking about it, so it was an easy promise to make. It seemed to appease him. "Let's head back to the hotel. I'm tired."

My phone rang as we walked into the hotel, and Jayce spotted my caller ID. With a saddened look on his face, he said, "I'll give you some privacy."

"Hi, Brady," I answered. My voice stayed low until Jayce stepped onto the elevator to go upstairs alone. Taking a seat in the lobby, I tried to focus on the call instead of what had happened a moment ago.

"I wanted to hear your voice. I hope it's all right I called."

"Of course."

He grew quiet before admitting, "I miss you so much, Marie. I haven't seen your face in weeks. I miss you in my bed. I miss your lips." Instantly I was transported back to the kiss in the streets with Jayce.

"I miss you too, Brady, but I hate to say it… you should move on with your life. It's better that way. We live too far apart, and I'm traveling. It's just a bad time." All of this was said with as much sincerity as possible. It felt wrong to lead Brady on, especially with these strange new thoughts about Jayce and that kiss.

"Maybe you're right. I wish you weren't, but you might be. It's harder than I expected it to be."

Long distance relationships seemed difficult but doable until you got involved in one. When we were together in Michigan, I never thought about anyone else. With Brady's arms around me, or his hand in mine, I felt alive and didn't need anything else. Talking to him on the phone without being able to touch, gave me an empty feeling inside. Before I met him, I felt less lonely and, although I would never regret our time together, I missed feeling excited about my trip. Instead, I had this feeling of missing a man next to me.

"Call me sometime and let me know how you're doing. I'm here for you, Brady. I hope you understand." He said good-bye in a barely audible tone before hanging up.

Upstairs, Jayce sat quietly watching some zombie movie on television. Without turning to look at me he said, "Constance left a few minutes ago with Clay. They're going on a date. She's going to text us to check in later."

"Oh, good! I like Clay. Normally I would insist we go along with her, but I promised not to baby her. A little taste of freedom will be good." Speaking to me was a good sign I hadn't destroyed our friendship forever.

"Yep," he responded curtly.

Jayce's short answer stabbed me right in the heart. Sitting next to him on the bed, I leaned against his shoulder.

"I love you, Jayce."

"How's Brady?"

"I'm not in love with Brady. I asked him to move on, and he's as hurt as you are. I'm not ready to settle down with him or to take big chances with you. I'm scared."

"Life is all about taking chances, Mo. Hell, this whole trip of yours is one big chance."

"I know, but I'm not willing to take a chance on losing you. You're the most important person in my life. Please tell me you understand?" He had to grasp what I was saying without taking offense.

"It's all good, Mo. We're good. Just admit one thing for me," Jayce requested.

"What's that?" I asked.

"I'm an awesome kisser, right?" A lopsided grin paired with wiggling eyebrows made me giggle.

"You are." If only he knew how much I truly meant it. Thinking about the kiss warmed my body in places never before affected by Jayce.

The rest of the night, we carried on as though no romantic gesture occurred. You could say things got back to normal in a New York minute.

Constance filled me in on her date as soon as she returned to the hotel.

"Clay chose a nearby pizzeria for our dinner date. We wanted a place to sit and chat for a while, to utilize the short amount of time we had together." Constance bounced on the mattress as if she couldn't contain her excitement while she narrated each moment.

"Nerves were getting the best of me and at one point, I glanced down at my phone to check the time. Clay thought I wanted to leave, so I confessed to him I'd never been on a date before. How my parents are overprotective, and they wouldn't let me out much. That it took a miracle to get them to agree I could go on this trip. Being a virtual stranger still, I wasn't ready to admit my heart problem as the reason. I didn't expect a long-term relationship with him, but in case there was a chance of something, I didn't want to scare him off."

"How did he take that information?"

"Better than I feared. He said there's nothing wrong with starting late in life and we'd have to get a few firsts out of the way tonight. Then his tongue swiped across his lips and my knees buckled."

My eyes bulged wondering if he'd tried to take advantage of her innocence. I was relieved when she continued the story.

"Clay stared at me for a moment before his eyes widened in horror and he assured me he wasn't implying sex. I told him I never thought that, when in truth it's the first place my mind went!"

"I'll admit it was my first thought as well," I said, now relieved we were mistaken.

"Then his lips brushed mine, lightly at first. No awkward tongue lapping or drooling happened. It was a soft, sensual kiss of seduction." Blushing, she giggled a little at her own choice of words.

"Sounds pretty amazing," I commented as she sighed with contentment and a giant grin on her face.

"It was. He dropped a tip on the table for the busboy, grabbed my hand, and said, 'Let's get you back to the hotel before I try to take back my word on all the firsts.' The thought of having spontaneous elevator sex with him like in a dirty, adult movie way definitely crossed my mind on the way."

"Since when do you watch adult movies?" I asked, interrupting the flow of her story.

"Well not triple-X features or anything. Just some good

solid R ratings." Her cheeks flamed, and she quickly went back to the story. "So, anyway… Clay pressed the up button for the elevator. Once inside, the doors closed, and we found ourselves riding up several floors alone. Reaching out, he held the close door button to keep us from being interrupted on the way up. Clay pressed me against the wall and kissed me. When I twisted my fingers through his hair, I tugged him closer." Sighing contently, she continued, "His hand grazed down my body, stopping when it reached my thigh. His fingers massaged my leg as his tongue slid across my lips." Nothing could wipe the dreamy grin off Constance's face at this moment. "Another mind-blowing kiss like that and I would have been putty in his hands."

"Wow. That sounds like a pretty amazing first date."

Constance's shoulder shrugged as her cheeks filled with pink. "It was. I had so many nervous butterflies in my stomach at the beginning, I was afraid I would throw up on him if I ate anything. I thought about telling him we'd eaten a late lunch just to avoid any embarrassing regurgitation, but the pizza smelled so damn good I decided to stuff my face to avoid talking and saying something stupid instead."

"You seem to have done a pretty good job considering the elevator ride."

Pink cheeks turned a crimson red as she bit her lip.

"Not that I have much to compare it to, but he's a fantastic kisser. I felt tingles in places I never knew could tingle."

Jayce walked into the room and groaned. "La la la. I do not want to know about my cousin's experience or lack thereof or about places tingling. I think I'll run down and use the workout room for a little bit. You two can have your girl talk." Most of what he said went in one ear and out the other as I took in the half-naked man in front of me. With a towel thrown over his shoulder, he stood before us shirtless with shorts hanging low enough to reveal the sexy cut trailing down below. The temperature in the room jumped at least ten degrees as I felt my cheeks redden, and I sucked my lip between my teeth.

As soon as the door shut behind Jayce, I shook my head free of the naughty thoughts of what I wanted to do with Jayce's muscular body. I curled up in bed with Constance. We spent a while watching a show before we started talking.

"Are you going to see him again before we leave?" A gentle shoulder shrug was the only answer she could give to that one. "Did he ask you out or say he'd call you?"

"He said he wants to see me again, and I told him I'd text him when I knew what our plans were."

"Tomorrow we're going to Central Park. You should ask Clay to come."

Grabbing her phone, she sent a text.

Me: Central Park for a breakfast picnic? Jayce and Marie will be there too.

Clay responded instantly.

Clay: I'll bring bagels and cream cheese for four. See you tomorrow.

Jayce walked back in the room as Constance relayed the message with a squeal. His repeated eye roll warned us he was ready to leave until we assured him our girl moment was over for the night. It had been a long day, and we were all exhausted. Jayce gave us a kiss on the cheek before crawling into his bed and turning out the lamp.

In the middle of the night, I rolled over, finding it hard to fall back asleep. My eyes met Jayce's, and he smiled as he held the blanket up, inviting me over. Gently rising from my bed, I moved carefully to keep from waking Constance. Crawling in bed with him, I lay with my arm beneath my head.

"You can't sleep either?" he whispered.

"Can't stop thinking about you leaving tomorrow. I wish we had more time."

Jayce reached forward to brush a hair back from my face. Closing my eyes, I relished the brief contact of his skin against mine.

"Me too. The last few days flew by too quickly. After your trip, we'll have to set up an annual one with Constance so we can both keep in touch with her."

"I'd love that," I exclaimed in an excited whisper. "She's going to be the part of this trip I miss most when it's over."

"Not Brady?" Jayce asked curiously. Possibly seeing my discomfort, he went on to say, "I will be glad when you come home for good."

"In all my planning, I never imagined I'd be so homesick. I thought staying in hotels would feel luxurious, but it's a little annoying. Some beds feel like home and others are like bricks. I'm grateful for the opportunity, but it's not as glamorous as I hoped it would be."

"And I never knew how much I would miss you," Jayce admitted quietly. Eyes fixated on each other, the heat building between us was intense. Gradually he leaned forward, licking his lips. As much as I wanted to kiss him, I willed myself not to.

Yawning, I covered my mouth with the palm of my hand. "I'm getting sleepy. I need some rest if I'm going to drive tomorrow." As I started to roll over, Jayce gently grabbed my wrist.

"You could sleep with me tonight." Eyes widening, he quickly rephrased. "Cuddling, like old times."

Soft, awkward laughter lightened the moment. Rolling over, I placed my back up against Jayce as he wrapped an arm across my stomach. We had lain this way many times before, but tonight was more intimate. When he pressed his lips against my shoulder, I closed my eyes and swallowed back the emotions building.

"Good night, Mo."

"Good night, Jayce."

JOURNAL ENTRY

We spent time at Central Park and the 9/11 Memorial. Clay joined us every moment. He seemed downtrodden toward the end of our last day together. He and Constance seem very happy. For the last few hours of our final night, he got a hotel room on the same floor, and Constance spent the night with him. I don't know if they did anything or just stayed up and talked all night.

This morning, as we packed the car with our bags, they both looked exhausted as though they hadn't slept a wink. I hoped that it was because they had a fun-filled night and not one of tears and sadness. Jayce and I stood watching them as they embraced for a long period. We hated to break them apart, but Jayce had a plane to catch.

We stood at the security gate for what seemed

like hours. It was only about ten minutes. For those ten minutes, we held each other and cried. Mostly I cried, and Jayce soothed me. It hurt so much to say good-bye to him once more, but we will be together again in three months. Our next meeting place will be Myrtle Beach in South Carolina. It will seem like an eternity before I see him again.

Connie and I stood watching until his plane took off before we left the airport and got back on the road.

Tonight, we're in Pennsylvania.

ꝏ*Marie*

10

Constance kept an eye on my phone while I drove.

"It's Jayce. He landed safely, and he's on his way home. He said he can't wait to see us in Myrtle Beach."

"Tell him we can't wait either, and I miss him already." Three more months would pass before I would see Jayce again. Having Constance with me would be the key to keeping me sane.

"So are you keeping in touch with Clay?" She hadn't mentioned him since we left New York.

"No. We both feel that we had fun together but don't think the long distance thing will work. He's a nice guy, and while he's a great kisser, and we had a spark, we didn't have much in common."

"Love isn't always a big dramatic spark of electricity. It takes time. And they say opposites attract. You don't want to give it a chance?"

"Not really. We spent most of the night talking about life in general, and we have different goals. We're friends on Facebook now, but that's as far as we'll ever take it."

Constance sent the text and set the phone down. "I don't understand why you don't give a relationship with Jayce a chance. You two are adorable together."

"Connie, our agreement was for you not to mention feelings or triangles or any of that mess."

"Sorry."

Silence filled the next hour of our trip. Constance used the quiet time to listen to an audiobook of one of her favorite fantasy novels. She turned her iPod up all the way and laid her head back to enjoy the story of the magical school she dreamed of attending as a child.

Flashes of the kiss I shared with Jayce danced across my thoughts. The intense passion I felt with Brady didn't match what I felt with Jayce, and my heart was as confused as my mind.

Whatever played through Constance's earbuds had her enthralled. Why did Constance have to be so intuitive when it came to my attraction to Jayce? I needed it to go unnoticed because I was not ready to admit to myself there may be something there.

Answering the hands-free button on the steering wheel, I said, "Hello?"

"Hey, beautiful, where are you?" Brady asked curiously. A comforting warmth embraced me with the sound of his voice.

"Not far into Pennsylvania. Trying to find a place to shack

up for the night. I'm glad you called."

Through the change of tone in his voice, I could picture him smiling. "I had a kind of crazy idea I wanted to run by you."

"What is it?" Admittedly his happy demeanor had me curious.

"Manny and I have some time off coming up, and we wanted to do a short road trip. Can we meet you and Constance in DC?"

For some odd reason, it surprised me at how excited I was at the idea.

"Yes! I think it would be good for Connie too. Plus, I miss you, Brady. I still think it would be better for you to move on, but I would love to spend some time with you if you're okay with no strings attached for now?"

A soft chuckle sounded, and I could hear his smile as he said, "You just made my day, sweetheart. I can't wait to see you. Can I ask one thing?"

"Sure, anything."

"Would you be offended if I reserved a hotel room for you and me? I want as much time with you as possible."

His request filled me with warmth, and I felt a pull of desire in my stomach. "I want that too."

"I'll text you the details as soon as I have them all then. Marie...." He paused for a moment, his voice sounding a bit nervous. "I love you." As soon as the words were out, he hung up the phone. My eyes widened and my jaw dropped open. Brady may have said he was okay with no strings attached, but his words just told a different story.

One thing I knew, hearing those words made me happy. To be loved by a man as honorable and kind as Brady meant I was a lucky woman. The goofy grin on my face wouldn't quit shining.

Constance pulled her earbud out and sat up. "What are you cheery about?"

"Did you hear any of my phone conversation?"

"No. I didn't even know you were on the phone. Who was it?"

"Brady. He and Manny are going to meet us in DC. You'll like Manny. He's very sweet. Brady is going to get us a room to share, so I'll pay for you to have a single room if you don't mind?"

Constance bounced in her seat while peering out the window. "Sounds great. I can't wait to meet him. Where are we now?"

"Hershey, Pennsylvania. I thought we could both use a chocolate binge day. We'll start at Chocolate World and then go to Hershey Park. Are you feeling up to an amusement park? We can stick to the simple rides so—"

Constance interrupted me. "Of course I want to go to the park. Roller coasters have never interested me, but there is plenty more I can do. Could we get a hotel room first and wash up?"

"Absolutely."

We arrived at the camping resort associated with the park. The hotel rooms we'd been staying in had been nice, but I wanted to change it up a bit and stay in a cabin for three nights instead. A beautiful, light oak covered every part of the cabin interior, exterior, and the kitchen cabinets. It was small, two bedrooms with a petite living room and kitchen combination. Thankfully, the resort had one of the deluxe cabins available because the others had no indoor plumbing. I couldn't fathom traipsing outside in the middle of the night to use the bathroom.

We sank down onto the plush couch and let out a sigh of relief in unison. "Maybe we should stay in for the rest of today and get a fresh start in the morning?" I suggested selfishly, wanting the rest. Constance silently nodded, and we curled our feet up in the middle of the couch and laid our heads on opposite armrests to sleep.

The first to wake up, I glanced at the clock to see three hours had passed. Constance snored lightly on the other end of the couch. The only other noise in the room was the loud growl resounding from my stomach. Scribbling a quick note to Constance, I snatched my keys up with as much stealth as possible. My mission became finding something delicious close by, preferably not a fast food hamburger. Constance would be starving when she woke, and she'd need food to take her medicine with.

After driving only about a mile away, I found a restaurant with takeout. Chinese food was cheap, and you usually got more than you could eat. Stepping up to the counter, I ordered a pint of honey chicken, a pint of sesame chicken, and pint of chicken lo mein, plus a couple of egg rolls and an order of crab rangoon. There would be a good variety for us to choose from, and we had a refrigerator in the cabin to store leftovers for other meals.

Constance bobbed her head to the music blaring through

her earbuds. Kneeling down, I tapped her on the shoulder. She smiled and pulled the earbuds out. "You are the best. I woke up starving and was so excited when I saw your note."

"I got a little bit of everything from a Chinese place not too far from here. It smelled delicious in the car. I can vouch for the egg rolls. I ordered an extra one, so I could eat it on the road. Let's get some plates down and dig in."

Constance grabbed the box and a set of chopsticks and said, "Forget the plates. We'll pass the pints back and forth until we're full."

After clicking the chopsticks together as though we were toasting, we each dug into a separate pint. Constance set her chopsticks down for a moment and swallowed before she reached over and placed her hand on my arm.

"I wanted to thank you again for letting me come along on this trip. These last few weeks have been some of the best of my life, and I owe it all to you."

Eyes growing misty with tears, I set my food down to reach over and hug her.

"I love you. You're the sister I always wanted."

After a strong hug of comfort, we pulled apart and swiped the tears from our eyes. "Enough mushy stuff. Let's talk boys. Tell me about Manny. Is he cute?" Constance asked as she picked her food up again.

The sudden change in subject had me laughing at her curiosity and eagerness. "Cute is not the word I would use to describe Manny. Sexy, muscular, suntanned god is more appropriate."

Constance nodded in approval.

"Maybe we'll share a room in DC. You know, to save money." She winked at me and we both burst out into hysterical laughter. Constance hadn't done anything more than kiss Clay, but I knew she was getting curious about going further even if she was only joking about Manny.

Two days at Hershey Park exhausted us after riding as much as we could, sometimes twice. In between rides, we took breaks and I made sure Constance stayed hydrated as well as fed. At the end of the second day at the park, we went to Hershey World to stock up on chocolate for the rest of the trip. Our next destination, Philadelphia, proved to be a great spot for patriotism. The Liberty Bell, Independence Hall, The Betsy Ross House, and Valley Forge Historical Park were just a few of the spots we enjoyed.

The first few days focused on history. The second few were spent checking out the nightlife and other fun hot spots in the city. After Philadelphia, the journey took us into New Jersey where we stopped in Atlantic City for a few nights. We checked into a casino nearest to the ocean and spent the days lying out on the beach soaking up rays and the evenings at the casino trying to win a little money. Budgeting thirty dollars an evening for gambling, we ended up coming out a few dollars ahead in the end.

On the last day, we strolled the Jersey shore filling up a jar with seashells and sand as a souvenir of our first stop seeing the ocean on our trip.

"Next stop, Wilmington, Delaware," I exclaimed putting the car in drive.

"What will we be doing there?"

"You plan it. Start googling and see what you can find for us." Constance let me do most of the planning, but I wanted her to have a say as well since this was her adventure too.

She began eagerly searching her phone for activities in the city. The drive wouldn't take long, a little more than an hour was all.

"Ooh. I know it's not historical or something only found in Delaware, but what about a day at the spa?"

"That sounds perfect!" My enthusiasm was as genuine as it could be. A day of pampering was exactly what we both needed. "Call and see if you need an appointment, and find one who can get us in within the next day or so. I don't plan on spending more than a few days there."

Luckily, Constance was able to find one of the spas with an opening the next day. We located a hotel a few minutes away and spent the next few hours exploring the local museums and the Brandywine Zoo.

Our spa day would be a full eight hours of massages, mud baths, facials, and lastly mani-pedis. The past few weeks on the road had made our muscles sore and our skin dry. At the end of the next day, we both felt refreshed and ready to set out on the adventure once more.

JOURNAL ENTRY

Tomorrow I get to see Brady again. We haven't seen each other for nearly three months, and we've barely spoken on the phone a handful of times. I'm nervous, to put it mildly. The thing I'm most nervous about has to do with the last three words he spoke to me. Those big three words every woman wants to hear from a sweet guy like Brady. So why am I no longer not elated by his proclamation?

Connie is anxious about meeting Manny. I think she's hoping to connect with him the way she did with Clay. I think she may be hoping to take it a step further. She's been asking me lots of questions lately about what it feels like, etc. She's been taking more breaks lately. I think she's afraid she's getting weaker and wants a chance to experience more of life.

Part of me hopes she hits it off with Manny. During my time in Michigan, I got to know Manny a little, and he's a bit of a player, but he wants to find a special someone. For now, I have to go to bed. It's only a short drive to DC tomorrow, but we're meeting Brady and Manny for lunch. I hope I can sleep tonight.

The anticipation of tomorrow is pulling at every emotion I have. What will it be like to see Brady again? Will I find I return his feelings, or will I wish he were Jayce instead?

♥Marie

11

____

BRADY

Manny and I waited for our luggage to make its way around to us. "You barely said two words on the plane. Are you nervous about seeing Marie again?" Manny asked.

"A little. I told her I loved her last time we spoke. Right after she told me she wasn't ready for a relationship, which was stupid of me." The words had sort of spilled from my mouth without thought, and I didn't know how Marie felt hearing them.

"Whoa, that's serious. What did she say?"

"I didn't give her a chance to respond. I said it and then hung up. I was afraid of the silence that would have followed. I'm a wuss, aren't I?" I lifted my luggage off the turnstile, and Manny did the same without answering.

"You've texted her since then, and she still wanted you to come out, right?"

"Yep, she seemed excited about it, too." What I didn't tell him was I ignored the first text from her for several hours because I'd been nervous she would tell me not to come. After I finally read it, I felt more at ease. Normally I didn't get this way in a relationship, but this girl had me wrapped around her finger.

"Well, there you go. Sounds like it didn't scare her off. I like Marie, and I like the two of you together. I'm pretty stoked about seeing her again myself."

Manny whistled for a cab. He gave the cabbie the address to the hotel as I loaded the luggage in the trunk. The hotel had rooms for us on the same floor but they were a few doors apart. I dropped the luggage in my room, refreshed my cologne and deodorant, and stepped back in the hall to find Manny.

"I'm going to go down to the lobby and walk around. You want to join me?" Sweaty palms and a racing heart had me on edge as I thought about my reunion with Marie. A nice walk around the lobby would help to calm me a little.

"I'll be down in a few. I'm going to get a shower." Manny leaned forward and sniffed in my direction. "Good smelling cologne, man. Now stop freaking out, and take a walk."

As I stepped off the elevator, I heard a gasp from my right.

"Brady!" Marie exclaimed as she dropped her bags next to who I assumed was Constance and ran toward me. All the anxiety went away as I wrapped my arms around her, lifted her into the air, and spun her in a circle.

"I missed these arms," she said with a giggle against my ear. Her breath against my neck caused my body to react instantly to her.

Setting her down, I placed my palms against her cheeks pulling her in for a kiss. I felt the quick beat of her heart, the warmth of her skin. She moved her hands down my side and up into my shirt sliding her fingernails along my abs. I groaned against her lips as I ground my hips into hers with subtlety. "We're in the lobby. We might want to save that for upstairs."

Marie's cheeks reddened as she looked around. She'd momentarily forgotten we were in public. She also forgot Constance stood behind her with their luggage.

Reaching out, I introduced myself.

"Hi, Constance, I'm Brady."

"I hope so, because otherwise this would've been a more awkward moment." She winked at him. "Where's your friend?"

"Manny's upstairs getting a shower. Did you get a room yet?" I directed my question at Constance, hoping Marie still wanted to share a room with me.

"I'm on the ninth floor," Constance replied.

"Great, we're on ten." I turned to Marie. "Would you like to see our room while Constance gets settled into hers, and then we can meet up afterward for lunch?"

"Sounds good," Marie said. If she had the same thing in mind I did, then things were about to get hot and heavy. As Constance stepped off the elevator onto the ninth floor and the doors shut, I pressed Marie against the wall and delved into a feverish kiss. She whimpered as my hands roamed under her shirt against her soft skin.

The doors opened on the tenth floor, and grabbing her

hand, we took off in a sprint to our room. Slipping the key card into the door, I waited impatiently for the green light. Once it opened, I grabbed her in my arms and our lips crashed together. Pressing her against the wall, hands above her head, my mouth made a trail down her neck.

"I missed you," I growled against her skin.

Releasing her hands, I jerked her shirt over her head, then moved back to her neck as she unclasped her bra from behind. Once her breasts were free, my thumbs moved to her nipples, rubbing circles across the taut nubs. Her moans were soft and begging. I ached to taste her. Flicking my tongue out, I elicited a more audible moan, which turned into a muffled scream as I increased the pressure of my sucking. Marie's fingers combed through my hair as she sighed at the sensations invading her body.

Frantically removing the rest of our clothes and tossing them into a pile, we moved to the bed. Just before I moved above her, I slipped on a condom. Pressing my lips to hers, I felt the vibrations of her moans as I pressed into her. Moving together in perfect harmony, it was as if we'd never been apart. It was as passionate as all those months ago when we first met. Her body tightened around me as she approached her orgasm. On the brink of my own release, I thrust into her one last time before we came together.

"So what do you think of the hotel room?" No vacation could be better than lying there together naked in my opinion. If I hadn't come upstairs first before seeing Marie, I wouldn't even have noticed anything about the room yet. Her beautiful smile, the blush in her cheeks, the gleam of sweat on her skin, those were all the things on my mind.

Marie glanced around seemingly for the first time.

"Hmm, not bad."

"I like it much better now. Especially the view," I flirted, lifting the blanket to check her out.

She yanked the covers down laughing. "My view isn't bad either." With a peck on my cheek, she added, "I missed you, a lot."

"Me too." If she missed me half as much as I missed her, it would make my day. Since the moment she'd left, I could think of nothing but the next time I'd see her. Even when she suggested we end things and move on, I couldn't bring myself to want another. The smell of her lingered on my sheets for days after she left. I didn't want to change them; except I was afraid they'd walk themselves to the washer if I waited too long.

"We can do more of this later, but we might want to get our friends and introduce them as well," Marie suggested.

When we stepped out of the room, we spotted Manny in the hallway by the elevator with the down button pressed. Turning as I called out to him, Manny grinned when he saw Marie. She ran down the hall, and he lifted her up in a hug.

"It's good to see you, chica." They stepped into the elevator and pressed nine to get Constance. Marie had texted her to let her know we'd be on the elevator. When the doors opened, she eyed Manny for his reaction. He was most definitely checking Constance out and looking pretty pleased. Constance's cheeks reddened as she noticed his admiration.

"Connie, this is Manny." Marie introduced them. The two

exchanged pleasantries and Constance stood next to him on the ride down. She stared at the floor trying to bite back a grin while Manny took the opportunity to give her another look.

Glancing down at the proximity of our hands, I took a chance and wrapped my hand around Marie's, with fingers intertwined. She peered up at me with an approving smile. I'd never been a guy to go crazy over a girl, but something about Marie had me whipped. She had been standoffish about wanting a full relationship, and I wanted to respect her need for that, but it made me wonder why if there was not another guy. It couldn't be lack of attraction to me based on how fantastic the sex was between us.

When we stepped into the lobby, Constance pulled Marie aside.

"Your description of him was appropriate." Based on the girlish giggles they exchanged, I assumed it meant Marie spoke highly of Manny.

MARIE

Stopping at a diner down the street from the hotel, we found a corner booth for four. Constance and I groaned in unison at the awful noise the slick upholstery made as we slid over. The waitress wore a uniform like you see in the movies with a name tag that had lace around it. It was as though we'd stepped back in time. The items on the menu had cutesy names for the meals such as The White House Special, the Pentagon Pancake Platter, and the Washington Monumental pie.

"What do you two usually do on your first day in a city?" Manny questioned.

"Spend the day in the hotel resting and checking out the amenities. Day two is when we go out exploring."

Brady grinned in response to my answer. "I like the plan of staying in today."

Manny rolled his eyes and then turned to Constance.

"You're lucky I came along on this trip, so you didn't end up alone while these two make up for lost time."

"I'm feeling luckier every minute." She winked at him, and he appeared to be thrilled by her flirting. "I have my laptop with me if you'd like to come to my room and watch a movie on Netflix."

"Are you asking me to Netflix and chill?" Manny leaned forward, eyebrow cocked, smile playing on his lips.

Constance looked around nervously wondering what she had said. "I guess. Does that mean something other than what I said?"

Manny chuckled and placed his hand over hers.

"Sorry, I was only teasing. It sounds like fun."

Brady and I exchanged a smile and gave each other a low five under the table. A few days before the trip, we'd texted about how we hoped they'd hit it off because both Manny and Constance needed a good person in their life.

Throughout the meal, we watched Manny and Constance flirt back and forth. At the end, Brady paid the bill for lunch and we walked back to the hotel.

"They have a pretty nice pool if you want to check it out later."

Manny answered for the others by suggesting, "Why don't we all meet down there in a few hours and take a nice swim. That will give you two a little time together, and Connie and I will have time to get to know each other."

We agreed to meet in four hours. As soon as Brady and I returned to the room, we made love and then spent the next few hours talking about everything we'd missed over the past few months. When I talked about the time spent in New York with Jayce, my guilty conscience took over. Brady had laid his feelings out on the table for me, and I hadn't addressed it or reciprocated. Although we hadn't officially called ourselves a couple, it seemed to be assumed based on our actions. As much as I wanted Brady, I wasn't ready to settle down. I wanted to maintain my independence for now.

BRADY

Marie's head lay on my chest against my heart. Methodically I ran my fingers through her hair, listening to her sigh every so often. Soft sighs had been the only noises in the room for the last few minutes. Since I couldn't see her face, I thought she'd fallen asleep.

"I missed this the most the past few months," Marie stated, breaking the silence between us and startling me slightly.

"The hot steamy sex or the snuggling?"

"Both." She laughed. "But mostly the snuggling and talking. Besides Jayce, I've never really had a guy I felt as comfortable around as you."

The moment Jayce's name left her lips, my whole body tensed. She bit her lip and scrunched her eyebrows in thought. She suddenly reeked of guilt, and I didn't like the smell of it.

"Are you and Jayce more than friends?"

"No, not really." The words came out wide open for interpretation.

"Not really?" My fingers stopped moving through her hair as the fear of her clarification choked me.

Marie sat up.

"I'm not sure what I meant by that," she admitted.

"Did something happen?" Pulling myself into a seated position, I leaned my head back against the wall. Based on her guilty look, I already knew the answer. We never promised to be exclusive. We never defined what our relationship was, so I couldn't hold it against her. She could have stabbed me with a hot fire poker straight through the chest, and it might have hurt less than thinking of her with him.

Marie closed her eyes and blurted out her confession.

"He kissed me in New York. I'm sorry, Brady. I didn't tell you because I didn't want to hurt you. I stopped Jayce and told him I didn't want to ruin our friendship by—" She stopped when she realized how she sounded, like the only reason she picked me was out of fear for losing Jayce.

"You don't owe me an apology. We agreed to see people if we wanted, but I do have a question. The other day, I said I love you, and I didn't give you a chance to respond. If I hadn't hung up, what would you have said?"

Marie froze, her eyes wide as her face paled. A few moments went by with no answer, so I rolled off the bed. Marie continued to sit there with her mouth open in surprise as I dressed.

"Brady, wait." Standing up, she sauntered over to me. Before she said anything, she glanced down at her naked body. "Give me one second to put on a T-shirt at least."

While she dressed, I checked my phone for the time.

"I shouldn't have put you on the spot that way. I'm going to put my shorts on and go for a swim. Manny and Constance should be down there now."

Marie's fingers wrapped around my elbow as I tried to walk away.

"Please don't be mad."

"I'm not mad." My palm gently caressed her cheek.

"I don't know how to put into words what I feel for you. I can tell you what I do know, though. I know when I saw you downstairs earlier, my heart started racing, and I couldn't control the smile on my face. I know when I'm with you, I feel like the most beautiful woman on the planet, and when I'm away from you, I miss you. I can't say those words back to you right now because those words terrify me. Please give me time. Please, Brady."

Reassuring her with a soft kiss first, I said, "We're good. Grab your suit and let's go downstairs."

Making Marie feel guilty or make excuses wasn't what I wanted. If and when she wanted to say the words back to me, she would. I knew this. Part of me feared she'd never say it back because she wanted to be with Jayce. Until she admitted this to me, or herself, I'd keep trying to win her heart. She was worth the fight. Jayce had years to make his move on her and didn't until after she'd met me. Although she asked for no strings attached, I professed my love for her to make sure she understood I wanted more.

MARIE

Down in the pool area, Constance pulled me aside to tell me about her time with Manny. She started rambling off details, barely taking a breath in between sentences.

"At first, I wore a black lace bra and a hot pink tank top with straps the same thickness as the bra straps. My cleavage had been adjusted to the fullest potential I could manage without surgery or padding my bra. I looked like Trampy McHookerson!"

I laughed as she didn't skip a beat with her story. "Luckily I realized how crazy I looked. The tank came off, and I replaced it with a T-shirt with *Just look at the flowers* and a few daisies surrounding the words. I opened the door and you should have seen how Manny's eyes traveled over my new attire. He laughed when he saw the T-shirt and told me he's a Carol and Daryl shipper."

Listening intently to Constance, I kept glancing over to

check on Brady and Manny, but they looked like they were both having a great time. Brady really didn't seem to be upset, which made me feel less guilty.

"I suggested we watch The Walking Dead, and he was all for it. Then I was bold and suggested I'd let him kiss me before the night was over! I have no idea how I got the courage."

My mouth dropped open.

"So, did you kiss?"

"During a difficult scene, I almost cried. I hoped it would go unnoticed until I Manny held my hand. His palms were sweaty, and I'm sure mine were as well. Manny then caressed my cheek as he wiped away the tear. For a moment, his eyes locked on my lips. His tongue swept across his bottom lip before he leaned in. After a moment, I relaxed into the kiss, and when Manny's tongue met mine, I melted."

Peering over at the guys talking, I wondered if they were telling the same stories or if they were talking about something completely random. I'd liked to have heard how the men would relay these stories. Would Brady tell Manny about our conversation earlier? Or did they keep all their emotions locked inside?

"He's a true gentleman, Marie. When I wanted to stop, he pulled away immediately and even apologized, worrying he'd taken things too far. I filled him in on my lack of experience from being homeschooled and basically sheltered all my life. He was incredibly understanding. I'm glad he tagged along on this trip." Constance's eyes lit up as she spoke of him. It was nice to see her experiencing new things and enjoying life.

"Me too. I had a feeling you and Manny would get along

nicely. He's a good guy. I haven't been around him very much, but Brady talks about him constantly. They've been best friends for quite some time."

Constance grabbed my hand.

"I'm sorry, I didn't even ask about your time with Brady."

"Amazing, mostly."

"Mostly?" Constance questioned.

"We had a wonderful time, until I opened my mouth to screw it up. I told him about Jayce kissing me in New York. He says it's fine because we weren't exclusive, but I know I hurt him." Hurting Brady was the last thing I wanted to do. The amount of self-loathing I had due to my warring emotions over Brady and Jayce made me sick to my stomach at times. Selfish was the word that came to mind anytime I thought about it. Stringing two men along had never been something on my bucket list.

JOURNAL ENTRY

We're spending a little extra time in DC with Manny and Brady. Manny and Constance have become inseparable. I asked Connie if they slept together, but she said there had been nothing more than a bit of kissing the first day. He has been a total gentleman ever since. Brady hasn't pushed me anymore to repeat the words he's said to me. We've avoided talking about it by wearing ourselves out with sightseeing during the day (the White House, the Washington Monument, Holocaust Museum, the Smithsonian) and making love at night.

The scary thing is that I think I may be falling in love with him. The closer we get to the end of this trip, the sadder I become to let him go again. I'm not sure what will happen if I do love him. I don't know that I could leave my life in Tennessee behind to move to Michigan for him.

Constance and I had a moment alone the other night, and she told me now that she has seen me with Brady, she does notice a difference in how I am with him versus Jayce. I guess it's a good thing. She seems to be Team Brady at the moment. Whereas before, I thought for sure she was pushing me toward Jayce.

I took a big step last night, called my parents, and introduced them to Brady via FaceTime. Afterward, I listened to my mother go on and on about what a sweet guy he was and how very attractive too. My dad didn't have much to say, but then again, most dads don't like to meet the man in their daughter's life. I'd never brought someone home to meet my parents before. It felt like a huge step, which made me more confident about my feelings for Brady. Perhaps my feelings for Jayce were all in my head. Maybe missing him so much is what elicited the dreams and thoughts I've had lately. While Brady was around, I kept in touch with Jayce through texting only.

As I'm writing this, Brady's lying beside me on the bed reading an article for one of his college classes. He's wearing reading glasses like an old man, but he's shirtless, and I can't stop staring at his well-defined chest. He's the male version of the sexy librarian. I'm going to miss him so much when he goes back to Michigan.

∞*Marie*

12

BRADY

The clock next to me mocked me with its bright red numbers. It was our last night in Washington, and sleep was the furthest thing from my mind. Marie, snoring lightly, was curled up in front of me, my arm draped over her. The past few days with her reminded me of our time in Michigan. Although the conversation about Jayce lingered in my mind, it was hard not to wonder what the kiss they shared meant to her.

Marie stirred, and I whispered groggily, "You okay, baby?" Answering with a nod, she couldn't control the shiver passing through her body. Switching on the lamp beside me, I sat up.

"Marie, talk to me." When she rolled over to face me, my bottom lip jutted out as I spotted the tears. "Sweetheart, why are you crying?"

"Finish the trip with me?" In Michigan, she'd made the same request. Although we both knew that it wasn't possible, the fact that she asked both pleased and hurt me at the same time. If I could drop everything in life to spend my days with her, I'd do it in a minute. But reality kept us from living life in such ecstasy.

"You know I'd love to." The tip of my thumb caressed her cheek. "I don't want to leave you tomorrow either. I love you."

"Do you have any more vacation time coming up? Maybe we could check my itinerary and meet again in another state?" Again, she ignored my declaration of love. The realization stabbed at me like a dagger to the chest. She asked me to be patient. I had to remind myself of the promise I'd made to do so.

To avoid her seeing my hurt, I embraced her. "We can look and see. It may be next year before I can meet up with you again, though."

———————————

MARIE

Brady requested we didn't follow them to the airport. They wanted to say their good-byes at the hotel to make things easier on everyone. Manny had grown fond of Constance in the two weeks they'd been together. After finding them in a compromising position, I asked him about his feelings for her. He said he'd never met someone with whom he had so much in common. It was refreshing, and the fact they had such great chemistry was a plus as well. Her heart condition scared him, though. He feared falling for her would cause him greater heartache than he could handle.

Witnessing their good-bye told me he was already pretty far gone for her. Manny brought her hand up to his mouth and kissed her knuckles.

"It's been a pleasure spending the last fourteen days with you. You're unlike anyone I've met before, Connie. I'll text you when we get home, and I'll call you in a few days. If you agree, I'd like to meet you and Marie in another state on your trip."

"I'd love it. I'm sure Marie won't mind either, and you could bring Brady too."

In the other corner of the room, Brady twirled me around and our lips connected. After an intense amount of kissing, Brady pulled me into a strong embrace.

He whispered, "I love you," and kissed my forehead before picking up his bag and walking away without looking back. Ripping the Band-Aid off quickly was the easiest way to get through the pain.

Fighting to keep my emotions intact, the sobs overpowered me in a total knockout punch. Arms embraced me. If they hadn't been so small, I'd have thought Brady had come back to me. Constance worked to console my broken heart.

Once we were back in the car, I needed something to take my mind off missing Brady.

"Tell me what I interrupted earlier." When I woke up that morning, I'd gone down to see Constance only to find an empty room.

"Well, Manny and I had kept to our separate rooms for most of the visit, but last night, I knocked on his door around midnight. He came to the door wearing black boxer briefs and nothing else. I swallowed back my nerves and told him I wanted to overstep my boundaries and do something I've never done before. That's what this trip was all about for me, life experiences."

Constance's confidence in herself had blossomed during this trip. I envied how courageous she was to put herself out there and go for what she wanted.

"Manny pulled me into his room and he asked, 'What is it, chica?' So I dove straight in for a kiss. I then drew the courage to walk past him into the room, when I dropped my robe."

A gasp of shock escaped me.

"Connie, you are my hero!" I held up my hand for a high five. She giggled as she smacked my palm.

"Manny stood googly-eyed like a teenage boy about to lose his virginity as he stared at my naked body. It gave me tingles to see how turned on he was! He made the entire night so special for me. I can easily say it was the best night of my life so far."

"I hope I didn't ruin it this morning when I came by. I couldn't find you and was scared something happened. I had no idea you hadn't told him about your heart condition." After dropping that bomb, I had excused myself to let them have that conversation in private.

"It's not your fault, Marie. I should've told him. Once you left, Manny sat down. He was clearly frustrated. I knelt down to make eye contact, but he wouldn't raise his head up for our eyes to meet. After a moment, he asked if the doctor ever said how long I have. I explained that the doctors has said I should've died years ago according to most medical books. I could die tomorrow, or I could live for twenty or thirty more years. He wanted to know if I could have a transplant."

"I've wondered as well. Wouldn't you be a candidate?"

Constance smiled sadly. "Technically, yes. But because my parents shelter me and I stick with my meds, my health is above average to be the next on the list. My heart is defective, just not defective enough apparently. Each time my heart function falls below a certain degree, I'm put on the list. I've been called up twice for a transplant and when I go in for tests, they proved my degree of medical urgency was much lower than another candidate who was a match. In truth, my parents have taken great care of me. Even with a heart transplant, there's no guarantee of a long life."

Details of Constance's condition always hurt my heart to hear. We'd grown so close on this trip; I couldn't imagine my life without her in it.

"Manny said he hoped for at least thirty, hopefully, more. He told me how gorgeous I am and how he loves the way I experience things. He said I soak them in as if I've never seen anything so amazing."

Manny had put into words exactly what I envied most about Constance, her ability to revel in her surroundings.

"Was he mad at all?"

"No, thankfully. He said after we leave here, he wants to keep in touch and hoped to repeat last night one day."

Not that I didn't trust Manny, because I did based on Brady's word, but if he hurt Constance I might have to kick his ass. So much joy and happiness filled her eyes, and the smile on her face would not be easily erased. Any worries I had about him ditching her disappeared when she received a text from him a few moments later. Taking a lesson from her, I stopped feeling sorry for myself and decided to enjoy the trip.

JOURNAL ENTRY

Brady and Manny made it home safely. We left DC and spent the next week in Virginia exploring historic towns like Richmond, Williamsburg, and Roanoke. We spent a few days relaxing on the beach, walking barefoot in the sand, and swimming a little while we still had some warmth.

North Carolina had a lot of beautiful scenery. We stopped in a ghost town where they filmed scenes for the first Hunger Games movie. It was surreal to see the different spots from the film, and it was sad to see a town abandoned in such a way.

Constance has been different since DC, in a good way. She seems hopeful and excited at the prospect of what we'll see next. She always seemed cheeriest after a talk with Manny too. They speak every other night. I think they're falling pretty hard for each other.

Before we said good-bye, I asked Brady to text me when he got home, but after, to give me a few weeks before contacting me again. I needed to put space between us. Occasionally I pop by to say hi to Manny and ask him to give my best to Brady. Most nights, I leave them alone and spend time reading or writing in my journal as I am now.

We're going to South Carolina next, and it's time for Jayce to meet up with us. We haven't spoken since New York. I've hated going so long without talking to him. It seems unnatural and wrong. I'd sent him a few texts but nothing more than letting him know we were safe.

Each time I tried to call, he'd been busy with work. He'd been taking on more responsibilities at the shop according to his texts. Promising to explain when he had more time, he apologized for missing our talks. I wonder if it will be awkward when we're face-to-face again. He e-mailed me the information, and he'll meet us at a condo he rented on the beach. It's October now, and the weather is beginning to cool slightly on the east coast, but the farther south we go, the warmer it's getting. We're looking forward to the cool breeze of the ocean again. Our goal now is to get to Disney World in time for Christmas.

Yikes. I just glanced at the clock and noticed it's four in the morning. I'd better get to sleep because we have to check out of the hotel by eleven.

Hopefully, I'll have some fun stuff to write about after visiting with Jayce.

Marie

13

MARIE

A three-bedroom condo on the beach, fifteenth floor with a balcony looking straight out into the ocean. Awestruck, we left our bags in the floor to run for the balcony view.

"Hello, beauties!" Jayce screamed out after we stepped onto the balcony.

Grabbing my chest with one arm and the railing with the other, I yelled out, "You about gave me a heart attack!" Still holding the railing, I used the other arm to smack his chest playfully.

Gripping my wrist, he jerked me forward.

"I missed you, Mo," he exclaimed as he scooped me up into his arms. Arm in arm, we stepped back into the living room of the condo. "I brought you both something." Jayce picked up his suitcase and flopped it onto the bed.

"Constance, this is for you. It's homemade jelly from my

mother. She said you loved it as a kid."

Next came a handful of letters.

"These are letters your parents have been writing you. They said you didn't call nearly enough, so they have to write everything down to remember it. They asked me to deliver them each time we meet up. Your mom wanted something more personal than e-mail."

Finally, he pulled out a leather bound book.

"I noticed you were writing in a journal the last time, and it was getting close to the end. I bought you a new one, so you can write down even more of your adventures. Maybe you'll even share them all with me one day."

Constance stretched her arms above her head and gave an overdramatic yawn. "I'm going to lie down. It's been a long day, and I need a nap." Translation: she wanted to give us some time alone.

"You need to take your medicine and eat dinner," I reminded her.

"I'm not hungry, but I am tired. I promise I'll set an alarm for two hours, and we can have a nice dinner then."

Jayce and I went to his bedroom and closed the door to keep the noise down for Constance.

"Zeb is sick," Jayce said as he took a seat on the bed.

"Your manager? What's wrong?" Sitting next to him, I placed my leg on his thigh as I listened.

"Cancer. Throat cancer, which makes sense because he smokes like a chimney. He's asked me to take over the auto shop." Jayce's hand came to rest on mine, filling me with warm tingles at the contact.

"Really? Are you going to do it?"

"I think so. Since I've been there, business has been booming so it can make me a lot of money. I wanted your advice, though. I'd have to slow down on school for a while. My parents think I'm crazy." His eyes searched mine for the answer to his problems.

"They've always thought you were crazy. It's one of the things I love most about you. You take chances. It's in your nature, Jayce."

He laughed.

"Sometimes taking chances doesn't go my way. Like with you. I hate that we haven't been talking."

"I'll be honest. It's because of the kiss. Not that I'm mad or anything, but I felt we were going in a direction neither of us was ready for at the moment. I'm terrified if we go down that road, and it doesn't work out, our friendship will be over. I don't want to lose you from my life, ever."

Jayce's shoulders dropped with relief.

"I agree, Mo. I can't imagine my life without you. Let's forget about that stuff right now. How was Washington?"

"Fine. Constance and Manny hit it off well. They talk all the time. I think he likes her, like a lot."

"And Brady? Are things still good with you?" Jayce asked with an awkward tone to his voice. Talking to him about Brady felt strange. The short and sweet version of "everything was fine" was all I said about the matter.

"I've been seeing a girl in Chattanooga," Jayce remarked. "We met before I went to New York but didn't start dating until I got back. You'd like her I think. Her name is Reese. We met at the shop. She's a college student who brought in an old Ford Escort that needed a complete overhaul. Zeb thought she was sweet, so he offered the work at thirty percent off. She's majoring in criminology and wants to be an FBI profiler. Doesn't that sound cool? She's smart, beautiful and…" His words trailed off.

A twinge of jealousy tugged at my heart hearing him gush over this girl. He'd never spoken so fondly of anyone.

"She sounds wonderful."

"She wants to meet you. Of course, I've told her everything I can about you. I told her about our trips, and she asked if she could come along when I meet you in New Orleans. What do you think?"

"I'd love to meet her." One thing crossed my mind, and I spoke it out loud before considering it further. "I'll see if Brady and Manny can meet us too. We could make it a couples week. It would give you the perfect opportunity to meet Brady." Seeing Jayce with Reese may be exactly what I need to know where my feelings stood. Jayce's happiness was of the utmost importance to me. Perhaps if I saw him with Reese, it would help me move forward with Brady by making me realize my feelings weren't romantic toward Jayce. All of this could be a case of homesickness; it did all start as soon as my trip began.

Jayce twiddled his thumbs and cleared his throat, no longer making eye contact. Wise thinking went out the window, because next I blurted out, "I'll call Brady now and set it up." It only took two rings for him to answer.

"Hello, sweetheart. Is everything okay?" Brady asked,

eyes wide and panic in his voice.

"Everything's fine. Why?"

He exhaled with relief. "You didn't want to talk for a few more weeks. I was afraid Connie was sick." Speaking via FaceTime, I shifted the phone and Brady's smile faded. "Who's your friend?"

"Oh! This is my Jayce," I exclaimed, pulling Jayce closer, so we fit on the screen together.

"Hi, Brady, I've heard a lot about you." Jayce and Brady had the same stiff, fake smile on their face. The tension in the room grew thick.

"Likewise. It's nice to put a face to a legend." After they told a few funny stories to break the ice, I asked about New Orleans. Brady's mood lightened, either due to the mention of Jayce's girlfriend or the prospect of more time with me. I hoped for the latter.

"I should have more vacation time built up by then. I'll check with Manny too. I've never been to New Orleans. Plus I'd love to see you." Pink filled my cheeks as I glanced at Jayce who looked away anxiously.

"I have an early day at work tomorrow and class in the evening. Can I call you in a couple of days?" Relief washed over me as he gave me an out on this conversation. Next time we talked, Jayce wouldn't be around, and it would be much less awkward.

"Yep. Talk to Manny and let me know."

"I will. I love you." The three words made my head turn to gauge Jayce's reaction. Looking back at the screen, I caught the hurt on Brady's face.

"Good night, sweet dreams," was the response I gave before hanging up. Even if I were ready to say it back to him, it would be inappropriate to tell him in front of Jayce for the first time.

Jayce seemed to be happy when he spoke of his new girlfriend, which in turn made me smile. All I wanted for him was to be content, and it wouldn't be fair for me to expect him to be alone in case things didn't work out with Brady. It would be terribly selfish of me to hold on to him that way.

JOURNAL ENTRY

Jayce and Brady met via FaceTime, and it was the most awkward moment of my life. The next uncomfortable time will be in New Orleans. I'm not sure what I thought when I came up with the plan to have a couples' week. Part of me wants to meet Jayce's girlfriend to make sure she is good for him. The other part of me feels that maybe the kiss in New York meant more to me than I realized.

Constance woke up from her nap, and I filled her in on the plans and the whole phone call. She couldn't understand why I'd gone crazy either, but she loved the idea of time with Manny. She wasn't up long before she went back to bed for the night.

I had a restless night, and when I couldn't lay there anymore, I went outside to listen to the ocean.

It soothed my mind, clearing the warring thoughts of Jayce versus Brady. At times, I thought it would be easier to be friends with both of them and live the single life a little longer. There's something to be said about being an independent woman. It's definitely not a life to look down on.

I finished watching the sunrise from our balcony. Off in the distance, I could see a pod of dolphins swimming. I could get used to a view like this and feel lucky to be able to experience it for the next several days. Constance was asleep when I got up. I checked to make sure she was breathing because she had slept for so long. We may have done too much lately, and her body is exhausted. I decided we'd spend two days of relaxation before doing anything requiring a lot of walking.

Lounging on the beach and ordering takeout are the only things planned for today and tomorrow.

∞Marie

14

MARIE

"I packed a bag of towels and another bag full of snack foods. We need to put water in the cooler, and we'll be ready to go." Shortly after waking up this morning, I took a shower and put on my swimming suit, excited to get on the beach again. Constance still appeared to be a bit weak and tired. She'd slept for over fourteen hours. Once Jayce woke up, I explained my concerns, and we agreed to keep a closer watch on her that day.

Jayce grabbed the rolling cooler, placed the bag of snacks on top of it, and rolled it out to the elevator. We grabbed towels, a bag with sunscreen, and other essentials for the day such as magazines and iPods. The beach wasn't very crowded, and it was a bit on the cool side, weather-wise. Choosing a spot up away from the tide, Jayce spread a blanket on the sand, and set everything on it.

Constance eased herself down onto the blanket. With more effort than usual, she said, "I'm going to lie out for a little bit. I'll watch our stuff while you guys swim."

Her words came out slow and breathy. Jayce's eyes met mine as we silently worried if she needed to go back inside.

Constance picked up on the concern and said, "I'm fine. I know my body, and I need to lie here. Go, enjoy yourselves."

Jayce linked his fingers through mine and led me down to the water. The tide came rolling in, and we braced ourselves to test the temperature. The cold water lapped over my feet and as high as midcalf making me squeal.

"I don't think I'm going into that water. It's freezing!"

Jayce ducked down, wrapped his arms around my waist, and lifted me over his shoulders. I drummed my fists against his back begging him to let me down as I squealed with laughter. He finally agreed to let me go by dropping me into the cold water in front of him.

Chills invaded my body. Through chattering teeth, I managed to say, "You're evil!"

Embracing me, he used the friction of his hands against my back to warm me up a bit.

"Sorry, Mo."

"Yeah, sure you are," I teased. Leaning into the embrace, I enjoyed the comfort of being in his arms. All it took was hearing he had a girlfriend for me to start questioning where my heart belonged. If I didn't take a chance with him, he could fall in love and be lost to me forever. Could I handle seeing him with someone else? My head against his shoulder, I brought my hands up his back, resting my palms on his shoulder blades.

Kissing my hair, he murmured, "What's wrong?"

"Nothing. Trying to stay warm is all."

"This is nice," he whispered. "Out here in the ocean, where you can't see any land in sight, it's as though we're in a different world. It feels like *our* world out here, and it feels good."

Eyes closed I let myself enjoy the moment. "I'm scared, Jayce."

His hands rubbed my back in soothing circular motions. "Scared about what?"

"Constance. She's getting worse, I can tell. Maybe I should take her home." Having Constance on this trip had made things more enjoyable for me, but I didn't want to enjoy myself at the expense of her health.

He pulled away to face me, and instantly I missed the contact.

"She needs this trip, Mo."

"What if she never sees her parents again because of me?"

"She knows her limits. She proved it today. Look at her up there." On the shore, Constance tapped her toes to whatever music was playing through her earbuds. Jayce was right. She knew her limits, and she was taking care of herself.

"Let's get back to shore," Jayce said all of a sudden. Noting the worry in his tone, I followed him as he moved rather quickly to the beach.

"What's wrong?"

He didn't answer until we were back on the sand. "There was a smack of jellyfish floating straight toward us. I didn't want either of us to have to pee on the other."

"You're such a gentleman." I cringed at the thought of being stung.

Constance sat up when she spotted Jayce standing above her.

"How's the water?" It seemed the rest had done wonders as her voice was practically normal again, not breathy and low.

"Cold! Jayce saved me from sudden death by jellyfish and urine, though."

"Urine?" Constance inquired with a scrunched up face.

"Don't ask. You want a chance to experience the water with Jayce now?"

"Well, your story makes me want to jump at that." Constance put her hand out to Jayce, who helped her get on her feet. "But I'll take my chances."

Occupying the now free blanket, I lay back letting the sun warm my body. A call from my mom entered my moment of peace.

"Hi, Mom."

"Wow, I barely recognize your voice anymore since you never call us. If I didn't have Jayce's number, I'd never know if you were alive or dead."

My mother had a way of being overdramatic.

"I called you a week ago. I'll try to do better. With Constance for company, I tend to lose track of time. Please don't bug Jayce too much because he has a life and a girlfriend."

"Yes, I know. I met Reese. She's a sweetheart and a real beauty."

Jayce introduced Reese to my family? I wondered if he'd introduced her to his own. *Could they be more serious than Jayce let on?* My mother's somewhat nagging voice brought me back to reality.

"You're too quiet, Marie. I know you've been to several states for the last few weeks, and you should have plenty to talk about."

"I'm in Myrtle Beach, Mom. You know because Jayce told you. If you have some time off coming up, you could arrange to meet me for a short vacation. Take the time to meet Constance and see I'm doing great. What do you think?"

She didn't hesitate to jump on the idea.

"I'll call you in a few days when I have my schedule in front of me, and we can figure it out."

"Sounds great, Mom. I love you."

"I love you too, sweetie. Be careful."

Later, back in our room, we worked out the details for the next day of the trip. Since we were going to do a little shopping and sightseeing, we slept in for a little longer than usual. The first stop was an outdoor mall with several tourist attractions around it. A small lake occupied the middle of the mall. As we were walking across a bridge, we noticed a few machines that said *Feed the fish* and took a quarter for a handful of fish food. I stopped and grabbed a handful before looking into the water. Leaning over the edge, ready to throw it in, I gasped at the sight below.

"Look at all of them!"

In the murky water below were at least thirty catfish with their heads above water and their mouths open waiting for the food. As I tossed a few pieces in, the ducks across the way swam forward fighting for the fish for the food.

Jayce leaned over and looked down to the right where another machine was and saw more fish doing the same thing.

"Damn. They've all become conditioned to waiting beneath the machine for food. That's freaky and kind of sad too."

"Every time I drop food, these dang ducks attack and the fish can't get anything." I handed a quarter to Jayce. "Get some food, and go to an area away from the machines and distract the ducks. I'll try to feed the fish."

Jayce humored me and tried the little trick. It had distracted the ducks for only a moment before they realized the fish might be getting more. We included Constance in the game, and they tested feeding the fish with how long it took the ducks to follow. After a few minutes, all of us were laughing at the crazy ducks and ourselves.

"I give up. We can't beat them," Constance said with a chuckle. "I say we drown our defeat in ice cream over there." She pointed at a shop called The Fudgery, which sold fudge, hand-dipped apples, and ice cream.

"I noticed on the way in there was a Hollywood Wax Museum. Maybe we should check that out?" Constance suggested.

"You want to look at a bunch of realistically creepy-looking celebrities made of wax? How is this fun?" I'd never been in a wax museum, but I'd seen the movie *House of Wax*.

"Selfies with celebrities. I've seen pictures of people with these figures, and they look incredibly real. Wouldn't it be a great addition to your scrapbook to have us doing silly poses?"

Jayce shrugged his shoulders.

"She's right. It could be fun."

Two hours later, we had several pictures posing in photos with wax sculptures of celebrities from some of our favorite movies. A few inappropriate ones for fun. Standing behind a figure of Dolly Parton, I placed my hands in front of the sculpture as if I were cupping her breasts. Jayce chose to pose with Matthew McConaughey with his leg lifted in front and his tongue out as though he were licking his face. However, Constance had the best pose. The wax sculpture of Hugh Hefner was laid out on a red velvet circular bed. Constance sprawled out next to him on the bed and exposed her shoulder, peered over it, and covered her mouth as if caught in a compromising moment with him.

After so much laughter and running around, Constance's energy level was draining. She fell asleep in the car, and Jayce carried her up to the room so she could continue to rest. He tucked her in and kissed her cheek.

"We'll check on her in a few hours. Since I've been here, I've watched her take her medicine like clockwork."

I stared at Jayce with squinted eyes and a wrinkled forehead.

"I know you better than anyone, and I can see worry etched across your face. She's been taking care of herself for years. She's fine, Mo."

"When did you introduce Reese to my mom?" The question had been bugging me ever since the day before.

"Usually I find you predictable. I wasn't expecting that

question. I took Reese to the Aquarium on a date. We were at the penguin exhibit when I ran into your mom. Did she say something about Reese? She seemed to like her."

"She did like her. I brought it up, and I was only curious. She lives in Chattanooga, right?"

"She's in college. She's originally from Nashville. She loved penguins and hadn't had a chance to visit one of the most popular attractions in the area, so it seemed like the perfect date." Crinkling his nose, he eyed me inquisitively.

"You seem more than curious. What's going on?"

"Nothing. You're paranoid. I want to know about your life." Regret at not pursuing a relationship with Jayce slowly began to creep in.

Jayce walked to the fridge, and he grabbed a bottle of wine and two glasses.

"Let's go out on the balcony and enjoy the evening."

Jayce popped the cork on the bottle, poured me a glass first, then poured himself one. Taking a long sip, I leaned my head back and sighed.

"We should live on the beach. Every night, we could sip wine on our deck and take in salty air."

"I remember when you first talked about taking this trip. I said I didn't want you to because you'd want to move away. You said you'd never find somewhere you loved more than Tennessee. Guess I was right," Jayce commented with a wink and a smile.

"You'd love for me to agree with you. I included you in the move, so it doesn't count." Another sip of wine quenched my palate. "I've only seen a fifth of this country so far, and there are so many beautiful places I'd love to live."

"Is Michigan one of those places?" Jayce asked curiously.

"Yes. And not only because of Brady. It's gorgeous there. You'd love it. The Great Lakes are as clear as the ocean and the temperature in the summer is perfect."

"Have you and Brady talked about what happens when this trip is over? Do you think you'll move to be with him or vice versa?"

"I think I need more wine." Holding my glass out for a refill, I avoided his question. "Are you going to move to be with Reese?"

Jayce laughed.

"Reese and I are nowhere near there yet. We haven't even agreed to be exclusive."

"You must have talked about it, right?"

"Have you and Brady?" Jayce asked pointedly.

"Touché," I responded before taking another drink of wine. We remained silent for a moment, looking away from each other and out into the vast span of the ocean in front of us. The moonlight reflected light onto the water, and beyond that light, was darkness as black as pitch.

My mind wandered back to the moment we shared in the ocean. The moment where Jayce hinted that he wanted us to be alone in the world. Images of rolling around naked in the sand under the moonlight tormented me. Why had my mind betrayed me with these visuals?

"I think I'm going to call it a night. This wine is making me sleepy." Jayce reached forward to slide the door open for me. His hand grazed mine, and it sent a jolt of warmth through my body. Following me inside, he kissed my cheek before we went to our separate rooms. When his lips touched my skin, I wanted to turn and experience a kiss like in New York. The guilt set in when I checked my phone and saw a text from Brady.

Brady: Counting down the days to New Orleans. Miss you and can't wait to see you.

Marie: Me too, all of the above.

Brady: Wish you could see the smile on my face right now

Marie: I wish I could too.

The phone lit up with a FaceTime request from Brady. Quickly I smoothed my hair back and checked my appearance in the mirror before answering. Tingling with excitement, I pressed the button.

"Ask and you shall receive, beautiful lady," he said displaying the handsome grin on his face.

"I love that smile and everything about you, Brady." Nothing about that statement was a lie. I felt it in my soul when I said it. No guilt, no regret.

He closed his eyes, still smiling.

"Are you having fun with Jayce?"

"We were on the balcony overlooking the ocean and having wine and just a moment ago. It's been great so far. I was about to go to bed when I saw your text."

"I wish I could join you in bed right now. But I don't want to keep you awake. I only wanted to show you how happy you make me. Sweet dreams, baby."

I blew him a kiss good night before turning the phone off.

Reaching over, I turned off the lamp next to the bed and stared at the window across from me. Nerves twisted my stomach, keeping me awake.

I thought I told Brady I loved him, but wasn't sure exactly what it meant. Was I in love with him or did I love him as a dear friend? The same questions applied to Jayce. All I wanted on this trip was to see places I'd never been before. If I'd known how much things would change, I'm not sure I'd have worked so hard to get here. Brady had become an important part of my life, and I didn't regret meeting him, but I wished things were simple. Nothing in life was simple, though, and that had been my greatest life lesson on this trip so far.

JOURNAL ENTRY

Jayce left this morning to head back home. We will see him next in New Orleans. He's decided he and Reese will drive instead of fly. Constance and I packed up the car and entered our next destination for the trip, Savannah, Georgia, into the GPS. We'll be exploring Savannah, Atlanta, and a few smaller cities in the state before leaving. It's getting closer to the holidays. We're a week away from Thanksgiving, and for Christmas, we'll be in Disney World. Both of us are missing our families, but we're sticking to the plan. We're going to find a nice restaurant in Georgia for our Thanksgiving dinner.

Staying away from Brady and Jayce for the holidays, I hoped, would make me enjoy myself better instead of worrying about one or the other. I think it will be a nice break to spend time with

Constance. Girl time is what I need right now.

Constance and I have both been particularly excited about our time in Atlanta. We are going to visit some of the places where they film The Walking Dead and go to the Aquarium and World of Coca-Cola as well. It's going to be a busy part of our trip. We're both anxious to get to Disney and see it for the first time. We'd head straight there if we weren't set on spending our Christmas there instead. We've been researching it, and there are so many fun things to do during the holidays in the park. We rearranged our itinerary a bit so we can stay for a full month and do everything we want.

Constance is getting tired a lot quicker these days. We've been taking breaks more often, and my concern is heightened. I've been watching her like a hawk, and she is taking her medications at the exact time she's supposed to.

I'm scared she won't make it to the end of this trip.

ꝏ Marie

15

"Get a picture of me in front of the prison!" Constance requested enthusiastically. The prison was a backdrop for the show *The Walking Dead*. After getting a picture, I stepped up and shot a selfie of us together.

"I could die happy now," she said with a grin looking at the photo on her phone. The simple phrase used innocently made me cringe. Constance's condition was still new and scary for me, but I understood it had become a way of life for her and not something she dwelled on constantly.

"We can ride through the town of Woodbury next. I read there is a coffee shop there where the locals have cool stories. There's supposed to be a gift shop as well. Do you want to check it out?"

"Hell yeah!" Constance yelled. Beating me to the driver seat, she googled the address and entered it into the GPS.

Bouncing in her seat, she couldn't contain her excitement. Within a few minutes, the bouncing stopped, and her breathing became a bit labored.

"Maybe we should rest for a bit?" I suggested.

"No way, I'm fine." It took an unbelievable amount of effort for her to get those few words out.

"There's the coffee shop straight ahead. Find a spot to park, and let's go in there for a few minutes." It was a nice subtle way of convincing her to rest without noticing I was being protective. She didn't argue with me on that one, and for that, I was grateful. "I don't know about you, but I'm starving. Let's order a little something to eat and relax here. I didn't sleep too well last night and could use some rest."

I ordered a cappuccino for myself and a sweet tea for Constance, along with a variety of treats for us to share and taste test.

We sat next to the window and looked out at the surrounding buildings.

"It feels like we're on the show right now. I half expect to see the Governor or Andrea walk by," I teased. "It's surreal."

"You two have the best seats in the house. Do you mind if we join you?" an attractive young man asked.

"Sure, you can sit. I'm Constance, and this is Marie." Constance seemed more welcoming than I felt at the moment. Something about these men seemed off to me.

"I'm Nathan. This is my friend Pacey."

Nathan, the taller of the two with spiky blond hair sat next to me. Pacey, lightly tanned with thick black hair neatly trimmed, took the seat next to Constance.

"We're passing through on our way to Florida. What about you two?"

"Passing through as well," was the only detail I gave. Constance's mouth hung open, apparently to give our destination, but closed when I answered for her.

"If we're headed the same way, you could join us," Nathan suggested with a grin, causing a look of unease on Constance's face this time. She grimaced when he ran his finger across the skin of her arm.

"Thanks, but our boyfriends probably wouldn't approve. They're expecting us to meet them in the morning. Where in Florida are you heading?" I didn't want to be rude, but my gut screamed these men weren't trustworthy. With my body language, I tried to relay this to Constance. Arms crossed over my chest in protection, my eyes darted around for a way out of this situation.

"Miami," Nathan said curtly. He glanced around the room and then said, "We better get going, Pacey. I think I found a better view."

The men stood up and walked away from us to begin their spiel on a different couple of girls. The girls glanced in our direction, and I slowly shook my head to warn them off the men who seemed to have an agenda.

Soon after, the two men left the coffee shop, and we watched as they walked to their car and drove away.

"I shouldn't have asked them to sit. They seemed nice at first, but then they gave me the creeps. It could be I've been watching too many *Criminal Minds* episodes on my iPad at night."

"They rubbed me the wrong way too. Look at my arm." Laying my arm on the table I showed off the goose bumps that had formed. "Let's stay here a few more minutes to make sure they're gone."

After leaving the coffee shop, we went to the Woodbury Shoppe to explore all the merchandise for the show. For pictures, we took advantage of a couple of props from the set you could use as backdrops. We took turns on the back of the replica of Daryl's motorcycle and captured photos from within a couple of the jail cells and in front of the door spray painted with, "Don't Open. Dead Inside."

"I need to lie down. Can we find a hotel?" Constance gripped the railing of the stairs next to her.

"There's a couch over here. Let's sit down there for a moment, and I'll find a hotel nearby for us." I asked the cashier for the closest possible hotel while keeping a close eye on Constance to ensure she didn't pass out. Laying her head down on the arm of the couch, she closed her eyes.

"Is your friend okay?" the cashier whispered to me.

Leaning forward I whispered back to her, "She has a heart condition, and I think she's overdone it today. Can you tell me the closest hotel with a hospital nearby?"

The woman worked with me to google that information based on the towns closest to us. We weren't able to find much nearby in the small towns that surrounded us. "How far is Atlanta?"

"A little less than an hour from here. If she is comfortable in your car, it would be your best bet for getting her the best medical care. I hope you don't need it, though."

"Thank you," I replied with sincerity. Kneeling down in front of Constance, I gave her shoulders a gentle shake. "Can you make it to Atlanta? It's about fifty minutes from here. We can check into the hotel and relax for the rest of today and all of tomorrow."

Supporting Constance with an arm around her waist, we walked to the car. Constance took the passenger seat this time and I grabbed a pillow from the backseat for her. "Put this against the window to rest your head. Try to get a little sleep."

Speeding was not something I did often, but in this case, I broke the speed limit a few times and made it to Atlanta in less than forty minutes. Once I checked in to the hotel, I led Constance up to the room and into bed.

On the opposite bed, I lay down and watched Constance sleeping. I wanted to be sure to see her chest rise and fall with each breath. Sleep wouldn't come for me until I made sure Constance didn't need a doctor.

Needing a distraction, I picked up the phone and texted Jayce.

Marie: Checked into the hotel in Atlanta. Constance seems to be getting exhausted quicker these days. I'm worried.

Jayce: Can I call to talk or is text better?

Marie: Text for now, she's sleeping. I'm scared, Jayce.

Jayce: Watch for her breathing. If it slows down too much, call 911. Is she taking her medicine?

Marie: Yes. I've been very watchful lately.

Jayce: Good girl. You're doing everything you

can. Remember in Myrtle Beach, she just needed to rest her body. If you have to, stay in the hotel for two days this time to recharge.

Marie: I think that will be best. We're staying in all day tomorrow for sure. Constance can be stubborn, so I may not be able to keep her in much.

Jayce: I know what it's like to deal with a stubborn woman (Wink)

Marie: lol. I know you do. I'll call you tomorrow with an update.

Jayce: Please do.

My iPad accompanied me to the bathroom. Behind the door was a large garden tub. With the water as hot as I could stand it, I poured in a bit of bubble bath purchased the last time we'd gone to the store. Slipping down into the water, I sighed as the warm liquid soothed my tense muscles. I brought a chair into the room with me to set up my iPad. Netflix had a good selection of chick flicks I could watch as I relaxed.

On the screen, the couple pronounced their affection for each other in gooey details with extravagant words and promises of love ever after. *Does that really happen in real life?* If it did, then I hadn't experienced it. In my mind, love wasn't about long-winded pronouncements of forever and mushy admissions of never finding anyone else as beautiful or handsome as one person. Even if you were in love with someone you could find other people attractive. It was acting on the attraction you had to avoid. Perhaps that was my problem. I loved Brady but found myself attracted to Jayce. It was possible I was having dreams about Jayce because I missed him. Maybe I was confusing unconscious thoughts with feelings. What if I ended things with Brady to explore my feelings for Jayce, only to find out at the end of this trip that I simply missed his company and the comfort of home?

I ignored the last half of the movie contemplating these thoughts on true love. In one of the final scenes, the couple was making love, and instantly my mind went to the last time with Brady. Tension over the last few days had done a number on my body. The movie didn't help but I knew what would. I sent a FaceTime request to Brady and waited for him to answer. When he did, he was sitting in bed with no shirt.

"Am I interrupting anything?" I couldn't remember him ever sitting around without a shirt on before. If he had another woman there, it would break my heart.

Brady cocked an eyebrow and leaned forward toward the camera.

"Looks like I'm missing a nice bath. I have a confession. I had a shirt on until I saw you wanted to FaceTime, and I took it off."

The relief at his admission burst out of me in laughter. "I appreciate the gesture and the honesty. I was thinking about you and hoping you had a few minutes."

"For you, naked in a tub and wearing only bubbles, always. And may I say that I seriously wish I was there with you now."

"I wish you were too. I called hoping you could help me relieve some tension." After finishing the seductive request, I bit my lip knowing Brady would go crazy over the action.

Brady took the bait and replied, "If I was there, I'd slide in behind you in the tub. I'd place my hands under the water, guiding them along your hips, up your stomach, until I'm cupping your breasts. I'd massage your nipples with my thumbs and index fingers."

Locking eyes on the screen, Brady watched as I mimicked the trail of his hands. Lust filled his eyes as his tongue swept across his lips. He removed his pants as his erection pressed against the zipper. Wrapping his hand around the length, he began to stroke. His voice lowered in a seductive tone just above a whisper.

"Next, I'd keep one hand on your breast as I moved the other back below the water. My hand would delve between your silky thighs, finding your core and rubbing your clit slow at first and then faster." His name came out in a breathy moan. "That's right, baby. I'm there in the tub with you. Can you feel how much I want you? I want to fill you completely."

Moans grew louder as my fingers quickened their pace. "I'd lift you up and slide into you, filling you with every inch of me." Three fingers slid inside me and my body bucked at the sensations. With my eyes closed, I could sense Brady's actions as he described them.

He whispered, "Come with me, baby."

It sounded so close, I could swear he whispered it directly in my ear. My hand cramped as the intensity of the orgasm rocked my body. Brady experienced his release at the same moment.

"Did I mention I wish I were there?" Brady asked as we both came back to reality.

Leaning over the tub, I pressed my face closer to the screen. "I wish you were here too. That was pretty amazing, though, even with you so many miles away."

"It's almost Christmas. Are you and Constance going to be alone?" Brady made an abrupt subject change, which I welcomed. As much as I wanted to continue sex talk with Brady, my body ached for the real thing.

"Yep. We're going to be in Disney World though, so we'll be fine."

"I have a gift for you. I guess I'll save it for New Orleans."

"Perhaps we can find a hotel there with a tub like this one and reenact this moment for real next time?" I suggested.

"Woman, I love you," Brady said with a growl of lust. "We have to get off this topic, or I'm going to go crazy."

"Maybe I should get out of the tub."

"You are killing me." His eyes trailed up my body as I stood up. The bubbles covered me in all the right places, but they slowly began to drip off my body. "If someone could hurry up and invent teleportation, I'd be there before the next bubble fell from your luscious body."

Desire filled Brady's eyes as he watched me. Wrapping a towel around myself, I closed the lid on the toilet seat and sat down. Brady laughed. "Okay, seeing you sit on a toilet kind of killed the mood."

Chuckling I stood, picking the iPad up with me. "Sorry, I wasn't thinking. I need to get off here. I want to check on Constance, and you relaxed me enough I'm ready for bed now."

"I'm ready for bed, too, but in a different way I think. Get some rest, beautiful. Tell Constance hello for me. Sweet dreams."

Constance was still sleeping as peacefully as when I left her. Changing into my pajamas, I curled up into bed. It seemed I'd barely pulled the covers up over me before I fell asleep.

My eyes opened and then closed again. I placed an arm over my face. The sun shone directly in my eyes. The clock beside the bed showed I'd slept until nearly eleven. Constance wasn't in her bed, but the bathroom door was closed. A few minutes later, she stepped out, carrying my iPad with her.

"Good morning, sleepyhead. I hope you don't mind I was using your iPad to look something up. Mine's on the charger."

Groggily I sat up, rubbed my eyes, and stretched my muscles. "No, I don't mind. Do you feel more rested?"

"Definitely. What are we doing today?"

"Nothing. We're staying in for the day and relaxing. Maybe order a vegetarian pizza and watch a few movies on pay-per-view."

Constance's bottom lip poked out.

"Boo. I want to explore Atlanta! We spent our time in Savannah resting. We barely saw any of Atlanta yesterday."

"And last night you were exhausted. Humor me, Constance. Spend one more day inside, and I promise we'll explore the city tomorrow."

After much poured on guilt, I was able to get her to cave to my request. We spent the day curled up in our pajamas charging movies to the room. My body seemed to appreciate the rest as much as hers did.

In the morning, I woke up at 8:00 a.m. sharp, as promised, and readied myself for the day.

"Where are we off to today?" Constance asked as she

plopped down on the bed next to me.

"Downtown Atlanta. The Aquarium, World of Coca-Cola, and anything else you feel up to doing. There are a few spots for *The Walking Dead* sights, too, if you wanted to drive by Rick's house or see where they shot the CDC scenes."

"All of it sounds like fun. I called Manny this morning and told him about our adventures in Senoia. He was jealous of all the things we'd seen. He's looking forward to meeting us in New Orleans, though. He's excited we're going during Mardi Gras."

"I talked to Brady. I think I told him I love him, finally. Well, I told him one night in Myrtle Beach."

Constance gasped and sat next to me. "Wait, what do you mean you *think*?"

"Well, I said I love everything about him. That's close enough, right?"

Constance shrugged. "Depends on who you ask. I'd be happy to hear it, I think. I mean if you love everything about him, it pretty much means you love him I guess."

"You guess?"

"Do you love everything about me?" Constance asked, making her point.

"Of course. Oh, I see what you mean. Brady seemed pretty elated over it."

"Then great! I think Brady is an amazing guy." Constance had a point. Brady was a catch. Why couldn't my heart and my mind wrap around that fact and stop the guilt over Jayce?

———————

The Aquarium was busier than expected for a day during the week. Thanksgiving was only a few short days away so kids must have been out of school and on vacation.

Someone walked up behind me as we were admiring a display.

"Well, look who we ran into again."

Nathan and Pacey, the two men we'd met in Senoia, were standing behind us. Fear gripped me. The men were attractive and looked normal, but some of the most renowned serial killers were attractive. Something about them gave me the heebie-jeebies.

"What were your names again?" Nathan asked, running his finger along my arm. I jerked away from his reach as it gave me chills. He put his hands up in surrender, "Whoa, slow down. I didn't mean to offend you."

"If you remember correctly, I told you we have boyfriends, so please do not touch my friend or me. If you'll excuse us, we would like to enjoy our time together." I grabbed Constance's hand and pulled her toward the next exhibit. Nathan and Pacey kept close behind.

Constance leaned over to whisper, "They're creeping me out."

"Me too. If they don't leave us alone, I'll find a security officer."

The men trailed close behind from one exhibit to the next without speaking again. I wished Jayce or Brady were there. Jayce could be there in a couple of hours, but I hated to have him come if it ended up being nothing more than paranoia.

We sat in the food court to have a quick bite to eat. Nathan and Pacey followed us and sat a few tables away. Constance walked up to get some napkins and plasticware when Pacey approached her. Keeping my eyes glued on her, I listened to their exchange to determine if I needed to rescue her.

"Hello, gorgeous. I hope you're a little friendlier than the other chick. We're just interested in making new friends."

"You need to work on your strategy for making friends. Stalking people who don't want to speak with you is not the way to go. If you two do not leave us alone, we're going to call security."

Pacey faked a gasp and put his hand over his mouth in faux terror.

"Please no, not security." He laughed. "Forget it, we'll find some women who don't have a stick up their ass."

Constance scoffed. "I feel sorry for the women who fall for you, scumbag."

She mumbled it but not low enough, because he turned back and cornered her against the counter. "Little girl, you might want to be careful how you speak to people. A little thing like you could get hurt quite easily."

Constance stood tall and didn't show fear. "Are you threatening me?"

Pacey grinned and stepped back. "Of course not. Have a nice day."

Pacey walked back to Nathan who blew me a kiss when he spotted me glaring at him. When Constance sat back down, I suggested we wait until the men were out of sight before continuing.

"I'm going to ask a security guard to walk us to the car."

At the front entrance, I explained the situation including our recent experience with the two men. The woman said she'd gladly call an officer to walk us out and apologized if we received any harassment in the Aquarium. The guard kindly escorted us to the car and waved good-bye as we left. We glanced around but never spotted the two men. A moment later, in my rearview mirror, I spotted them two cars back.

"Constance, they're behind us. I'm getting scared. Call the police."

Constance called the local police, but they said they were unable to do anything. The men had done nothing wrong. They had ended up in the same place as we were, and nothing was unusual about them leaving at the same time. They couldn't arrest someone because they creeped a person out, or they'd be arresting people all the time.

To determine if they were following us, I took several left turns, and they stayed exactly two car lengths behind each time. Panic rose in my chest, and I reached over and grabbed Constance's hand. "Google the closest police station and enter the address in the GPS. That's our next stop."

The police station wasn't far from us. We parked and waited for Nathan and Pacey to pull in. Instead, they kept driving. As they passed, they waved at Constance, who stared them down. We sat there for a few minutes before leaving and driving in the opposite direction.

Back at the hotel, we quickly ran up to our room. We closed the curtains, put the extra lock on the door, and collapsed onto the bed.

"I'm beginning to regret this girls' trip. You think Brady or Jayce could quit their jobs and travel with us for the rest of it?" Constance said somewhat joking.

"Maybe this traveling wasn't a good idea. We could finish the trip now and go back home. I can return the money to my grandparents."

Constance patted the bed next to her, and I moved over to lie next to her. "We're not letting those jerks ruin this for us. Let's leave first thing in the morning and get out of this state. We'll head on down to Florida and relax on the beach for a week."

JOURNAL ENTRY

Georgia was the worst part of the trip thanks to Nathan and Pacey, the two guys who decided to stalk us. We didn't see them after they drove away from the police station. The next morning, we woke up earlier than usual, so we could get as far away from that place as possible. Since the beginning of this trip, I've met wonderful people. I should've known that eventually there would be some bad seeds thrown in. Neither of us slept very well after the encounter. We double locked our room as a precaution. Constance apologized again for inviting the men to sit. In a way, I think she blames herself for giving them an opening. I tried to reassure her as best as I could that we weren't to blame for anything they did. We never led them on or gave them any kind of reason to continue following us.

We chose Panama City Beach as our next location. It was off-season for the beach. The end of November is a little chillier than most people prefer. We were able to get a room directly overlooking the beach with no problem and little expense. I called Jayce and Brady both to let them know where we were. I didn't tell either about what happened in Atlanta. Constance and I decided it would be best not to make them worry.

Brady keeps asking me questions about Christmas. I think he's worried about us being alone. After asking me every question about our arrival in Disney and what hotel we'll be in, I assume he's going to send my gift to the hotel. I have to find something special for him and mail it as well, or I'll feel like a terrible girlfriend. We're scheduled to be in Orlando in the next few days. Constance and I are both looking forward to a month-long vacation in Disney World. To make things cheaper for us, we bought season passes instead of day tickets. We've considered going down a few days early and staying in a hotel off site, but we've decided to relax at the beach for the next week. Constance needs as much rest as possible before we spend day after day at a theme park. We plan to incorporate many breaks as well, but also want to enjoy our time there.

Tonight, Constance is asleep as I sit on the balcony watching the waves crash against the shore. This trip seems to be causing a lot of problems for her and I blame myself. We had the run-in with Nathan and Pacey, and it's taken a toll on Constance's health more than once. Not to mention the tug of war I know I am putting Brady through. This dream trip of mine is starting to become a nightmare.

I have to find a way to get back to what the goal of our trip was or decide if we should end it early.

ooMarie

16

MARIE

We spent the first part of December staying at one of the value resorts on the Disney property. We'd wanted to experience a few different hotels, so now we were moving on to the Coronado Springs Resort. The hotel was centered around a lake making it easier to park at the main building while we checked in.

Constance went to the gift shop as I went to the registration desk. Folder in hand, containing all our tickets and other information, I ran smack into my mother.

"What are you doing here?" Immediately I noticed she wasn't alone. "Dad!" While embracing my dad, I felt my mom's arms close around the two of us.

"We didn't want you and Constance to be alone for Christmas. Your very special man came up with the idea, helped make the arrangements, and found your dad and me the best possible deal. He's a keeper."

My very special man stood behind them. Without thinking, I ran to him.

"I love you so much! I can't believe you planned all of this."

Jayce pulled away. "I didn't plan anything."

The next sound was Constance squealing, "Manny!"

Turning around, I watched Manny and Constance embrace just as my eyes found Brady and saw the hurt wash over his features. Jayce cleared his throat and said, "Brady did all of this for you."

Brady strolled over to my mother and extended his hand. "I'm Brady. It's nice to meet officially."

Ignoring his hand, she yanked him forward into a hug. "I've heard wonderful things about you."

Brady's smile never reached his eyes.

All I wanted to do was grab Brady and kiss him, but the hurt in his eyes stabbed at my heart. He barely looked at me, let alone touched me. In fact, Manny hugged me first. Manny kept me company as I waited for Brady to return with their hotel keys.

Constance handed Manny a key card. "Brady said to give you this, and he'd see you in there. I was hoping we'd be sharing a room together."

Snatching the key from Manny's hand, I decided to put an end to this silent treatment. "You will be. I need to talk to Brady."

Everyone promised to meet up in two hours. The messy ponytail in my hair came down. I flipped my hair forward to give it some body. Checking the mirror in the lobby, I examined my face before leaving to find Brady. He'd told Constance the room number since it wasn't on the card.

In case he wasn't decent, I considered knocking, but then again he was expecting Manny. And in truth, his being indecent wouldn't be a bad thing. Sliding the key card into the slot, I waited for the green light and the click before turning the handle. The king-sized bed had a bouquet of roses tied with a red ribbon decorated in Mickey silhouettes. Next to the bed, on the nightstand, was a bottle of wine chilling in an ice bucket along with two wine glasses etched with Mickey heads. A note next to the bucket read, "To the happy couple, may your evenings be filled with romance."

Brady stepped out of the bathroom, startled when he saw me. "Where's Manny?"

Index finger pointed toward the display, I teased, "Does Manny know you two have become more than friends? Or was this your big moment to confess your intimate feelings for him? I'll admit Manny is quite gorgeous, but I thought we were dating here?"

Brady's response was dry and full of annoyance. "Are you asking if Manny is the *special man* in my life?"

My cheek stung from being slapped by his accusing tone. "I'm sorry. I assumed it was Jayce because he knows my parents."

"Does your mom always call him that?" Brady asked with genuine curiosity, probably thinking he overreacted.

"She never calls him that." Of course, I instantly realized I made things worse with such an idiotic response. "How did you even know how to contact everyone?"

"I had Constance get all the numbers off your phone. I didn't want you to miss Christmas with your family, and selfishly I wanted to be with you for Christmas. I suppose it's a good thing I thought to include the special man in your life as well."

"Please stop. You're hurting my feelings, Brady. We've been in the same place for almost an hour, and you haven't even touched me. Please." Taking a chance, I reached for his hand and expected him to pull away, but he didn't. He dropped his head down until our lips met. The kiss was different, though, as if he had to force himself to kiss me. It ended much quicker, too, with Brady pulling away first for a change.

"You should probably make sure your family got settled in." Brady sounded cold and unlike himself. He turned his back on me, and I fought to hold back tears.

"Please don't let this be our first Christmas together. I don't want to fight. You know Jayce is my best friend."

"I'm in this all the way, Marie. Are you?"

"I love you," it came out as a whisper. I meant it. I just wasn't sure how I meant it. *Was my love for Brady a forever kind of love?* Nothing changed. He simply stared at me. In case he didn't hear me, I spoke louder this time. "I love you, Brady."

Almost knocking me down, he kissed me with the passion I craved. He lifted me up and I wrapped my legs around his waist, and my fingers clung to his hair as our mouths danced.

Carrying me to the bed, he flopped me down onto the soft mattress. My body bounced, and I gasped as his mouth trailed across my jaw, down to the nape of my neck. My shirt came over my head as I carelessly flung it across the room.

The intensity of the moment gave me new perspective. Perhaps this was the forever kind of love. Our underwear still stood between our full connection, and already I felt on the brink of orgasm. Brady rocked me to the core with barely a touch. Fingers latched around the top of my panties as they slowly slid down the length of my legs. Grabbing my feet, he palmed each one, pushing my legs forward. Placing a foot over each shoulder, he freed his hands to slide on a condom. My back arched as our bodies came together as one. I bit my bottom lip to muffle the scream as the intense quivers overcame my body.

Collapsing against his chest, I curled up in his arms. Tracing my index finger along the muscular ridges of his chest, I gazed up at Brady with a grin.

"I hope Manny isn't mad at me for ruining his romantic weekend with his boo."

Brady's stomach shook with laughter. "I think I'm going to break up with him. The guy is way high maintenance."

Sitting up, I glanced at the alarm clock. "Shoot. We're supposed to meet everyone in the lobby in twenty minutes."

Brady groaned. "Can we stay here instead? I want you to myself."

"You invited them," I teased.

Brady rolled on top of me, holding me in place. Although we didn't have time for it, I hoped he wanted a second round. Instead, his eyes softened and his voice lowered.

"Before we go, I owe you an apology for earlier. I'm not

normally a jealous person, and I shouldn't have overreacted."

"No apology necessary. It was a misunderstanding. Let's get dressed and have dinner, and then we can come back here and make up again."

"Deal," Brady said with a grin.

After meeting in the lobby, we all agreed on Downtown Disney to have dinner and shop a little. Planet Hollywood seemed a great choice for a tourist destination. My parents were living vicariously through me since they hadn't traveled much in life. Photos from every stop I'd made had been sent back home to them, and my mom made the decision to start her own vacation fund they could begin utilizing in a few years.

"We're treating everyone to dinner tonight. It's our way of thanking Brady for arranging for us to be together," my dad said at the beginning of the dinner, offering up a toast to Brady in thanks.

Afterward, the girls wanted to do a little shopping, so the men agreed to check out Legoland and a few sports shops.

JAYCE

Brady had been obviously avoiding me since the moment Marie mistakenly thanked me instead of him. Patting Brady on the shoulder, I extended an olive branch of sorts.

"Hey, man. We haven't gotten to talk much. Marie has told

me a lot about you, and I can see how happy you've made her. I'd like for us to be friends."

Brady didn't hesitate or act angry. He simply shook my hand. I sensed that he too wanted things to be copacetic for Marie. It had to be difficult for her to split her time between her boyfriend and her best friend. Seeing Marie with Brady stirred up jealousy I never knew was possible, but seeing her happy was enough to quell the hurt. As long as he was good to her and kept that smile on her face and the pep in her step, I'd be his best friend too. Her happiness meant more to me than anything else in the world.

"Check out this statue. I had Legos as a kid, and I could only build things like a square house, a square car, or if I got really creative, a square tower." Brady stood in front of a life-sized statue of The Incredible Hulk, well as life-size as a person, not the actual Hulk.

Chuckling, I responded, "I know the feeling. Kids now can build the tower of Sauron and have Gandalf riding a horse up to it."

Brady smiled. "You're a *Rings* fan?"

"Yep, the third movie is my favorite. What about you?"

"Loved them. And the Hobbit movies were pretty freaking spectacular too. Do me a favor and don't tell Marie I'm such a nerd."

Holding my hand in the air, I swore an oath of secrecy. "Although, Marie is cool. If she ever went to a Comic Con, she'd never stop going. She's a nerd at heart. Reese took me to my first convention recently."

"Reese is your girlfriend, right?" Brady's eyebrows rose

with interest.

"We haven't really defined things. We're not exclusive yet."

His face fell in disappointment. A change of subject kept me from worrying too much about what the look meant. "Would you mind helping me find Marie a perfect Christmas present?" Brady asked.

Even with Reese in my life, I couldn't stop my mind from focusing on Marie. Helping Brady find her an amazingly romantic gift didn't sound even remotely fun to me.

Brady must have sensed how I felt because immediately he tried to backtrack. "I shouldn't have asked. Forget I said anything." My shoulders dropped in relief. I hadn't realized I'd tensed so much at the topic.

"So, why didn't you bring Reese along on the trip?"

"It seems too early for us to spend the holidays with family."

"Family? Are your parents not around?"

"Yeah, they are. Marie's parents have been like my family too, though." Everything I said made Brady's face crinkle with worry. I felt like I'd permanently lodged my foot in my mouth.

"You don't spend Christmas with your actual family?"

"My parents are workaholics, and they're divorced. They don't do much for holidays. It isn't unusual for me to spend them with Marie and her parents." Wheels of doubt were turning in Brady's head. I could almost see the insecurity. "Look, Marie talks about you all the time. She told me she was in love with you."

"Was that after you kissed her?" Brady inquired.

"What are you boys up to?" Marie walked up saving me from the terribly awkward question.

"Getting to know each other a little bit is all." Brady draped his arm across her shoulders. Pulling her close, he kissed her forehead. "What did you buy?"

"Not as much as Connie did. I don't know where we're going to put everything in the car." Marie's body leaned toward Brady. Although things had changed for Marie and me since she began this trip, one thing I knew for sure was how important she was to me. Seeing her so elated made it difficult to dislike Brady.

"Where is Connie?" I glanced around for the rest of the group, desperately hoping for an escape route away from the happy couple. Being happy for her was one thing. Watching them in love was a bit harder to cope with. It was a work in progress dealing with these emotions.

"She and Mom went to check out another store. It was a bit too much girl time for me, and I missed my boys." Grabbing my wrist, she pulled me closer and wrapped her free arm around my waist. "Tomorrow when we hit the parks, I'm hoping you two will be my riding partners for all the best roller coasters."

"I love roller coasters. I'm in," Brady exclaimed.

"Count me in too," I chimed in. I'd need to work on progressing a bit quicker on accepting the two of them together. Maybe spending more time with them would make it easier to see. Or it would kill me. Either way, I knew I'd find out.

BRADY

Back at the hotel, Constance and Manny went to what had originally been her room with Marie. Marie gave her parents and Jayce a kiss good night before following me to the room. The rest of the night was ours together, and in the morning, we'd meet up to catch the bus for the Magic Kingdom.

Too much garlic on my dinner had made my mouth taste horrible. Rushing off to the bathroom, I brushed my teeth and swished a bit of mouthwash around for extra effect. Marie was in the other room changing into what I hoped would be one of my T-shirts. In Michigan, she wore one every night we were together. A wide grin spread across my face when I stepped back into the room. "You wearing my shirt is better than any lingerie."

"So you don't want me to wear the black lace number with the matching thong later?" Marie teased.

"Well, now. I wouldn't want it to go to waste either." Between the thought of her in black lace and the reality of her wearing nothing but my shirt and possibly panties, I was hard instantly.

Marie giggled. "Oh really? Sorry to disappoint you, but this will have to do for now." Fingers gripping the edge of her shirt, she lifted it to prove she wore nothing else. Only a glimpse was given before she covered herself again.

My hands grazed down her sides until I reached the hem of her shirt. Placing my mouth next to her ear I whispered, "I think it will look better crumpled in the corner over there." I nodded to the right of the room, lifted the shirt over her head, and tossed it away. "Yep, much better."

She squealed with laughter as I lifted her up and we fell to the bed together. Hands locked around her wrists, I lifted her arms above her head. "I'm going to make this all about you. I want you to sit back and enjoy. Just make sure you make those sexy noises that let me know how much you like it."

The moans began in a soft whimper as my lips traveled along her jawline, down to her neck, across her collarbone, and started a trail down her stomach. At her belly button, my tongue dipped in, and then I moved away. Marie made a sound of protest. She sat up, and I was on her again pushing her arms above her head once more. "Stay there."

Finding what I needed in her luggage, I returned to the bed with a scarf and placed it over her eyes. Nibbling her bottom lip, she lifted her head, so I could tie it in the back.

"What are you doing?" Marie asked.

"Now you won't know where I'm going next. Just feel me." I growled in her ear, flicking my tongue against the lobe before biting down gently.

An audible gasp blew through her lips as my tongue caressed her nipple. The warmth of my breath caused it to pebble. Kissing her stomach, I gave the impression of going lower. Instead, I sucked the neglected nipple into my mouth, swirling circles around the taut nub, making Marie squirm and whimper beneath me. The sounds of her pleasure heightened my excitement.

Fingers walked along her abdomen, hovering beneath her belly button. She bucked her hips, begging for my touch. "Not yet." Desire in her whimpers gave me confidence and pushed me forward.

Moving to the end of the bed, I wrapped a hand around each ankle and spread her legs. Tasting her sun-kissed skin, I moved from her ankle and then up her calf. Silky smooth thighs invited me to explore them further.

Marie whined, "Please, Brady. Please."

Another gasp as my tongue found the sensitive nub between her legs. Her sweet nectar on my tongue drew me closer to losing myself. Each movement was methodical and thought-out. Each moan amplified as I increased my speed. All at once, I moved away from her.

"Brady?" she asked in a panic. In order to slow my own release, I had to pull back for a moment.

She tried to remove the blindfold, and my hands covered hers.

"I'm here," I murmured in her ear and then flicked her lobe with my tongue. Stepping away from her for a moment, I slipped on a condom.

A cool breeze lapped at her body from above, and I could hear the soft whine of the ceiling fan. Both nipples pebbled as the cool air touched them. The bed shifted under my weight. My leg brushed against her thigh, I slid my hand beneath her and lifted her leg into the air, draping her ankle over my shoulder. Pressing the tip of my erection against her opening, I teased her by not going in. "Brady, please, I want you." Relishing the feel of her, I slid myself in slowly at first, enjoying the tight fit of her body around mine. Emotionally and physically connected, I wasn't ready for the moment to end.

Thrusting into her, our bodies moved together until we both reached that sweet release. Afterward, we lay in bed panting with beads of sweat dampening our skin.

"Our neighbors are going to hate us," I remarked.

Marie chuckled. "Let's hope they took advantage of the magic hours at the park tonight, and the room is empty."

I snorted. "What if they have kids in there? We might have ruined them for life, you know?"

Marie placed her hands over her face and groaned. "I'd die of embarrassment!" Her awkwardness was adorable. As her cheeks pinked up, her mouth screwed up in a half frown, half smile.

A group text from Manny asked us to meet at the pool for a late-night swim. As much as we both wanted to stay in bed, we decided a swim would be nice and relaxing. We put on our swimsuits, and Marie sent a text to Jayce to invite him as well. Two towels thrown over my shoulder, I opened the door for Marie. Our neighbor's door opened and Marie's mouth dropped open as her eyes met Jayce's. She blushed and covered her mouth horrified.

"I didn't realize you were right next to us, Jayce," I commented, hoping not to turn this into a more awkward moment. "We would have invited you over to hang out." I was being polite; I would never have given up the time I just had with Marie.

"I'm not a threesome kind of guy, and you two sounded like you were doing much more than hanging out. Thank goodness a family wasn't in this room. Those kids would have been wondering why you were calling out for God so much."

Again, Marie's eyes bulged, and her face was beet red, but I found it difficult to hold back my amusement. "I'm sorry, Jayce. It isn't what it sounded like." My head whipped around as my face scrunched up with utter confusion as to what that even meant. Apparently Jayce was befuddled as well because he looked at her like a monkey doing a math problem. She covered her face in embarrassment once more and said, "Forget it! Let's go swim."

Down at the pool, Manny had Constance pressed against the side with his arms somewhere beneath the water. Marie cleared her throat loudly. "This is a family pool."

Manny glanced around at the empty waters surrounding them. "There's no family around right now. Come on in, guys. The water is perfect."

Kissing the spot of skin below her ear, I said, "I love you."

She grinned and said, "Good, so you won't be mad when I do this," and she pushed me into the pool causing a large splash to wash over the rest of the group. Coming up for air quickly, I sought revenge by wrapping my arm around Marie's waist and yanking her into the pool.

We spent the next few hours swimming to the point all of us were exhausted. Manny was toweling off when he saw Constance begin to fall. His quick reflexes saved her from hitting the pavement. Manny and Marie traded concerned looks. Constance could barely keep her eyes open.

"Chica?" Manny called out softly. "Can you walk?"

Constance mumbled an answer that was incoherent. Manny lifted her into his arms and kissed her cheek. "I'll carry you."

Marie leaned into Manny and said, "Make sure she's taken her medicine today. Keep an eye on her tonight, and if she doesn't get better, call me immediately."

JOURNAL ENTRY

Constance showed signs of deep exhaustion again last night after we went swimming. Manny carried her to their room, and I texted him several times throughout the night to check on her. I know she's in good hands with him, but it doesn't keep me from worrying.

I couldn't sleep, so I watched Brady sleep last night. His mouth hangs open, and he snores a bit loudly, but he's adorable. One time he woke up and caught me watching him. He helped tire me out for sleep after.

This morning, we're going to go check out the parks for the first time as a group. Manny wanted to let Constance sleep as long as possible, so he said he'd text us later. I'm elated to see the place I've only ever seen on TV and in movies. Brady woke up as excited as a child on Christmas morning. He prodded me awake wearing a Santa hat with Mickey's ears attached he bought at the gift shop in the hotel.

Right now, he's in the shower, and I should be thinking about him and his nakedness, but I can't stop thinking about Jayce in the pool last night. I've never felt such lust toward him. It's beginning to scare me because he seems to be more comfortable with Brady's and my relationship, as though he's over the idea of us being together.

I want to be over it, but for some reason my feelings are getting stronger by the day. It's frustrating. I feel like one of those girls who I read about in books. The girls who aggravate me so much, I scream at them about what idiots they are. I'm not sure what I'm going to do. Each time I start to fantasize about Jayce, I end up making a move on Brady to forget about it. That isn't a healthy way to be in a relationship. It's also causing an extreme amount of guilt to eat away at my conscience.

Maybe.

 Marie

17

Picking up the phone, I called to check on Constance.

"Good morning." Her voice was scratchy from sleep.

"Morning?" I said confused since it was afternoon. "Did you sleep well?"

"I think so. I slept hard at least. What time is it?"

"Two in the afternoon."

I heard Constance gasp and shout to Manny, "We were supposed to meet everyone at eight this morning!" Sitting quietly, I listened as their conversation continued.

Manny replied, "I asked them to go without us. You needed rest. I told them if you felt up to it, we'd meet them this afternoon."

"You've missed half a day at the parks because of me. You came all this way—"

He cut Constance off. "To spend time with you. The park's

not going anywhere."

The subtle meaning in his words cut through me.

"And I am." Suddenly her voice took on a somber tone, and I heard shuffling as she moved away from Manny.

His voice started out far away and moved closer. It felt like I was intruding on an intimate moment.

"I only meant we don't get a lot of time together, because of how far apart we live. If you want, we can stay in the rest of the day, and I'll be happy."

Constance's voice sounded more hopeful now. "I'd love to spend the rest of my life in bed with you, but I think I could handle a few hours at the park."

Manny took the phone from Constance and said, "Hey, Marie, we're going to get a shower, and we'll be there soon. We'll text you when we get to the park."

"Sounds great, Manny. Thanks for taking care of her."

The phone call had been a distraction while I'd been waiting for Jayce and Brady to get off Space Mountain. It was their third time on the indoor coaster. Once was enough thrill for me. Jayce called out for me as I stepped onto the moving platform to jump aboard the "people mover" ride for relaxation. They ran to catch up and politely asked to pass the people behind me. Being a continuously moving track, it wasn't as if they'd have to wait in line longer.

Just before we jumped into the car in front of us, Brady gave me a quick peck on the lips.

"Did you talk to Constance?" he asked taking the seat next to me while Jayce sat across from us.

"Yep. They're coming out to meet us. Connie is feeling

much better this afternoon. She was little annoyed to have missed almost a full day at the park. I asked him to text us when they get to the front gate, and we'd meet them in the Pirates ride." Taking in the background imagery as we rode, one part took us through a background view of Space Mountain stirring up stories of the adventures Brady and Jayce had on the ride with some of the crazy people who rode near them.

"You two seem to be getting along well." Bouncing stories off each other and teasing jabs were much better than the awkward silences from when we first arrived.

"This guy is awesome. I can see why you're best friends. We've bonded quite a lot today. Plus he's informing me of some of your deepest darkest secrets," Brady teased.

Jayce held his hands up in mock surrender. "I have not betrayed any secrets, I swear."

Eyes dropping to slits, I stared him down. "You better not have."

Brady draped his arm across my shoulders and leaned in. "Now I'm curious about what deep dark secrets are hiding behind those sweet green eyes of yours."

Mocking a maniacal laugh, I replied, "Wouldn't you love to know? They're going to the grave with me, buddy."

Jayce chortled. "Seriously, though, Brady is a cool guy. We've been having fun. Tonight we may grab Manny and your dad and have some drinks at the bar, give you and Constance a little girl time with your mom."

"Sounds pretty good to me. I got a text from my parents earlier. They were going to spend the day at Epcot and meet us back at the hotel later." Just as the ride came to an end, we received a text. Manny was at the front of the park, so we needed to get to the Pirate ride to meet them. We tried to walk quickly while searching a park map for the shortest route, but it proved a difficult task.

"Do you need help finding something?" a blonde female park employee asked with a Southern cadence to her voice.

Glancing up from the map, I asked. "Can you tell us the quickest way to get to the Pirates ride?" The badge on her chest read Mary Jane, and beneath her name, it said Nashville, TN.

"Are you *from* Nashville?" I inquired with a finger pointed at her badge.

"Yep. Lived there most of my life," Mary Jane answered with a smile.

"I'm from Chattanooga. We're practically neighbors!"

"Very cool! I love Chattanooga. I visit quite often." Mary Jane stopped and glanced around a moment. "Tristan!" she called out to a handsome-looking male employee just across the way from her.

Dodging guests like a pro, Tristan sprinted over. "What's up, beautiful?" Based on the way Tristan stared at his coworker, I wondered if they were a couple.

"Can you lead these guests over toward the Pirates ride? Show them the short cut."

"It would be my pleasure." Elbow bent, I linked my arm through his as he led the way. "Is this your first time at Disney?"

"Yep. I'm traveling around the country, and my boyfriend arranged to have my family and best friend come here for

Christmas to meet me. "

"That's a pretty awesome boyfriend." He bent down to whisper. "You can correct me if I'm way off on this, but based on the way you eyed them, I'd say the boyfriend is the one on the right, and the friend is the one on the left?"

Turning to see if he was right, I was shocked to see he thought Jayce was my boyfriend. "Other way around." Now I wondered if I showed too much affection toward Jayce. Brady didn't seem to act any different so he hadn't noticed. It almost seemed silly to dwell on what a stranger says. Then again, maybe an outsider was the best judge.

Tristan winced. "Ooh, glad I whispered to you," he continued speaking quietly. In a loud, yet terrible, pirate accent he exclaimed, "Here we argh, maties. Hold on to yer belongings and drink ye some rum before ye leave." Tristan winked.

"Now ye understand why they don't have me working this ride. Argh." Tristan took a moment to laugh at himself along with the rest of us. "Enjoy your visit," he called out before walking away.

Spotting Constance up ahead, I ran toward her. Manny kissed her cheek.

"Are you feeling tired?" he asked her as I approached them.

Removing his arm from her shoulder, she stepped away from him. "No, I'm fine. Please don't spend the day babying me."

It wasn't anger but frustration in her voice. Self-loathing ate away at her again, and I knew she was thinking she was ruining the vacation for everyone. I knew this because I'd seen the look from Constance more than once on this trip. "I'm sorry. I shouldn't be so snappy with you."

"No apology necessary, chica."

Avoiding any special treatment for Constance, I called out to them. "How are you guys? We missed you this morning. These two"—I pointed at Brady and Jayce—"have been tearing up Space Mountain."

"Sounds like fun. I'm anxious to get my adrenaline flowing!" Manny exclaimed.

———

For the next few hours, we sprinted from one ride to the next. Low-key rides were all Constance could handle, but they were as fun as any coaster. Most of the coasters had warnings to people with heart problems.

As darkness fell on the park, we located a nice place to watch the nightly show. In the middle of the park, Cinderella's castle acted as a movie screen as lights displayed scenes from movies and even seemed to transform the building. At the end was a fireworks show putting any we'd seen elsewhere to shame. Everyone left in the park was at the front at closing time. The crowd was thick and slow-moving. Keeping an eye on Constance, I was relieved to see the tight hold Manny had on her.

Back at the hotel, the guys went to the bar while Constance and I met my mom in her room. She had bought a bottle of wine to share. Constance couldn't drink with her meds, so I grabbed a bottle of water from the mini fridge for her.

"Did you two have fun?" Mom asked.

"So much fun. I felt like a big kid. Brady and Jayce acted like big kids too."

"They appear to be getting along better," Constance acknowledged.

"At times, I felt like the third wheel on their man date." Rolling my eyes, I shook my head and laughed.

"They are both very attractive. You might want to watch those two. You may end up single at the end of this trip." All of us laughed, covering our mouths to keep from losing the drink we took. "Your dad squealed when he saw Minnie Mouse today. He literally *squealed* like a little girl!" Doubled over in laughter, trying to hold back the tears, our faces were red as we held our bellies. Scrolling through her cellphone, she showed us the picture of dad with Minnie. The smile on his face was priceless.

It had been a long day, and I could see the exhaustion weighing heavily on Constance. Instead of drawing attention to her, I gave an exaggerated yawn.

"I think this wine is going to my head. I hate to do this, but I think I'm going to lie down. You guys could come to the room, and we could watch TV or something?"

"I'm going to head back too," Constance said, making my plan successful.

Left holding the bottle of wine, I curled up in bed and had two more glasses after flipping through the channels and finding an old movie. As I drifted to sleep, my dream started out vividly with Jayce stepping from the pool in slow motion, water dripping from his rock-hard abs. Water went everywhere as he whipped his head from side to side. I was on a chair sunbathing when he leaned down over me. Tipping my sunglasses down, he pressed his lips to mine. Standing up, he dropped his swim shorts to the ground. Before my eyes could see him naked, a knock sounded at the door.

Stumbling out of bed, I swung the door open to find Jayce grinning. "I came to tell you good night and let you know Brady will be here in about an hour."

A black T-shirt stretched across his abs, straining midarm over his muscles. I bit my lip. Anything goes in a dream, so I pulled him in for a kiss. Together we fumbled toward the bed after I slammed the door shut behind me. Falling back on the mattress, I groaned as Jayce fell on top of me. Hands slipped beneath my T-shirt until they were cupping my breasts roughly. Lips created a heated trail over my neck. Flipping him over, I removed my shirt and straddled his waist, stubbing my toe against the dresser in the process. Aware this wasn't a dream, I realized I was very much naked and grinding against my best friend in the room I shared with my boyfriend.

Gasping, I jumped up covering my chest. "I've had a lot of wine," I stuttered.

Jayce cupped his hands over his pants as he stood up. "I drank a lot of vodka down there. I have to go." Jayce fumbled with the handle of the door and ran over to his room.

Face covered in shame, I stayed on the bed. It had never taken a sexual turn before when I'd gotten drunk with Jayce. Everyone was getting along too well at the moment, and I didn't want to be the one to ruin the holiday or the trip. Before

I had time to get dressed, Brady opened the door. Finding me in nothing seemed a happy surprise. Licking his lips, his eyes filled with lust.

"I thought you were going to be a little longer."

Brady moved next to me, brushing his lips against my bare neck. "I missed you and wanted to catch you before bed. Looks like I came at the right time."

As his tongue worked on my neck, his thumb brushed across my nipple before he cupped my breast. It took me back to a few moments ago with Jayce and I had to push him away.

"I thought it was you at the door a moment ago." Brady nodded, waiting for more of the story. "I answered like this and kissed the person standing there and got on top of them in bed."

Brady's eyes darkened with jealousy. "Jayce?" he asked, already knowing the answer.

"It was my fault. He stopped me as quickly as it started." Which was worse? The fact I almost had sex with Jayce and got caught by Brady or making up a new story to cover the mistake? Regretting the wine earlier, I wanted to be able to blame it all on a drunken mistake. The hurt in Brady's eyes made the guilt double. How could I have let things go so far with Jayce? After the day we all spent together, I thought things had changed.

Picking the T-shirt up off the floor, he handed it to me. "Why would you answer the door naked or without seeing who it was?"

"I had three glasses of wine. I don't handle my alcohol well." It was a sad excuse, but I had nothing else to justify my actions. Even blaming the wine seemed lame. Brady could see right through me.

"I need another drink now," Brady stated sadly. With slumped shoulders and a sullen expression, Brady went into the bathroom. Watching the clock tick away time, I waited for him to return, eventually falling asleep.

The bed dipped under Brady's weight, stirring me awake. Curling up against his back, arm draped over his middle, I kissed his shoulder blade. "I love you," I whispered to him. Desperately I wanted him to forgive me for the stupid mistake.

Hand covering mine, he intertwined our fingers. "Good night."

A painful stab in the heart gave me an understanding of how Brady had felt the times he'd said he loved me, and I didn't respond. It sucked. Another rotten thing that crossed my mind was how things would be with Jayce the next day. Tonight I may have ruined things with both of them in one unguarded moment.

JOURNAL ENTRY

Brady has been distant ever since I told him what happened with Jayce. He holds my hand and acts like he's happy, but he hasn't tried to be intimate more than kissing. He has assured me he's tired from the long days at the parks, but I know it's not true. My heart is breaking because I hurt him so deeply. Jayce doesn't seem to remember what happened or chooses to ignore it because he's been acting no different than usual. If he's ignoring it, I owe him my gratitude. I'm too embarrassed to talk to him about it. We wouldn't be able to ignore it forever though. Everyone is leaving in two days. Constance and I will remain for an extra week. I must make amends with Brady before he goes back to Michigan.

As for Disney, it has been a magical trip as

expected. I've done well to enjoy myself without letting the issues with Brady and Jayce affect my time here. We've watched the nighttime show for each park, and I think my favorite would be the Fantasmic show at Hollywood Studios. It was an amazing display of lights, magic, and water displays. Rides made for children and adults have been some of my favorite. In the Peter Pan ride at Magic Kingdom, essentially you fly above everything and watch the story unfold below you. We all have favorite rides of our own, but in truth, I haven't found one I didn't enjoy enough to do at least twice.

Constance has had a blast. It's the happiest I've seen her. It truly is the happiest place on earth for her. She and Manny have been on cloud nine and inseparable since he arrived. I love watching them together. He's a perfect match for her.

Now if I could decide who my perfect match is, it would be great. Brady's distance has made me ache for him more.

♡Marie

18

MARIE

My parents said their good-byes and caught their shuttle to the airport. Manny, Brady, and Jayce were leaving the next afternoon. Laughing at whatever they were conversing about, the men seemed to enjoy themselves while we sat in silence. Wordlessly I cursed myself for causing a rift in my relationship. It was time to force Brady to talk to me.

Looking at Constance, I said, "Brady has barely spoken to me the last few days. I need to find out where we stand before he leaves tomorrow. Do you mind if I ask him to go back to the room for a while?"

"I don't mind at all. Jayce and Manny will keep me company. Go. Fix things."

Taking a deep breath for courage, I stood up. "Wish me luck."

"Good luck," Constance said with her hands held up in the

air displaying crossed fingers.

As I approached, Brady looked up with a sweet smile. "Do you mind helping me with something back in the room?"

"Um, sure. Are we coming back later?"

"Yep. You two stay down here and keep Constance company," I instructed Manny and Jayce.

Rising from his chair, he reached for my hand. Silence filled the air around us as we walked. Opening the door, his hand pressed against my lower back as I stepped inside first. Together we sat on the bed, and I spoke first on the difficult subject.

"You haven't been yourself the last few days."

"It's our first Christmas together, and I wanted this trip to have happy memories for you, so I've held my tongue and tried to act as normal as possible. Now, I'm going to be brutally honest. You broke my heart, Marie. Your admission the other night was crap. Something else happened to make you kiss Jayce, and it wasn't the effects of the wine. At most, it lowered your inhibitions."

There had already been too many lies. I couldn't lie to Brady any more. A tear rolled down my face as the guilt overwhelmed me.

"I love you. That part hasn't changed. What has changed are your conflicted feelings for Jayce and me. I think we need time apart. When I leave tomorrow, I'm going to stay away from you until New Orleans. Two full months without contact. No texting, no Facetime, not even commenting on Facebook posts. I want you to have time to decide what you want without me interfering. If you want me, I'll meet you in

New Orleans as planned. If you want Jayce, I'll cancel my trip, and we'll part ways or agree to be friends. The decision is yours to make. Take the time to consider what you want, and make the choice best for you. Your happiness means enough to me I'm willing to give you up if it's what you want."

Tears burst forth, and I couldn't control the hurt bubbling inside of me anymore. The cold, hard truth was two months with no contact at all most likely meant the end. Brady would move on, and I would lose both men because Jayce had Reese. Making this decision terrified me more than anything. Did I need a man to survive? No. But I wanted both men in my life. It was selfish, but it was the honest truth. Pulling me into his arms, he smoothed my hair back.

"I love you," I said, and the truth came out in a trembling voice.

"I know. And I love you. I'm not ending this yet." He moved his hand across my cheek, wiping the tears. "I want you to be happy, and you need to figure out what that is. If it's Jayce, then you should be with him. I've gotten to know him on this trip, and he's a great guy. I don't want you to be with me simply because you're scared to hurt me or scared to see where things can go with Jayce."

"I like what we have." Not only the amazing sex, but my conversations with Brady, our time spent together in Michigan, our phone calls. Everything we'd shared was dear to me.

"I do too," he said, giving me a peck on the lips. "We need to determine if absence does make our hearts grow fonder."

Pressing his lips against mine once more, he took a deep breath as he intensified the kiss. We tugged at each other's clothes until we were both naked and rolling around on the bed. As he moved above me, Brady's mouth focused on my neck while I scratched my nails down his back.

This time was desperate and intense as if we felt it might be the last time together. We explored each other's bodies, trying to memorize them. We gripped each other as if we couldn't let go for fear of losing the passion. Never closing our eyes, we drank in the look on each other's face. Afterward, we cuddled, wrapping our bodies together closely to hang on.

Awaking to an empty bed, I glanced around the room. Everything had been packed up, and Brady's bags were gone. A note with his key said he thought it best to avoid the good-bye this morning.

No, we couldn't end this way. My hands shook as I texted Constance that I'd be back in a bit. I ran down to the car and broke every speed limit to get to the airport in time. It was unfair for Brady to leave without a proper good-bye, not that I'd been very fair to him lately. Nerves wracked my body as I prayed I'd get to the airport in time to catch him.

I sent a text to Manny begging him to keep Brady from going through security until I arrived. He replied he would do his best. Every traffic light was red along the way as they mocked my impatience. Manny kept me updated on where they were so I could find them quickly. Only an hour was left before his flight according to my phone. Manny wouldn't be able to keep him away from security much longer.

Finally arriving at the airport, I jumped from the car, almost forgetting to put it in park, and ran into the building. Sprinting through the airport, I found the coffee shop they'd stopped in. Manny spotted me, and I saw him nod his head and say something to Brady. Brady turned around and gave a sad smile. He met me halfway. Stopping to catch my breath and control my emotions, I allowed him time to catch up to me.

"How could you leave without a proper good-bye?"

"I thought it was easier."

"It wasn't for me," I admitted sadly.

"I found it wasn't easy for me either. I watched you for over an hour this morning. I wanted to wake you but didn't know what else we could say to one another," Brady admitted.

"How about, I love you. I'll miss you. I can't wait to see you again. Last night was amazing."

Embracing me, I pressed my nose to his shoulder breathing in his scent. "You have to take this break seriously. Consider us as not a couple anymore for now and find out what makes you happy." My body tensed as the tears were ready to spill. "Please don't cry."

"Who, me? No tears on this face." It took every ounce of control in me to hold back the tears threatening to fall.

Brady smiled when he saw my face was dry although his eyes were misty as if he could break at any moment. If I chose Jayce, this would be our last moment together. After what we shared, I didn't see friendship being an option.

Gently, he pressed his palms against my cheeks. "I love you, Marie. Take care of yourself." Kissing me softly, he turned and walked away.

Manny eased his arms around me, replacing Brady's. Unable to hold back the tears, I made a snorting sound as I released the sobs.

Manny kissed my cheek and whispered, "I won't tell him you cried."

So many emotions tore through me: guilt, sadness, love, and regret. Brady had been so thoughtful to put this trip together for me, to make my Christmas away from home a special one. Truly, I loved him for it, for many reasons. Though he said he loved me, I had this undeniable fear that I'd never see him again.

"Thank you." As my body shook with the sobs, Manny held me until I could calm down.

"If you need anything or want to check up on my man, just give me a text. Take care of yourself."

"Thanks, Manny. I'll tell Constance good-bye for you."

"No need. We said our good-byes this morning, and I'm going to call her later. Watch out for her, will you? She doesn't want an overabundance of protection, but someone needs to keep an eye on her."

"I got your back," I said with a wink. "You better go before you miss your flight."

Manny ran to catch up with Brady. I watched them walk out of sight before turning to leave.

JOURNAL ENTRY

Constance and I are leaving Florida today and heading up toward Alabama. No word from Brady since he left. We're sticking to the no contact thing. My opinion is it sucks. The last few days in Florida were great with Constance. We went up to St. Augustine, an old town that had originally been a Spanish settlement on the coast of Florida. To see such history had made it one of our favorite parts of the trip. We found a unique bakery that made the best cookies either of us had ever had.

Jayce and I have been talking a lot. I told him what happened with Brady and me, and he felt unbelievably guilty he'd broken us up. I reassured him it wasn't his fault. He said he wanted to pursue his relationship with Reese because it's good for him. I suppose now I have to determine if Brady and I will reunite or call things off for good. At least our friendship was still intact for now. Losing both of these men would've been too much to handle.

Next stop is Gulf Shores, Alabama. All these beach stops have given Constance and me a nice copper-colored skin tone. As much as I enjoy the beach time, I'm looking forward to eventually getting to see real snow. In Chattanooga, I've rarely seen more than a few inches of snow in the winter. At some point, I want to see at least a foot of snow and try skiing for once. Constance is asleep right now, and I'm barely keeping my eyes open. I haven't been sleeping as well the last few weeks. I think being on the road is getting to me.

I miss my bed at home.

ꝏ*Marie*

19

"Manny's going to Skype with me tonight. If you want to join us, you can. Maybe you can see how Brady is doing?" Constance hadn't brought Brady up for a few days after we left Florida. She knew I needed time to heal, so the waterworks didn't start all over again.

"You two need your time together. I may utilize the workout room at the hotel while you talk. You deserve some privacy."

"He wants kids one day," Constance said out of the blue.

"Brady does?" I questioned curiously.

"No. Manny."

"Is that a bad thing?"

"With my heart condition, I'm not even sure I can carry a child safely. Not to mention I could drop dead at any minute."

Groaning, I begged, "Please don't talk that way."

"Sorry. My point is I think I'm going to break up with him."

"What? Why?" If anyone deserved a happy ending after this trip, it was Constance and Manny.

"He deserves to be happy with a woman who can give him things he wants like a family and long life together."

"Why don't you let him decide what he wants? Don't make decisions for him. You wouldn't want him to call things off with you if the situation was reversed." Pausing a moment, I waited for an argument to ensue, but none came.

Changing into workout clothes, I ducked in long enough to say hello to Manny on the screen before I left the room.

The workout room was small, only containing two ellipticals, two treadmills, a weight bench, and a set of weights. Having the room to myself, I grabbed a treadmill and plugged my earbuds in turning on my favorite playlist.

Following the norm lately, my thoughts drifted to Brady. When I popped in to say hello to Manny, I hoped Brady would be there too. Aching to see him, I had picked up the phone several times to send him a FaceTime request and chickened out every time. He asked me to take the time to think, and I was honoring his request. And I couldn't say often enough how much it sucked not talking to him.

"Uptown Funk" drove the rhythm of my steps. As the beat picked up, I tried to swish my hips a bit and turn side to side. A fancy spin caused me to lose my footing. My eyes popped open when a pair of strong arms steadied me.

"Thanks," I stammered, staring into the deep brown eyes of a handsome stranger. His gleaming white smile made my knees weak.

"You have some killer moves there, but you should be careful." He leaned against the machine and said, "I'm Connor."

"Marie. I'll keep my eyes open and save my moves for solid ground."

"Good idea. Are you in town by yourself?"

"My friend Constance is with me. She's upstairs talking with her boyfriend."

"I'm on a business trip, and I hate traveling alone. You're lucky to have a good friend with you. If you're up for it, maybe you two would like to have dinner with me this evening?"

"I have a boyfriend." The words flew from my mouth, and the lie stabbed my chest with yearning for Brady. After what happened in Atlanta with Nathan and Pacey, I didn't want to take any chances with creepy men again.

Connor held up his left hand to show the gold band on his finger. "Happily married man."

Embarrassed at my assumption, I offered an apology. "Sorry. I'll check with my friend, but I'm sure we'd love to join you." Since he already knew what hotel I was staying in, it seemed harmless to meet him downstairs for dinner.

"What were you dancing to?"

"'Uptown Funk,'" I stated coyly.

"No wonder you were getting down with your bad self," Connor remarked with a shimmy of his hips.

"Wow."

Connor cringed. "My wife constantly tells me not to speak. I'm a big nerd."

Sucking my lips between my teeth, I held back my laughter. "It's endearing. Want to race on the machines? I can take the earbuds out and share my awesome dance mix with you."

"Deal," Connor agreed. He took the towel from his shoulder and slung it over the machine. Starting the song over, I turned it up to a decent level. We set the machines at comparable speeds and took turns challenging the other to something. Connor would turn the machine on the run speed to see who turned it down the fastest. Then I set the speed very low to see who grew impatient quicker. During the slowdown, we added a few dance moves in for fun.

An hour later, we'd gotten a great workout and laughed enough for me to forget my sadness. Promising to meet him in an hour with Constance, we parted ways. Upstairs I found Constance still on the computer with Manny and noticed Brady sitting behind him. Our eyes met briefly, and I quickly ran away from the screen.

"I look like crap," I hissed to Constance.

"Tell her she doesn't," Manny stated. "We can hear you by the way. Come back over here. It won't kill you two to say hello." To get rid of as much sweat as possible I dabbed the towel over my face before stepping in front of the screen.

Brady grinned widely. "Did you have a nice workout?"

"I did. I thought we weren't supposed to speak?" Still worried about my appearance, I kept running my fingers through my hair.

"Seems silly to ignore you. We just can't make an effort to reach out."

"Makes sense to me. It's good to see you." Brady looked

amazing, but he was always a sight for sore eyes. As good as it was to see him, it also hurt… a lot.

"You too. Manny and I are about to head out to see a movie. What are you two going to do?"

"I met a guy while exercising and he invited us to dinner." Brady's demeanor suddenly changed, and I realized I needed to clarify my statement. "He's on a business trip and misses his wife. When he found out Constance and I were together and had boyfriends, he asked us to join him."

Almost instantly, Brady's smile returned. "You ladies have fun."

Dim lighting in the hotel restaurant gave it a romantic setting. I pointed to Connor when I spotted him. Constance then leaned over and whispered, "Good grief, he's gorgeous! If I were his wife, I wouldn't let him travel alone."

"Hi, Connor."

Standing in a gentlemanly fashion, he motioned to the seats across from him.

"Please have a seat. You must be Constance?" Constance gave a shy smile and sat down. "I'm glad you ladies could join me. I hate eating alone. Most of the time, I order room service and talk to my wife on the phone, but tonight she's got a meeting at our daughter's school so she won't be home until late."

Ordering a sweet tea for myself and a Diet Coke for Constance, I did my best to keep the conversation going. "You have a daughter?"

"Two actually," he said as he pulled his phone out of his pocket. "Sasha is three and Lenox is eight." Scrolling through his phone, he pointed out pictures of his family.

"Your girls are beautiful. Is this your wife?" One photo contained a beautiful olive-skinned woman with shiny black hair and beautiful green eyes.

"That's my Cherish."

"She's stunning. How long have you two been together?"

Connor closed his phone and set it on the table. "We started dating in seventh grade, and I proposed on the night of our high school graduation, so we've been married ten years now. What about you two? Boyfriends, right?"

"Yes," we answered simultaneously.

"It's funny, we're best friends, and we're dating best friends."

Connor grinned. "That's pretty cool. How long have you two been best friends?" Spilling the story of how we met Manny and Brady was split between the two of us. The evening went well. Two hours had gone by before we knew it. When Connor got his bedtime call from Cherish and the girls, we called it a night.

Before leaving, we promised to see him at breakfast the next morning. The hotel had a hot continental breakfast that came with the nightly rate. In the morning, I was the first up. Waking Constance, we both fixed our hair but left pajamas on to traipse downstairs for breakfast. Connor sat at a table with two plates next to him containing waffles. "Good morning, beauties. I made you each a waffle while I waited."

"Thank you," I replied for both of us. Constance had walked over to get us each a glass of juice and a banana to go with our fresh waffle. "Did you sleep well?"

"I never do. I stay up most of the night working when I'm on the road. I have a hard time sleeping without Cherish in the bed next to me."

"What do you do for a living?" Constance inquired right before she shoved a large piece of syrup-covered waffle into her mouth.

"I'm a director for a hospital corporation. I work on the billing side, and I travel around to find new clients for us to do their billing. It's all pretty boring. It pays well, which helps send my girls to private school. And this year, I have a conference in Orlando to attend, and I plan to surprise them with a trip to Disney. I already cleared it with my boss to extend my stay."

Her eyes widened, head lifting confidently, and a grin filled Constance's face at the mention of Disney. "We spent almost a month there for Christmas. Your girls will have a blast!"

"My wife and I have never been either, so it should be quite the adventure."

"As someone who experienced it for the first time as an adult, you'll love it as much as your kids do," I interjected.

Leaning back in his seat, Connor patted his stomach with his palms. "I have eaten my weight in waffles this morning. You two have made this trip much better than any other. Unfortunately, I have to check out in an hour."

"We've enjoyed spending time with you as well. Give me your phone," I requested with my hand extended. Opening his

Facebook app, I sent myself a friend request, then went into my own phone to accept it. "We're friends now, and I want to see pictures from that Disney trip."

At the end of the meal, we each gave Connor a hug good-bye. In just a few short hours, we would be on the road as well.

JOURNAL ENTRY

Alabama was interesting. First, we met Connor, the truest form of a southern gentleman. Then we went to Birmingham where we toured the Museum of Art, spent a full day at the Birmingham Zoo, and went to the Jazz Hall of Fame. In Huntsville, we visited the U.S. Space and Rocket Center where we dined on astronaut ice cream and other fun treats.

After Alabama, we went to Mississippi. Jayce and I had gone to Tunica together, but I didn't want to keep Constance from enjoying the town. We spent two nights there without gambling. We used the time to people watch. It's amazing the things you see when you watch people interact in a casino. Emotions from utter defeat to never-ending confidence.

Brady and I haven't spoken since the Skype

session in Gulf Shores. I sent him a text to let him know Jayce and Reese are still a couple. He never responded, and it's been two days now. Since our trip to New Orleans is in two days, I wasn't sure if he was going to meet us or not.

Tonight we're in Baton Rouge, and we'll be here until we leave for New Orleans. Constance and I went shopping today to buy new outfits specifically for Mardi Gras. As I sit here writing this, my text alert goes off. Brady sent me his flight information. Suddenly I'm even more excited about Mardi Gras. Once Brady sees how happy Jayce and Reese are, and that it doesn't bother me, he'll understand I want to be with him. By the end of Mardi Gras, I'm confident Brady and I will be a couple once again.

∽Marie

20

MARIE

"The board showed their flight was on time, so where are they?" Bouncing back and forth on the heels of her feet, Constance anxiously awaited Manny's arrival. Suddenly lifted up from behind, she squealed when her name was yelled out.

Manny spun her around planting a passionate kiss on her lips.

"Chica, I missed you." He barely spoke the short phrase before they were tongue wrestling. Rolling my eyes in annoyance, I cleared my throat hoping to interrupt the gooey display of affection. My nerves were on high alert about how the reunion with Brady would be.

Turning around, I found Brady with a grin on his face.

"Hello, gorgeous," was the only thing he said before I cut him off with a fierce kiss. "Much better greeting than I expected."

Wrapping my arms around his neck tightly, I closed my eyes and breathed him in. "I'm so happy you're here."

"I promised Manny he'd go to Mardi Gras. I couldn't let him down." Such nonchalant words from him stabbed at my heart. Was he there to let me go in person, for good this time?

"Oh. Is Manny the only reason you're here?" Stepping back from him, my face fell into a frown as my excitement was deflated.

"You haven't told me your decision yet."

"Yes, I did," I argued.

"No. You said Jayce and Reese are still dating. All it tells me is you haven't had a chance to explore your feelings for him. As much as I loved the mind-blowing kiss, this trip isn't a romantic one. Manny got himself a room to share with Constance, and I'm getting a room as well."

"You and I can share a room and save money. It will give us time to talk." By talk, I meant horizontally convincing him of my decision.

"I can't share a room with you and not want to do things we shouldn't do as a non-couple."

"Brady, please."

"If this is too hard for you, I can get a return flight home tonight. I don't want to ruin the trip for anyone." Brady's tone wasn't angry. It was sincere.

Constance and Manny stood by, silently watching us go back and forth. Pulling Brady aside, I whispered, "I need you to know I love you and want you with me. But if it makes you more comfortable to have your own room, I'll respect your wish."

"Thanks, Marie. I think it will be easier this way." Disappointed was putting it mildly in how I felt, but I wanted this to go the way Brady wanted. He deserved to take control of what happened next after everything. Giving him the space he needed was the least I could do.

JAYCE

Arriving at the hotel with Reese, I texted Marie to find they were just leaving the airport. During the trip, Reese and I had gotten into a rough argument when she found out Brady and Marie weren't together at the moment. When she asked me why and I told her the truth, she flipped out. It wasn't my intention to start an argument. I only wanted to warn Reese there might be noticeable tension from Brady. After checking in to our room, I began the desperate attempt to gain forgiveness, so we could enjoy the time together without more awkwardness.

Because of the argument, Reese insisted on two beds at check-in. Once in the room, she lifted her suitcase from the cart and slung it onto the bed. Angrily, she unzipped the bag and began to hang her outfits in the closet to keep them from wrinkling. Walking up behind her, I placed my hands on her hips. Jerking away, she moved around to the other side of the bed.

"Reese-y, there is nothing to worry about with Marie.

Please don't ruin this amazing vacation."

Her steel gaze told me that terrible taste in my mouth was from my foot.

"Don't even try to blame this on me. If this vacation happens to be less than perfect, it's not my fault. Last night you told me you're falling in love with me, and this morning you tell me you kissed another woman a few months ago."

"I meant what I said last night. And the kiss doesn't mean what you think it means. Marie is my best friend. Neither of us wants to ruin our friendship by hooking up."

Reese whipped around, and her mouth fell agape in shock. "Oh, so you didn't have sex with her, so you could preserve your friendship? I feel so much better knowing it wasn't because you're committed to me. What a load off my shoulders!"

Damn foot was lodged in my mouth! I couldn't get the words in my mouth to come out correctly. It was never this difficult to talk to Marie—a thought I definitely wouldn't repeat in this moment. "Reese, please," was all I could say without screwing things up worse.

Through gritted teeth, she replied, "I'll be on my best behavior. I've been looking forward to this trip for a long time, and I'm mature enough to let this wait until we get back home."

Stepping out in the hall, I noticed Marie and Brady only three doors down. Marie spotted me and her eyes grew wide, her grin even wider.

"Hey, stranger!" My eyes lit up, and I felt the smile on my face trying to break my jaw. I was so happy to see her. A moment later, Reese stepped into the hall, and I had to control my happiness a smidge.

Taking Reese's hand, she half-smiled, half-grimaced at me. Brady draped his arm across Marie's shoulders and they made their way over to us. Introductions began. Pleasantries were exchanged. The awkward tension was palpable.

"Constance and Manny are going to be on this floor as well. Once they get up here, we should all head to Bourbon Street," Marie suggested.

"Sounds great to me," I responded. Brady and Reese stood there looking incredibly uncomfortable. Exchanging a sympathetic look with Marie, we were saved by Manny's voice as he walked toward us. Distance from Marie was supposed to quell my thoughts of her. So far it had only seemed to make things more awkward now that we were back in the same place again. I had to question every action and touch to be certain I didn't give Reese the wrong impression about my feelings for Marie. Although I wasn't sure it would be a wrong impression if she picked up on something between us. No matter how we tried to fight it, I still felt my heart pulling me toward her.

The first stop on Bourbon Street was a restaurant for dinner since we all agreed we were starving. Marie paid extra attention to Brady, possibly overdoing it for my benefit. After we ordered, Marie leaned over, kissed Brady's cheek, and said, "I love you."

Overhearing her declaration felt like a hot poker in my chest, though I tried to hide the hurt. Turning to Reese, I noticed her glaring at me, obviously gauging my reaction.

Putting on my best grin, I leaned forward to kiss her lips. Constance and Manny held hands beneath the table. At least one couple was happily at ease and enjoying themselves.

The moment passed as quickly as it came. Marie made a suggestion the girls spend a little time together. Without considering his tone, Brady remarked, "That didn't end so well the last time we split the guys and girls."

Marie stared at Brady in shock. His words seemed to throw her for a loop. Without knowing why, I could only assume she thought they'd moved past what happened between us in Florida. If the situation were reversed, I'd act the same way Brady just did. No one could blame him for feeling betrayed.

As his features softened, I could see he instantly regretted his snarky comment and added, "I'm sorry. I've had a long day, and I'm a little cranky. I think I'll go back to the hotel early." Marie's eyes glistened with sadness as she stared down at her lap. It was easy to see the guilt eating away at her, and I wanted to comfort her, but it wasn't my place.

Marie removed her napkin from her lap and placed it on her plate. She reached into her wallet, pulled out enough cash to cover the tab, and handed it to me.

"Dinner is my treat. I'd like to call it a night as well. I want to rest up for the Mardi Gras celebration tomorrow night." She stood up and held her hand out to Brady. "Walk back with me?"

MARIE

People crowded every inch of the street. Brady gripped my hand as he guided us through the raucous crowd. On the short trip back to the hotel, I saw more pairs of naked tits than I'd seen in my entire life. Beads were flying from balconies following catcalls. A few women grabbed Brady in spots he wasn't expecting, and it angered me. On the verge of protest, a drunken bald man bumped into me and started grabbing my breasts. Brady's face flamed in anger as he shoved the man backward into the crowd of gropers.

Toward the end of the street, the crowd began to thin, and we were able to get to the hotel without further molestation. Brady's face still showed immense anger as we stepped onto the elevator, and he hadn't spoken to me at all.

"If it's that crazy tonight, imagine what it will be like tomorrow." I attempted to break the tension between us. Brady scoffed and nodded but didn't speak. It was time to play dirty again.

Going to our separate, yet adjoining rooms, I grabbed a bag from the closet before stepping into the bathroom and shutting the door. A lace bra and panty set with a garter belt of black silk attached to sheer black thigh-high stockings were in the bag. After the last trip with Brady, I bought them when he became so excited at the mention of it.

After looking in the mirror, appreciating how sexy I looked in this lingerie, I knocked on Brady's door. Once we checked in and were given adjoining rooms, we agreed to keep the joint door unlocked as long as the other knocked before entering. After a minute with no answer, I stepped into the room and glanced around. Brady had written a note on the nightstand memo pad.

WENT TO THE HOTEL BAR. BE BACK IN A BIT.

Instead of admitting defeat, I went to the closet and grabbed a coat. It was long enough to go to my knees, and no one would know I had nothing underneath other than the lingerie. It would be like a scene out of a movie, and it turned me on to think about Brady's reaction.

Downstairs Brady sat at the bar with a gin and tonic and a frown. It wasn't exceptionally busy tonight surprisingly enough. Most people were probably out on the street partying since it was early in the evening.

A tap on the shoulder brought him out of his thoughts. Taking the seat next to him, I winked and asked, "Come here often?"

"Hey, I'm sorry about earlier." Brady began to apologize and stopped when he noticed my confused expression. "Are you angry with me?"

"Me? I think you have me confused with someone else, gorgeous. I stopped in for a drink and good company. Do you think you can give me both? My name is Marie. And you are?" Sitting on the stool next to him, I crossed one leg over the other, exposing most of my thigh.

His eyes moved up my leg, and his ogling warmed my body. Moving the coat aside enough to show him the top of the thigh-high, I asked, "Like what you see, gorgeous?"

"What am I missing?"

"I don't know, but I'm missing your name. Is this how you always act when you meet someone new?" Role-playing may not be my forte because it seemed he wasn't picking up on my naïve act.

Then the light bulb clicked on, and Brady's eyes brightened. He placed his hand on my thigh and leaned forward.

"I'm Brady. It's a pleasure to meet you, Marie. Why don't you take your coat off and stay a while?"

Eyes cocked to the side I pursed my lips. "I would, but I have a wardrobe malfunction of sorts." Perusing the room, I noticed my back was to everyone else. Quickly I opened the coat to show him the lace bra and garter with panties and then closed it.

Brady held his hand up and yelled, "Bartender, check, please!" The bartender alerted him it would be just a moment. Brady couldn't wait. "Keep the change," he said as he handed the man a twenty and grasped my hand. Sprinting toward the elevator, we dodged a few people in the lobby, and I struggled to keep my coat from flying open.

As soon as the door closed, Brady pushed the button for our floor and turned back to look at me. "Open that once more, please."

Slower this time, I untied the belt and held it open for his viewing pleasure. Brady groaned as his arousal strained against his zipper. The doors opened, and I covered up before the people getting on could see. Sliding behind Brady, he kept me covered for the rest of the ride. The other couple seemed oblivious to what was going on. They certainly didn't seem to notice Brady had his hand behind him and was fingering my clit. A few squeaks escaped, though I was biting my lip hard to stay silent. Brady smiled at the couple next to them.

"She's gotta use the restroom, and she always makes that cute squeak when she's trying to hold it."

Now I had to press my face against his shoulder to keep from laughing. Finally, the elevator dinged for our floor, and we ran straight for our room. We were pressed against the door when our mouths met in a fierce, passionate kiss while Brady fumbled to get the door open. Coat flung open, his hands slipped around my waist. I grabbed the key card away from him and got a green light on the first slide. Stumbling into the room, Brady used his foot to kick the door closed. We fumbled toward the bed, and I pushed him down onto the mattress. Legs on either side of his waist, I ground my heat against the large bulge in his pants.

Brady guided the coat off my shoulders, and his eyes raked over my body. Fingers trailed over the black lace bra, grazing my nipples, before cupping my breasts fully. I covered his hands with mine, urging him to grip harder. Closing my eyes, I relished his hands against my skin as he pushed my bra up over my breasts. Desire pulled at my stomach.

Unbuttoning his shirt, my hands slid over the contours of his abs. His muscles rippled as my fingers trailed over his skin. Tracing a line of kisses down to his belly button, my fingers grazed over the thin trail of hair leading beneath his trousers. Brady groaned when my knuckles brushed against the tip of his arousal while trying to undo his zipper. A gasp flew from my mouth as I felt his finger slip inside my panties. Wet heat welcomed his touch.

Although I didn't want to pull away, I wanted to make this about him. My fingers wrapped around his length and began making long strokes. When my tongue grazed the tip, he lay back on the bed and exhaled in relief. Brady had always put my needs first even in the bedroom. As much as I wanted him inside me, it was my turn to spoil him for a change.

As he reached the cusp, Brady called out, "Stop. Marie, wait."

Taking a few breaths to keep himself from climaxing, he leaned over to grab his pants off the floor. A moment of fear gripped me with the concern he'd changed his mind about sleeping with me. As he pulled a condom from his pants pocket and ripped it open, I breathed a sigh of relief, anxiously awaiting his return to me.

With raw and primal need, he grabbed me around the waist, pulling me against him. Knees pressed against the bed, I positioned myself directly above him. Hands on my hips, he pressed the length of himself into me, sliding deeper until I nearly lost control. Slow strides as I arched my back and pressed my palms against the bed behind me. After a few moments of taking it slow, I sat up and bucked against him fast and hard until we both quivered with release, sweaty and exhausted.

Brady kissed my temple. "I thought you were mad at me. I guess I was wrong. If I wasn't, though, then I need to make you mad more often."

Chuckling softly, I walked fingers across his chest. "You didn't make me angry." Chin resting on his chest, I gazed up at him. "I've made up my mind, Brady. I want you and no one else. Jayce is my best friend in the world, which probably will never change. Reese makes him happy, which makes me happy." Lips spread wide in a grin, he pulled my face up to meet his and kissed me.

When our lips parted, he asked, "What was your favorite childhood memory?"

"Weird segue moment." I laughed.

"I'm changing things up."

"Okay. Well, I would say… the day my dad took me to the aquarium for the first time. It frightened me, because you start at the top, and it's quite a few stories high. My dad held my hand and told me if I stood with my nose against the glass, I could pretend I was in the water with the fish. He lifted me up, and we pressed our faces to the glass. The cool glass against my cheek with a little condensation from the air conditioner gave the perfect effect of being in the water with them. It took my mind off being scared at how high up we were." It had been a long time since I thought about that day. "What's yours?"

"The day my parents divorced." That wasn't the answer I expected. "I know. It's weird to be a favorite memory. I told you before my dad was always 'business before family.' During my parents' marriage, my mom tried to get his attention all the time. As soon as she wised up and decided to leave him, she began to do more for my siblings and me. We started new traditions and grew closer as a family unit."

"I'd like to meet your family."

"When your trip is over, we'll make it happen."

JOURNAL ENTRY

Brady and I are back on track and better than ever. Discussing our feelings and working through our issues, we found a way to move past everything that happened before and decided to start fresh. I offered him the choice of no strings attached in case he meets someone else while I'm on this trip. Instead, he wants to be exclusive, and I think I'm ready for that as well. We only had three days together in New Orleans, but we used the time wisely. Mardi Gras was amazing. The amount of nudity on the streets was insane, but the music was fabulous, and the six of us had the best time.

Constance and I are taking Brady and Manny to the airport today, and then we're spending one more day in New Orleans with Jayce and Reese. I'm going to be sad to see them leave. Jayce and

I were supposed to meet every three months on the fifth day, but he has to renegotiate those terms. Zeb's health has taken a turn for the worse, and Jayce is running everything on his own at the shop. He can't afford to take too many more vacations until he gets things under control. I'll miss him, but in truth, it seems to make things easier on both our relationships.

He's going to meet us on the West Coast in about six months as we round out our journey. Constance and I have talked about cutting it short and heading straight for Hawaii. She's anxious to see a real volcano and visit the island state. Also, after the ordeal with Nathan and Pacey, we're both a bit afraid of running into shadier characters.

Most of the Midwest is flat country so the drive may be scenic but a bit tedious at times. I'm considering cutting the trip short myself. I've been looking at a map to figure out the cities I most definitely want to visit and trying to cut out some of the in-between stops. Not visiting all the states doesn't tarnish the dream I had, and in some ways, it makes it better. Not many people get to see as much as I have in the past year. I feel lucky for all the things I've experienced and the people I've met.

My trip is halfway over, and if I went home now, I'd still be content with everything I've seen.

∞ *Marie*

21

"Hello, Dad." I answered my phone on the first ring when I saw the number.

"Hey, sweetheart. Where are you now?"

"It's our last day in New Orleans. Constance and I were about to check out of the hotel and spend a few hours with Jayce and Reese before they get on the road."

"How was Mardi Gras? Please tell me you have no beads to show for it," my dad said with a cringe in his voice.

Uncomfortable with the idea of his daughter flashing her goods, I had to reassure him. "I have a bag full of beads, but don't worry. I didn't have to show anything but my smile for them."

"That's my baby girl. I have some good news to share. I got a gig singing at a bar here in town two nights a week."

"Fantastic! What bar?" Fake enthusiasm poured out of me

each time he had news that didn't include him moving back to Chattanooga with my mom. Each new job at a bar brought him more hope at a music contract, and each time it ended with disappointment.

"It's new, so new they haven't opened yet. It's called A Shot in the Dark. It's smack in the middle of downtown Nashville, so it should get a pretty steady crowd. A group of brothers owns it, and a friend of mine gave them my demo, and they loved it."

"When I get back to town, I'll come to Nashville and catch a show, and maybe I'll bring Brady with me." Making plans with Brady in mind didn't make me nervous or unsure for a change.

"Sounds like a plan. You know I never think anyone is good enough for you, but if I had to choose a man for you, it would be Brady. Of course, if you were interested in Jayce romantically, he would be my first choice."

My parents had always tried to make a love connection out of my friendship with Jayce. From the moment they met him, they thought he was a true gentleman, and I couldn't choose a better man. Now they loved Brady too, which made me happy.

After hanging up with my dad, I helped Constance get all the bags down to the car in time to check out and meet up with Jayce and Reese in the lobby restaurant.

"I can't believe this trip is over already. It seems our time together goes by quicker each trip," I mentioned solemnly.

"Tell me about it. I'm sorry we have to make it even less often now too," Jayce replied. "You make sure to call me as much as you can, though. I worry about both of you on the road alone."

"Did you tell him about Nathan and Pacey?" Constance asked.

I drew my lips in a hard line, silently scolded Constance's question. "No, I didn't feel it was necessary."

"Who are Nathan and Pacey?" Jayce inquired.

"We met these two men in Atlanta. We first saw them at the Woodbury location of *The Walking Dead* and then again at the Aquarium in Atlanta. They followed us around there and in the car until we pulled over at a police station."

Jayce's head reared up, his eyes dark with anger. "And you're just now telling me about this?"

"I didn't want to worry you."

"You need to end this trip and go home. It isn't safe for the two of you to be out here alone," Jayce demanded.

"Nothing happened. We're both safe, and we took the proper precautions. We had a security guard walk us to the car, and we went to the police. This kind of thing could happen anywhere."

Jayce stewed quietly in his chair as I tried to explain we weren't in danger. His abundant concern for my well-being had Reese on edge. Lips in a hard line, eyes rolled to the ceiling, she tapped her foot impatiently.

"Marie, I don't want anything to happen to you or Connie. You're my family, and I couldn't stand to see either of you hurt." As he spoke, he rested his hand upon my shoulder in a loving manner, and Reese let out an audible groan of annoyance.

"We need to get on the road," Reese stated sternly, teeth gritted in anger. After this trip, I wasn't as fond of her as I hoped to be. Although she seemed to make Jayce happy, she hadn't been very friendly toward the rest of us. Perhaps I should give her the benefit of the doubt. Still, she rubbed me the wrong way.

Jayce looked at his cell phone with his free hand. "It's still early."

When he looked up at Reese, he followed her gaze to see she had been staring at his hand on my shoulder. He let go instantly and checked his phone again.

"You're right. We should get going." It seemed Jayce and I couldn't even touch without someone getting jealous. I hated the impact this trip had on our friendship. Every time I turned around, things became more awkward for us. Some days, I wished I could start this trip over again and do things differently.

No long good-bye from Jayce, only a brief hug before moving to Constance. Reese kept a watchful eye on him the entire time. Constance hugged Reese good-bye, and I stepped forward when she turned and waved, then walked away. Jealousy didn't bother me. No one on the outside understood my close friendship with Jayce.

"Did the temperature go down in here or what?" Constance whispered as they left.

"Are you ready to get on the road and see some of the great state of Texas?"

Constance welcomed the subject change without arguing. "Yep. Where's our first stop?"

"Houston. We have a five-hour drive to get there. It seems like a good place to stop first."

Peace and quiet filled the next few hours as Constance plugged her earbuds in, and I drove without distraction. Three hours later, Jayce checked in.

Constance read it out loud, and I responded with a simple nod. "I'm sorry I brought up the Nathan and Pacey story. I made a stupid assumption."

"I'm not mad you brought it up. I should've told him when it happened. Now I need to tell Brady. When we stop tonight, I'm going to call him and fill him in on everything. I have a feeling his reaction will be worse than Jayce's. He'll probably want to quit his job and school to finish the trip with us."

Once in Houston, I called Brady. He flew off the handle, and like Jayce, demanded I end the trip immediately. Bringing his anger down to a dull roar, I finally convinced him we would be safe. Saving Constance from a repeat, I asked Brady to explain it all to Manny as well.

"What did you think of Reese?" I asked Constance, needing to know if I read too much into her actions.

"Not a fan. She barely spoke to anyone, and she rubbed on Jayce so much trying to lay claim to him to the point it became obscene. My cousin can do so much better. For some reason, though, he seems happy with her. I suppose as long as she keeps a smile on his face and doesn't hurt him, I'll keep my mouth shut on how I feel about her."

Constance's comments mirrored my thoughts, which put me at ease that I hadn't been viewing her out of jealousy.

JOURNAL ENTRY

For the past few months, we've stopped in several towns in Texas and then made shorter trips in Oklahoma, Kansas, Arkansas, Missouri, and Nebraska. Constance seems to be doing great. She hasn't had any exhaustion spells, and we've been taking our time and relaxing as much as possible.

Ever since they found out about us being followed, Jayce, Manny, and Brady text and call every chance to check in on us. Most of the time we don't mind; it gives us a chance to hear their voices and tell them about our day.

I haven't been documenting in my journal as often as I should, but I hope to get better with it. I'm taking pictures as my souvenirs, and I hope to write stories to go along with them later.

Things are changing for Brady. He keeps talking

about the future now that my trip is almost complete. He wants me to consider moving to Michigan. He's trying to coerce me by adding I would be closer to Constance.

All I can think is I'm not ready to live so far from Jayce. Which brings up my feelings for Jayce once again. If I'm not willing to give him up for Brady, then are my feelings as genuine as I think?

Marie

22

MARIE

Iowa offered local attractions including the *Field of Dreams* movie site, Greater Des Moines Botanical Garden, and Pikes Peak State Park.

Smaller cities gave Constance more time to rest. Lately her body had been wearing down quicker than usual, although she'd tried to hide it from me. Since we'd begun the trip, we'd both been looking forward to seeing Mount Rushmore, and we were so close. Checking the distance from Des Moines, we found it would be a ten-hour drive. Saving our energy, we broke it into two days of driving. For the first time Constance didn't argue; she needed to sleep.

When the day finally came, we arrived at the park and paid the small fee to take the thirty-minute walk to the grand monument. Eyeing her cautiously, I watched for signs of Constance overdoing it. Two oversized bottles of water to keep us hydrated were slung over my shoulder in a canvas bag.

Beneath the grand carving, Constance bent her neck back to gaze up at the amazing sculpture. Most people were stopping for only a moment to see it and snap a few pictures. She wanted to soak in the experience. Grabbing my arm, she pulled me aside to an empty spot in the grass.

"Besides meeting Manny, this is my favorite part of the trip now. It's incredible someone carved that. I'm in awe. The way it must feel to leave such a mark on the world."

"True, but who knows the name of the guy who carved it?" I never expected her to answer me.

"Gutzon Borglum and his son, Lincoln."

Mouth screwed up in disbelief, I asked, "How do you know that?"

Lifting her hand, she showed me the screen on her phone. "I googled it on the way up here." Bumping my shoulder against hers, I gave a stern look before laughing out loud.

"I wish Manny was here to see this. He has this monument on his bucket list. It's funny I'll probably be the one to kick the bucket before any of you, but you all have bucket lists."

"Not funny, Connie."

"It's fine, Marie. If I were to die now, I'd be content with my life. I have you to thank. I've seen more in the last year than I've seen in twenty-one years of my life. You're my best friend and the sister I always wanted. In case I forget to say it again before this is over, thank you, and I love you."

Wrapping my arms around her, I pulled her close to me. "I love you too, sweetie. Maybe when this trip is over, you and

Manny can visit again?"

"He's the absolute love of my life. I know it's true without a doubt. When you invited me on this trip, I never expected to meet someone like him. We were talking the other night, and he asked me if I'd come live in Michigan. He said if I can't, he would move to Canada for me. He keeps talking about the future, and it scares me and excites me at the same time. Am I making sense?"

"Completely. More sense than anything in my life at the moment. Brady keeps talking about our future, and I just get confused as to whether I want one with him or with Jayce."

Her head spun in my direction giving me whiplash. "I thought things were good with you and Brady?"

"They're perfect. Leave it to me to question perfection. I blame you. If you hadn't tried to convince me I had feelings for Jayce, maybe I'd have continued to ignore them."

Snorting with sarcasm, she said, "Poor, pitiful Marie who has two gorgeous men to choose from." Although she was joking, I knew she didn't envy my decision. "Brady is a good man, Marie, but Jayce is too. All I can say is make sure the decision is what makes you happy. Don't make it based on who might get hurt or because you're scared. Life is too short, take it from me."

Flopping back on the grass, I stared up at the sky. "Your advice is not helping make this decision easier."

Joining me on the ground, Constance stretched her arms above her head. "Sorry. I have an idea. Why don't we make a pros and cons list?"

"That worked so well for Ross on *Friends*," I teased.

"We'll figure this out for you one way or another." Standing, we brushed ourselves off, and started the trek back to the car.

Back in the car, Constance laid her head against the car door and took a nap. Beautiful scenery kept me entertained on the next leg of the trip. A sense of peace fell over me as I drove. We were in the last few months of the trip; things were going well with Brady, and Constance hadn't had any more episodes.

Weary eyes blurred the road alerting me to pull over for the night. Pulling into the turnaround in front of the lobby, I shook Constance to wake her. Nothing. Gently touching her face, I started to say, "Connie, wake up," but stopped as I noticed how cold her cheeks were. "Connie, please wake up," I begged, panic filling my chest. With trembling hands, I dialed 911 as I prayed she was still alive.

After giving my location to the operator and assessing the situation, he instructed me to try CPR. A bellboy had stepped outside to grab a cart; he rushed over when I yelled out for help. We pulled Constance from the car and laid her on the ground. I began chest compressions, and my fears rose when I saw no results. When the ambulance arrived, I had stopped and sat staring at Constance in disbelief. Paramedics checked her vitals and exchanged a look with each other before shaking their heads letting me know all hope was lost.

On my knees, I fell back to the sidewalk in shock. Bile rose in my throat as I wondered what I could have done sooner. Pulling my knees up to my chest, I let my emotions go. Sobs rocked my body and tears soaked my cheeks. The paramedics lifted Constance to the gurney and covered her face with a sheet before strapping her body down. Handing me a card for the hospital, I was told to go there to have her body released to the funeral home of her choice. Words barely registered with me.

Constance's phone rang from the cup holder of the car. In a zombie-like fashion, I answered without thinking.

"Who is this?" Manny asked. "Constance?"

I sniffed loudly before I choked out, "It's Marie."

Manny's voice cracked, and he spouted off questions in a panic. "What's wrong? Is Constance sick again?"

Emotions overwhelmed me, and I handed the phone to the paramedic still standing beside me. "Hello?"

Manny panicked again. "Who is this? What's going on?" Speakerphone must have been activated because I could hear the conversation from both sides.

"Sir, my name is Michael, and I'm a paramedic. Can you tell me the young lady's name you were talking to just now? She's been too upset to speak."

Manny replied, "Her name is Marie, and she was traveling with another woman named Constance. Why do they need a paramedic?"

The paramedic held the phone away from his ear. "Ma'am, I need permission to tell this person what happened to your friend." I nodded. Michael took a deep breath and said, "I'm sorry, sir, the woman named Constance needed the paramedics, but she was gone before we arrived."

"They're traveling the country, and I know they're somewhere in the Midwest. I need to know exactly where she is now, please." Michael gave a precise location to Manny, who asked him to let me know he would be here in a few hours. Apparently I drove myself to the hospital, but I don't remember even getting in the car.

The receptionist at the information desk pointed me to a waiting room until the rest of the family arrived. Constance's parents were flying out in the evening. Manny had texted to say he was on his way as well. His flight would arrive a few hours before theirs would.

Beige walls, bland pale-green chairs, and obscure paintings filled the drab waiting room. A news program was on with a ticker tape running across the bottom with headlines, but it was all a blur to me. The last few days ran through my mind on repeat as I attempted to figure out if I could've prevented this from happening. A large form stepped in front of me, bringing me out of the daze as Manny's face came in focus. Kneeling down, he embraced me, and I began to weep again.

"She hasn't missed a dose of her medicine in months. I've been watching. We took breaks all the time. I tried to take care of her."

Manny shushed me. "You did everything you could. There was nothing more any of us could do." He grabbed a tissue from the table next to me and handed it over. "Brady wanted to be here. He's going to fly out in a couple of days and meet you."

"I don't want to be alone tonight. Please don't leave me alone, Manny."

Back at the hotel, we spent the rest of the evening grieving together. He shared my room and promised to tag along to meet Constance's parents in the morning. During the night, I received a text asking me to open the door.

Jayce stood in the hallway. His eyes were red and swollen. No words were needed as we held onto each other. My head buried in his chest, he kissed the top of my hair and rested his head against mine. A moment later, I led him into the room. He spotted Manny asleep on the couch.

"Is Brady here too?"

"Not yet. He's coming in a few days. Stay with me tonight, please." Jayce nodded and shut the door behind him. After snuggling up against his chest, I was finally able to fall asleep. In the morning, I awoke to find Manny sitting up drinking a cup of coffee. A muscular arm draped over my stomach, and I smiled in contentment.

Manny frowned. "You should've woken me if you wanted the room to yourselves."

Feet on the floor, I raised my arms and stretched until my bones cracked and popped. "He showed up in the middle of the night. And we're friends, just like you and I are friends."

Manny smirked. "We didn't share a bed last night."

Rolling my eyes like a scolded teenager, I asked, "Did you want me to make him sleep on the floor? You took the couch. We needed each other last night."

Manny cleared his throat and asked the big question. "More than you need Brady?"

His accusations were too much for me to handle. "Not today, Manny. One of my best friends just died. She happened to be Jayce's cousin, and we're both grieving. Brady has nothing to worry about." What I told Manny was true, but I was still glad he'd been the one to see this and not Brady. I'd hurt Brady enough in the short time we'd been together.

"What are you going to do about your trip now?"

"I don't know." The thought of moving on without Constance was too depressing to consider. Although I'd started out on the trip alone, she'd been the best part of my journey.

Manny took a sip of coffee and thought for a moment. "You started it alone. You could always finish solo too. Or, if you want, I can finish it out in Constance's place."

Eyebrows scrunched in thought, I considered the proposition. "You'd want to travel with me for a few months? What about work?"

"I can take a sabbatical. I have a little nest egg built up." He peered down sadly at his coffee cup.

"What were you saving for? A rainy day?"

Manny stared off into the distance. "An engagement ring." Eyes misting over with tears, I watched the grief consume him as he tried to fight it.

Suddenly Manny's loss became so much worse than mine, and it stabbed at my wounded heart. I'd been so focused on my own grief and on Jayce's, I hadn't stopped to think about how much Manny had loved Constance. Constance would have said yes with no hesitation. I knew how much she loved him. Taking the seat next to him, I rested my hand on his shoulder.

"She would've been incredibly happy."

He smiled, and his eyes glistened with tears. "I'm grateful to you. I'd never have met her if you hadn't come into Brady's life. Even though we didn't have much time together, every moment with her was amazing. I'm not sure I'll ever find another soul like hers."

"She loved you more than you'll ever know, Manny. You two deserved your happily ever after."

"We were nothing but happy, so in a way we got it. Before I met Constance, I wasn't always a glass-half-full kind of guy. After learning how little time she had, it felt wrong to do anything but look on the positive side of things. I wish we'd had more time together, but I'm so thankful for the time we did have."

JOURNAL ENTRY

I miss Constance so much. She died three days ago, and her parents flew her body back to Canada. They were so kind when they saw me. I suppose I expected them to want to tear me to shreds or blame me for their daughter's death. Instead, they embraced Manny and me as if we were family. They were so pleased to meet him after everything Constance had told them. They invited him to spend the holidays with them, and he promised he would, for Constance.

Manny and I decided he should finish out the trip with me. Brady couldn't get the time off work due to a big company project, but he's called every day to check in on me. I hate to admit my first thought was that he's putting his job before family like he swore he would never do.

After hearing his voice that first night, I knew he hated every minute of not being there for me. I told him I was in good company and not to worry. He's going to meet us in Vegas next month when he's finished his project. I've barely had time to grieve between Brady and Jayce's calls and having Manny with me. I'm not sure if it's a good thing or a bad thing, but for now, I welcome the distractions.

Occasionally Manny and I will bring up stories about her, but for the most part, we only talk about what to do next. Our first overnight stay will be Colorado. We stopped in Nebraska to say we'd seen the state, and we had dinner at a small café. Then we drove straight through to Denver. The scenery was breathtaking on the drive down. We found a quaint hotel to check in to and call it a night. I'll try to write more after I experience my first time skiing. I can't wait to get to the slopes and give it a try.

I hope I don't fall on my ass.

ღMarie

23

MARIE

No position made me comfortable so I finally settled on my back and stared at the ceiling. The bed was fine, but for some reason I couldn't sleep. Writing in my journal didn't tire me out the way I hoped it would. Instead, there I was, wide-awake, listening to the soft murmur of Manny breathing in the bed across the room.

As a last resort, I grabbed my tablet and scrolled through, looking for a game, but nothing helped. None of the books on my "to be read" list sparked my interest either.

A stomach rumble reminded me I hadn't eaten in a while. Actually, I couldn't remember the last meal I'd eaten. Every time Manny ate something, he offered to get me a meal as well, but my appetite hadn't been there. Now suddenly I was starving.

On the dresser was a notebook full of the hotel information.

One of the pages was for a twenty-four-hour pizza place. My stomach growled in appreciation as I gazed at the pepperoni pizza with cheesy stuffed crust. If I were a cartoon character, I'd have hearts in my eyes and my tongue would be oversized and hanging out of my mouth. I ordered two large pizzas, one with extra cheese and pepperoni, and the other with the works. Only a piece or two would be devoured by me, but I knew Manny would be hungry as soon as he woke up, and we could eat the pizza for at least two meals.

There was a knock on the door about thirty minutes later, and the smell of the food made it difficult to pay the delivery guy without ripping the pizza from his hands and shoving it in my mouth like a rabid werewolf. *Do werewolves eat pizza?* I gave him cash and told him to keep the change, leaving him with a nice hefty tip and a grin on his face.

The slice of extra cheese and pepperoni had barely crossed my lips before Manny stirred in his sleep.

"What smells so good?" he grumbled as he sat up.

"Pizza. Sorry, I couldn't sleep, and I got hungry." Famished was a more appropriate word after noticing I ate that first slice in about three bites.

He slept with his hair in a ponytail, and it had come out of the hair tie a little and stood up in different directions giving him an adorably cute look. It was easy to see the instant attraction Constance had to him. Fingertips almost reached the ceiling as he stretched his arms above his head. His shirt rode up a bit just below his belly button as he scratched and walked over to the table to join me.

"Damn, it looks good. Mind if I join you?" Motioning to

the chair next to me, I lifted a slice of pizza out for him. He scarfed it down as if he hadn't eaten in weeks.

"Men. You piss me off with how you can eat so much. It's been like three hours since you ate a burger, which was at least a pound, and you had onion rings and French fries. How can you possibly be hungry?"

"Fast metabolism."

"Asshole," I muttered. Manny chuckled and grabbed another slice of pizza. "When I was in grade school, I was chubby. Kids made fun of me. One girl would make 'boom' sounds as I walked by as if I was shaking the ground. I went home every afternoon and cried, but I never let my parents see my tears."

"Kids can be such shitheads." Manny shook his head with distaste.

"Tell me about it. When I was twelve, I sat in my bedroom with a handful of pills because of those shitheads. I didn't let them win, though."

"Good for you." Manny held up his fist, and I bumped mine against it.

"I'm not sure why I told you about being bullied. Maybe it's because I almost let some mean kids take away my joy, when Constance never knew how many days she had left. Seems selfish almost."

Manny grabbed a napkin and wiped off his hands after closing the pizza box.

"I for one am especially glad you triumphed over those idiots, but you can't compare yourself to Constance. She wouldn't want you to. Let's make a pact for Connie. We tell only happy stories for the trip. No tears, no sadness. It's what she would want."

Shaking hands in agreement, I kept my word by saying, "Tell me something happy."

"My six-pack is totally rocking tonight," Manny said, holding up his shirt. We both burst into a fit of laughter.

"I needed a good laugh."

"Me too." Manny lay back on his bed and tucked his hands behind his head. "Constance used to do this thing with her tongue."

Smacking my hands over my ears, I chanted, "Da-da-da, I don't want to know dirty stuff."

Manny tossed a pillow at me. "Get your mind out of the gutter, pervert. She did this thing with her tongue where she could curl it but not like a normal person. It would bend in like waves. It was the weirdest thing. Did she ever show you?"

"No, but it sounds quite interesting." Watching Manny try to manipulate his tongue to demonstrate what Constance could do was giving me a fit of giggles. "She did show me the trick where she could tie a cherry stem with her tongue."

Manny's eyes widened. "Damn, I never saw the cherry trick."

"Did you ever hear her sing?"

"You mean the thing with the lyrics?" Manny started to sing, "Pour some shook up ramen!"

"Yes!" I exclaimed. "Or my favorite was 'Like a virgin, touched for the thirty-first time.'" After sharing a few more lyrics, we were in tears.

"I miss her," I choked out. Without a doubt, Constance

opened my eyes to more things during this trip than I'd have ever experienced without her. The several months we had together weren't enough, but I'd cherish them for a lifetime.

Manny moved to my bed and kissed my forehead. "I do too." We held each other and broke the no tears promise.

A few hours later, I woke up snuggled against Manny in my bed. I remembered we'd fallen asleep crying. Breakfast included a glass of water and two ibuprofens from my purse to help curb a headache coming on.

"Good morning," Manny said as he rolled out of the bed.

"Hey, sorry about getting emotional. I didn't even make it twenty-four hours on our promise."

Manny patted my shoulder. "We'll get there. It's still too fresh to think we could stick to it." He picked up his phone to check for missed calls, but there weren't any, only one text. "Brady wants you to call him if you get a chance today."

"Wonder why he texted you?" I answered my own question when I picked up my phone. There were several missed texts from Brady, and they became a bit more worried each time. "Shoot, I turned my phone off and didn't realize it. I'll call him."

Brady answered on the first ring. "Hello, beautiful."

"I turned my phone off by accident. I'm sorry."

"No need to explain. I only wanted to check in. I feel better knowing Manny is there with you. I know he won't let anything happen to you."

His concern and love for me gave me hope again and put a genuine smile on my face. "Can I call you back with FaceTime? I'd like to see you."

"Please do."

When the line connected again, I was face-to-face with Brady.

"Hey, sweetheart," Brady said with a grin.

Manny stuck his head in the frame. "Hello, darling." He kissed the screen and gave a fake girlish giggle. Laughing, I shoved him out of the way.

Brady snickered as he thanked me. "So, you're in Denver now?"

"Yep. We're going to try skiing today. Manny promised to be patient with me on the bunny slopes." Manny walked over again, this time with a slice of pizza in his mouth. He waved and held a thumbs-up in front of the screen.

Brady shook his head and chuckled again. "I hope you have the patience to put up with him on this trip."

"When he starts to annoy me too much, I've got a few tricks up my sleeve to annoy him back."

"Good girl," Brady remarked proudly.

We traveled in Athens the next day to enjoy a few days of skiing. Four times I fell, which wasn't bad, and the plus side was I didn't break anything. Three days were enough time to get our fill of the slopes.

Over the next few weeks, we made short stops in New Mexico, Arizona, Utah, and started up through Nevada. Arriving at the Grand Canyon early, we decided to stay in a hotel nearby and do a little hiking. It was a short drive from Las Vegas and two days away from when Brady would arrive.

Hiking was something Manny did often, and I couldn't think of a better way to see the Grand Canyon. When I suggested it, Manny said, "Constance and I had talked about doing that one day. After finding out about her heart condition, I knew it might never happen, but I assumed we'd have many more years to do other things. Keeping you company was my goal for this trip. In a way, it makes me feel closer to Constance somehow."

"I feel closer to her with you around too. Besides Jayce, I don't think anyone knew her better than the two of us." When Manny first offered to come along, it seemed awkward and that it would be uncomfortable. It didn't take long for us to get into a natural flow though.

Since Constance passed, I've barely wanted to take a day of rest. We've covered a lot of tourist sites, but the nature journeys like this one had been my favorites.

Being the more athletic one and a gentleman, Manny carried the backpack loaded with water bottles and snack foods. Trusting him to lead us in the right direction, I followed closely behind. Once we found a nice spot, we sat down to eat a snack and enjoy the scenery.

Tipping the water bottle back, Manny guzzled it down, leaving only a small portion in the bottom. Taking a bandana from his bag, he soaked it with the remaining water and tied it around his head to keep cool. Putting my hair up in a bun, I followed his lead and felt instant relief as the cool fabric touched my skin.

"I used to think I was in shape until we started this hike," I complained as I wiped the sweat from my brow.

"You're in great shape, Mo. It's a rough hike out here. You're doing incredible."

"Are you excited about seeing Brady in a couple of days?" His abrupt change of subject seemed to be something that had weighed on his mind a bit.

I contemplated the question longer than either of us expected, it seemed from the concerned dip of his head.

"I think so. I mean, of course I am. It's just different now, not with Brady and me, but with life in general. Sorry, I didn't mean to get all deep with you. Yes, I'm excited to see him."

Even through the crunching sound of the granola bar, he could hear the struggle in my spoken thoughts. Crumbling up the empty wrapper, he stuffed it in the backpack.

"If your feelings for Brady are conflicted, you can talk to me about it. We're friends, you and me. I can be neutral. I don't tell Brady what you tell me, and vice versa."

My ears perked up like an eager puppy as I wondered what he meant.

"Has he said something about our relationship?" Although I knew he wouldn't betray Brady's confidence, I hoped he'd let something slip and give me insight.

Chuckling at my sudden interest, he said, "Of course he has. I'm his best friend. I'm not going to tell you, though. It's not my place. It's how you know you can tell me stuff."

"It wouldn't be fair for me to tell you something like I'm having feelings for someone else."

"Fair or not, you just told me," he remarked. Valid point. Manny wasn't someone to sugarcoat things. It was one of my favorite character traits of his.

"I'm selfish. I want both of them in my life, but I don't want anyone else to have either of them, and I know I can't have them both romantically," I confessed, staring straight ahead, unable to look at Manny.

"No, you can't."

"Thanks for the tough love," I teased.

"I like Jayce. He's a good guy, but I'll admit I'm Team Mardy."

I snorted. "Team Mardy?"

"As in Marie and Brady? Well, it's easier to say than Team Brarie. You know it's all the rage now with celebrities to give them cutesy nicknames based on their first names. Nevermind, it's not important." Manny shrugged. "My advice to you is to make a decision. If you don't make one soon, you could lose both of them."

Manny's advice was what I needed. Even though he was loyal to Brady, he didn't try to push me one way or another. He knew this was a decision I had to make and no one else.

"And if I make the wrong decision, I could lose both of them too," I admitted.

JOURNAL ENTRY

Vegas, Baby. Vegas. We've been in Vegas for three days now and haven't gambled a dime. We've walked the strip and been inside every casino along the way. Some of the hotels are grand enough to have amusement parks in the lobby. It's been an insanely fun trip.

Manny and Brady are the best company. They've taken turns spoiling me with gifts and compliments. It has been the best part of the trip since Constance passed away.

After Brady leaves, we're not going to see each other until the trip is over. My last venture is going to be on a cruise to Hawaii. I want to ask him to go with me, but I'm going to wait until it gets a little bit closer. It seems too romantic a place to visit with a friend.

Manny and I are going to drive through Utah and Idaho next on our way to Washington state. We're going to spend a few days in Seattle at Manny's request. He has several points of interest he wants to explore.

After, we plan to spend at least a month in California. I'm especially looking forward to Hollywood. As much as I've enjoyed seeing everything on this trip, I'm ready to go home.

With all the good along the way, there's been enough bad to make me want to get back to reality. Part of me is anxious to get back to Jayce, too, and to see if things are back to normal once we live in the same town again.

∽Marie

24

MARIE

Idaho didn't have a lot to see besides flatlands and farmhouses. In my research, I came upon a town called Cascade with several waterfalls nearby. Cascade became our first stop in the state.

An alert light came on showing we had a low tire. A quaint little diner transformed from an old theater seemed the best place to pull over. The front passenger side was almost flat. There was a nail stuck in it.

"I best change the flat," he informed me.

"Great. I have a donut in the back, but no spare."

Manny queried Siri for a mechanic nearby. "I found a shop not far from here. Why don't you stay here and relax? I'll get you a new tire and join you when they're through."

People-watching and a bite to eat sounded like the perfect way to kill time. A girl, probably in her late teens, came through the door alone, and it captured my attention. She had vibrant red hair with springy curls and a bounce in her step. It appeared she didn't have a care in the world. She sat at the table across from me and ordered a cherry soda with chili cheese fries. She caught me staring and gave a nervous but friendly enough smile.

"Would you like to join me?" To me, she seemed harmless, but when I offered, she bit her cheek nervously.

Red glanced around a moment and said, "Well, I'm waiting for a friend, but he seems to be running late. I guess we could keep each other company for a bit."

After flagging the waitress down to have her order sent to the new table, she claimed the chair next to mine. "My name is Marie. I'm traveling with my friend, Manny. It's my first time in Idaho. Are you a native?"

The girl grinned. "Yep. My name is Parker. What brought you to the tiny town of Cascade of all places?" The waitress brought the chili cheese fries and drinks over, and my mouth watered as the meaty, spicy smell of the chili filled my nose. Parker pointed at the large plate of fries. "Please, help me eat these."

"Oh no, your friend might want some of them."

Parker snorted a laugh. "My friend, Mitchell, will order at least a double of these when he gets here."

My stomach growled in anger at my food refusal, and Parker laughed. "See, you know you want them." Swiping a fry with a hefty amount of chili, I brought it to my lips and savored the flavor.

"As for an answer to your question, I chose Cascade

because of the waterfalls."

Parker's face lit up like a child on Christmas morning. "They're amazing here. One of them is a special spot for my husband and me."

The word husband made me choke on the fry in my mouth. "How old are you?"

Parker snorted with laughter again. "I'm twenty-one, and I get the same reaction a lot. My husband, Quinn, and I have been married almost a year."

I didn't know what else to say but "Congratulations."

A guy with blond hair walked into the restaurant and seemed a bit concerned when he noticed Parker wasn't alone. He approached the table cautiously, almost purposely walking at a snail's pace as though it took every effort he had not to run forward. "Parker?"

She looked up at him with affection in her pale blue eyes. I assumed by the look that it was her husband. "Mitchell, this is Marie. She's passing through town and was asking about what she should see." He glared with concern and distrust like a mama bird looking out for her young.

I cleared my throat and extended my hand hoping to show I meant no harm. "Nice to meet you, Mitchell."

Mitchell sat down and called out to the waitress, "I'll have two of these, please!" He pointed at the half-eaten plate of fries.

"See, told you," Parker said, not taking her eyes off him. Gossip was not my thing, but something was definitely going on between those two. If she looked at her friend that way, how did she look at her husband? I wasn't sure it was possible to show any more love than she was showing right then.

Mitchell left them briefly to request something at the counter. While he was gone, I leaned forward. "Quinn is your husband, but I saw the way you looked at Mitchell. It's none of my business, but you're very young. Do you regret getting married so soon?" I slapped my hand over my mouth as soon as the words spilled out. "Damn, sorry. Ignore me."

She laughed, the smile lighting her face. "Honestly, it's fine. I love my husband. Mitchell is my very best friend, and at one point, I thought I was in love with him, but I realized I do love him, only not as much as I love Quinn. It's a different kind of love. Trust me. We tested it. The man can kiss like you wouldn't believe, but he still didn't compare to Quinn for me."

I spotted Mitchell staring at us, and he was grinning as if he could hear what she had said. It was impossible for him to hear it from across the room, so I had to assume the waitress said something to him.

"What if you couldn't tell a difference in the passion? How would you have chosen?"

"It wasn't a matter of passion. Mitchell and I could stir up some heat when we wanted to. In the end, Mitchell was my best friend, and we had only kissed. Quinn and I had shared so much more, and my decision came down to this. If I stayed with Quinn, I got both of them in my life. If I chose Mitchell, I'd have lost Quinn. It sounds selfish, I know, but I couldn't lose them both. It's worked out perfectly well in the end. Is your friend Manny the lover or the friend?"

Her intuition was spot-on, knowing I was asking from

personal struggle. Now to explain that he was a third guy in the mix. Not that there would ever be anything romantic with Manny. He was like the brother I'd always wanted.

"Neither. Manny is simply a friend. My best friend, Jayce, and my boyfriend, Brady, are the ones I'm confused between."

"Can you live without one of them?" Parker asked, to which I shook my head. "Then there's your answer, choose the boyfriend and you get to keep both."

"I'm only a few years older than you, but you are so much wiser than I am." Her logic made perfect sense on paper. However, I wondered how it worked when the two men were together. As a stranger, I could see the immense love in her eyes. What did her husband think when he saw the same look? Could a relationship between Brady and me work out if he was constantly worried about my feelings for Jayce?

It seemed as if having them both around would cause more strife, like when we'd been in Disney or in New Orleans and they were together. Parker's life seemed to work out, unless she met at the restaurant alone with her friend to avoid awkwardness with her husband. Whatever it was, it wasn't my business. I would give her idea a good thinking over.

"I'm wise beyond my years, they tell me. I have the mind of a thirtysomething instead of a twentysomething." Parker attempted to hold back a grin as though she had made an inside joke. It completely went over my head if there was one.

Mitchell returned to the table, and I instantly became aware of the qualities Parker loved about him. He was very protective of her and had a great sense of humor.

Glancing up, I spotted Manny walking over to join the

table.

"Glad to see you had someone to keep you company," he said.

Quick introductions were made and the four of us talked for a little longer before I insisted we get on the road again. Hugging Parker, I whispered, "Thank you for the insight. I hope one day to be as smart as you are about this stuff. If you turned this amazing guy down, I known your husband must be damn near perfect."

Squeezing me tighter before letting go, she winked. "Damn near."

"I bought you two new tires. Another one had a nail in it as well," Manny relayed as we walked back to the parking lot.

"How much do I owe you?" I grabbed a handful of bills from my wallet.

Manny pushed the money away. "My gift to you."

Kissing his cheek, I sincerely replied, "Thank you."

Washington state welcomed us with evergreen trees and distant mountains as a backdrop. Seattle's weather was the perfect temperature with a cool breeze and a light drizzle of rain. Pike Place Market was famous for fish throwers, so we stopped there first. It was several blocks from the hotel, so we walked to enjoy the scenery and get a little exercise after so many hours in the car.

The sidewalk in front of the market was full of onlookers cheering for the workers. Fish were flung over the counter to a man in an apron who called out "Hey, ya!" before tossing the fish back. Behind the counter, he moved the fish's mouth to make it look as if it were speaking before he shouted, "Hey, ya!" and threw it again. The same fish was thrown back and forth five times before it was laid to rest on the ice out front of the market. Each time they threw it quicker than the next. Bystanders watched in awe as they waited for the slippery fish to fall from their grasp.

"Lovely lady, would you care to sample a bite of fresh crab meat? It's so fresh, the crab is barely dead," he called out to me. He held up the creature, which was in fact dead, and cracked one of the legs off. He pulled out a chunk of meat and held it out for me in his gloved hand.

Biting into it, I licked my lips. Good thing I wasn't trying to be sexy since the crabmeat sent a dribble down my chin.

"That is delicious. Manny, you have to try this!" Grabbing a sample of his own, he seemed to appreciate the drool factor of the meat. Our stomachs demanded more as they growled in unison. In the restaurant attached to the market, we each ordered a plate of beer battered fish and chips and a bottle of beer to wash it down.

"To Constance," I said, holding the bottle up in the air. Bottles tapped together briefly before we took a long pull. "Damn, that's a good beer."

"Hell yeah, it is. Let's order another round of these." Manny gestured to the waitress and smiled. The waitress was an Asian woman with waist-long hair and beautiful, chestnut-colored eyes. She gave her best smile as she sashayed over. "You are not the dude we had a moment ago."

"He went on break. He'll be back though. What can I get for you?" she inquired.

"Two more of these beers, please."

"She's very pretty," I commented as the woman walked away.

"She's not bad." Another long sip of beer. "Don't try to get me to date, Mo. It's only been a few months. I have too much respect for Constance."

"You know she'd want you to be happy."

"I am happy. I'm happy on this trip, and I'm happy you and I have become close friends. When I get home, and I have nothing but work to look forward to, that's when I'll consider dating again." One more gulp finished the last of his beer, just in time for the waitress to deliver the next round.

Four rounds of the delicious frothy drink later, and we were both too tipsy to do much walking, so we caught a cab back to the hotel.

Once back in the room, Manny had to lie down.

I flopped onto my bed and punched a number on my phone. "Hello, cutie." I giggled into the receiver. Manny grinned at my drunken self. My words were slurring and giggles were on repeat. Hitting the speakerphone button, the voice coming out of the speaker startled Manny.

"Hey, Mo. Are you drunk?" Jayce responded.

"Why would you think I'm drunk?" I asked before emitting a loud hiccup. "Oops, excuse me." I cleared my throat and took on a serious tone. "Do you love Reese?" Manny moved closer, concern clouding his face.

Jayce remained quiet for a moment. When he didn't

respond, my voice lowered as I said, "You do love her. Why can't you love me? I don't want to be selfish and keep you and Brady in my life. I want to be selfish and have you all to myself."

Manny's mouth dropped open in shock.

Jayce spoke up. "Marie, what's going on?"

I sighed heavily. "Forget it. If I tell you I think I love you, then you'll get scared and run away from me. Maybe it's best if I keep it to myself and let everyone be happy. I met this girl named Parker, and she loves her husband, but she's also in love with her best friend, and it works for her. Maybe it could work for us too?"

My babbling continued as if it were a one-sided conversation. In the middle of the conversation, I closed my eyes.

"Jayce?" Manny asked, noticing the call was still active.

"Hey, Manny. How much did she have to drink?"

"Not all that much really. Just four or five beers."

"That's quite a bit for her. Do me a favor and see if you can wake her up and have her take aspirin and drink some water, so she isn't feeling like crap tomorrow," Jayce requested.

"Sure thing, man," Manny said trying to sound unshaken by the conversation he overheard.

"You heard what she said, didn't you?" Jayce asked, obviously noticing the odd tone to Manny's voice.

"I don't want to be in the middle. All I will tell you is if you have feelings for Marie, you need to tell her. Brady is my friend, and he doesn't deserve to be second best. Tell Marie how you feel when she's sober, and see if your feelings match.

That's my two cents, and now I'm broke."

"Thanks, Manny. Take care of Mo, and tell her I'll call her later."

<hr>

Over breakfast, Manny informed me Jayce said he'd call me back later. I must have looked at him completely nonplussed until he informed me of my "drunk dialing" the night before.

"Where is our next stop?" Saved by the map, I avoided asking more about the phone call. If I couldn't remember speaking to Jayce, and it made Manny uncomfortable, I may have screwed things up royally.

"We have a few more days to explore Washington. Then we'll park the car at the airport and fly out to Alaska. Before we leave, though, I think you should take a few minutes to talk to Jayce."

In a soft whisper, I asked the question that terrified me.

"What did I do last night?" Manny wouldn't answer me, but his silence spoke volumes. "I love Brady."

"Speak to Jayce." Manny grabbed his phone off the table and walked out of the room to give me some privacy and to save himself from hearing more things he had to keep from his best friend.

"Marie, hey."

"Sorry if I was weird last night. Manny and I had a few beers at the Pike Place grill. You know how I get when I've been drinking."

Jayce responded, "You get truthful," in a serious manner. I had an idea of what that meant. Last night I'd dreamed I told Jayce I wanted to be with him. *Was it a dream or reality?*

"I don't know what to say."

"Welcome to my world last night. The truth is I still don't know what to say. Reese is my girlfriend, and Brady is your boyfriend. We care about them, and we can't throw everything away on a whim. On the other hand, I do love you."

Four words made my heart swell. He'd said them before, but they had a deeper meaning this time. Endless possibilities of our life together scrolled through my mind as I couldn't stop the grin brightening my face. "So what now?"

"I need time to think. I want to figure all of this out."

"Okay. I can give you time. How's this? My trip will be over in three months. We'll talk then and see how we feel."

"And what about Brady?" Jayce asked.

"I'll make my choice about him as well. I'm so sorry. This whole situation is crazy." I sighed. "We both have a lot to consider. Brady and I aren't seeing each other until my trip is over. I'd want to tell him in person if we are going to break up."

"I can understand. I had better go, Mo. I'll talk to you soon."

Lying back on the bed, I covered my face with my hands. *What have I done?* If I had a genie right then, my wish would've been for someone else to make the decision for me.

JOURNAL ENTRY

Alaska was beautiful. We saw bears, moose, and bison along with many other kinds of wildlife. Manny and I ventured on glacier tours, and we took hikes through the wilderness. It was relaxing and tiring at the same time.

After flying back to Washington, we drove through Oregon and admired the scenery, stopping once to sleep. Our drive through California was both beautiful and exciting. We spent a few days on the beach. We saw the Redwood National Park, spent a few days in San Francisco, explored the Hollywood Walk of Fame and the famous Chinese Theatre. After California, we mapped our way back toward Tennessee. We didn't spend more than a day in any one place. At this point of the trip, we were both exhausted, and I was terribly homesick.

We'll be in Tennessee in about two weeks. Then

Manny will board a flight back home to Michigan, and I will spend two weeks in my bed before boarding a flight for my final stop, Hawaii.

Jayce and I are going to have a sit-down talk when I get home. I've been avoiding Brady lately, and I think he noticed because he stopped calling my phone. He asks Manny about me, and I get an occasional text saying he misses me and hopes we're having fun. I find myself missing him at times and relieved at other times. If I keep this up long enough, I can take the coward's way out and have him break up with me instead of admitting to him I might love Jayce too. I've been leading him on for too long. I don't want to be that person any more and hate that I have been.

Manny checked us out of the hotel, and I'm in the car waiting for him to return. Until I return home, this is my last entry. I'm going to utilize the two weeks before Hawaii to get my scrapbook in order with all my pictures. I'm looking forward to spending time with my family too. I miss everyone so much. Manny has been great company on this trip. I'm so thankful he came with me. If he hadn't, I'd have gone home months ago—shortly after Constance died.

ღ*Marie*

25

MARIE

"I have enough money to go to Hawaii with you if you want company," Manny offered as we took the ramp to the interstate.

"If you want to join me, you're welcome to."

"What about Jayce or Brady? Are you going to ask one of them?"

Gripping the steering wheel tighter, my knuckles turned white. "I haven't made up my mind."

"Brady's been asking questions lately I can't answer. He wants to know if you talk to me about things. He's afraid you're drifting apart. He asked my opinion on if he should break up with you. He thought maybe it would make you happy, and you wouldn't feel guilty about moving forward."

A tear slipped from my eye as I tried to focus on the road.

"What did you tell him?"

"You two need to talk. You can't text your way out of this

like two teenagers. You're both adults, and you have to make a decision. You can't have them both, no matter what decision you make. If Jayce loves you, he's not going to watch you marry Brady and be fine with it. And if you choose Jayce, you'll never see Brady again. Stop wasting time leading them both on, and make a choice." Tough love was the only way to get me to make a choice. Though it was hard to hear, it was the kind of advice I'd needed.

More tears fell from my eyes as I listened. Manny's words were said with love and not malice. "I will."

For the next several hours, neither of us spoke a word. I focused on the road, and Manny took a nap. I hoped I'd have a decision before we crossed into Tennessee.

———

Three days later, I drove over the Tennessee line, anxious to see my family and filled with hope at the decision I'd made. With two days until Manny's flight, I asked him to stay with me. Happily agreeing, he took the guest room in my apartment. I gave him a few moments to settle in.

On the couch reading a book, he startled me a few minutes later.

"I'm sorry about the other day," he began.

"Don't apologize. I owe you thanks for the speech. I'm an adult. I'm twenty-seven years old now, and you're right. I needed to make a choice. Don't hate me if the choice isn't one you agree with, please."

Manny nodded his head in understanding. "Do me a favor,

and wait until I get home before you break Brady's heart. I want to be there for him."

"Okay, but don't assume I've chosen Jayce. For now, I'm keeping it to myself. The person I choose will be the first one to know." It seemed there was an obvious choice all along. The more I weighed the pros and cons, the more obvious it became. In the end, I would hurt someone I cared very deeply for, but they'd heal, and we could all move forward with our lives instead of living in this limbo of sorts.

"Fair enough," Manny replied with a genuine smile.

I told Manny I needed to run some errands, and one of those was to see Jayce. Rapping my knuckles on his door, I stood fidgeting nervously until he answered.

"Mo!" he exclaimed excitedly before lifting me into a tight hug. "Come in," he said, setting me down.

"Are you alone?"

"Yep. Sit down. I'll make us something to drink."

He placed a glass of iced tea with a straw in it next to me on the table. Taking a long sip for courage, and wishing it were a Long Island Iced Tea, I placed it back on the table.

"How was the rest of the trip?"

"It was wonderful. Manny made it easier to get through without Constance." Jayce swallowed, dropping his gaze to his hands as he fiddled with a string on the couch cushion. "Did you decide what you wanted to do about Reese? Or me?"

Jayce raised his head. "I've been thinking, and I don't

understand what's changed since I told you about my feelings last year. You've been with Brady all this time, and you've been trying to convince me repeatedly you're in love with him, and we're only friends. When you called me the other night, and you were drunk, it shocked me. It came out of nowhere, Mo."

"It wasn't out of nowhere. I've been struggling with these feelings for almost two years now. I didn't want to lose you." Even I thought the explanation was weak.

"I'm still with Reese. You're not the only one torn between two people. I need more time. Can you take more time to think too?"

More confused than ever, I walked out the door unsure what to do. Jayce scrubbed his hands over his face in frustration. "I'll make a decision soon, Mo. I promise."

JOURNAL ENTRY

Jayce hasn't given me a decision. I told Brady I had to think things over because I was confused on where I wanted our relationship to go as my trip came to an end. It seems ridiculous. If anyone should know what I want, it's me. So why is this so hard?

I went through with my plans for Hawaii. Manny is meeting me at the airport. We're going to spend two weeks on the island in celebration of the end of our trip and to celebrate Constance's life.

Brady asked me to think while I'm away. He wants me to decide if I'm going to move in with him. I think I will tell him yes. I do love Brady, and I know I can be happy with him. If I move away, then I can leave Jayce in my past. It works out best for everyone.

Jayce and I will be friends through e-mail and text, I hope.

Seeing him, at least for a while, would be too hard and embarrassing.

∞Marie

26

———

MARIE

Manny said he would meet me at baggage claim at the airport in Hawaii. Before boarding the plane, I sent a final text to Jayce telling him if he changed his mind about him and Reese, he could meet me in Hawaii. I asked him to text if he did, and I'd wait for him at the airport.

Stepping off the plane, I followed the signs to baggage claim. Continuously checking the phone for a text from Jayce, I was repeatedly disappointed when there wasn't one.

Standing beside the luggage carousel was a familiar face, but it wasn't Manny. Brady was only a few feet away from me. I stood staring as he knelt on one knee with a small velvet box in his outstretched hand.

"Marry me," he said. Unable to speak or move, my mouth dropped open, and my breath caught in my throat. His smile began to fade with each passing moment of silence.

"What are you doing here?" I inquired. "Where's Manny?" How cruel was I to ignore his romantic gesture? Why did I keep hurting this amazing man? Brady deserved so much better than what I'd given him.

"He'll be here in a couple of days. I asked him to let me come first and surprise you. You seemed very surprised when you saw me. For a second, I thought you were disappointed it was me."

Caressing his hand, I said, "I've never been disappointed to see you." The words were true. I'd always loved seeing him. But at this moment, I'd been hoping for a different surprise visitor. Although, I had to admit that his proposal floored me to the point I almost shouted out "Yes!" without thinking. How many men would come this far to surprise someone with a proposal?

"You haven't answered my question," he commented, rising from his knee.

"Marie!" Jayce called out from across the way as he sprinted toward me and stopped abruptly. He bent over with his hands on his knees panting for breath. Once he could speak, he looked up at Brady. "I didn't know Brady was making this trip with you."

"He's not. I mean, he wasn't. Manny was supposed to meet me."

Brady still had the diamond ring in his hand, which Jayce spotted before he turned back to me. "Are you two engaged?"

"She hasn't answered me yet," Brady stated, becoming impatient.

"Do you want to marry him, Mo?"

"Can we have a moment alone?" Brady asked.

Jayce answered instead. "I'll give you two a minute. First, Marie, I came here for you. You know why."

Unable to speak for fear of shoving my foot in my mouth, I nodded. Jayce moved aside out of earshot to give us privacy.

"Marie, if the proposal is too much, we can take it off the table for now. I want you to know I want us to be together. I'm not trying to pressure you into something you're not ready to do."

Gripping his hand tightly, I covered our joint hands with my free one. "The proposal was surprising, but it was a romantic gesture, and I love you for it. Recently I've realized everyone was right about my feelings for Jayce. They've grown into more than friendship. I love both of you, and I don't know what I want."

Brady's eyes dipped to the floor in defeat. Eyes heavy with sadness, he peered up at me.

"I can't keep doing this, Marie." He waved Jayce back over. "I think Jayce will agree with me. You need to make a decision now. If you don't, it's possible you'll lose both of us. It isn't fair to keep us both hanging on. It's not fair to you to be at war with yourself over this either. You need to be happy, and you can't do that until you make a decision."

Jayce nodded. "He's right. We need an answer."

Nearby was an empty bench, I sat to gather my thoughts. It was finally time to make a decision that would change my life. It wasn't fair to either of these amazing men. Brady was right. They deserved women who could give them their full heart, not only part of it. In reality, I should've let them both go, but

I could never cope with losing them both. Taking a seat on either side of me, they each took one of my hands.

After a long, painful silence, I tilted my head up. Looking at Jayce first, I smiled and then turned the smile to Brady. With a deep breath and a squeeze of their hands, I said, "I've made my decision."

27

One year later

"Holy mother shit son of a fucking asshole!" I screamed at Satan's head that appeared between my legs. No, I didn't suffer from Tourette's syndrome. I suffered from labor pains. Satan was how I referred to my gynecologist as she cheered me on with a smile while I tried to push a watermelon out of my vagina.

When my contractions began five hours ago, my mother drove me to the hospital. As we walked into the emergency room, I was able to take some of the pain away by easing myself into a wheelchair. With my feet placed strategically on the footrests, my mother quickly wheeled me to the registration desk.

"My daughter is in labor. Her contractions are about three minutes apart now. Can you please page her doctor? Dr.

Grainger." The girl at the desk immediately picked up her phone and then typed something into the computer to dial the doctor directly. When there was no answer, she paged her overhead.

A few moments later, they wheeled me into the room and lifted me up onto the bed. Instantly, I grabbed my mother's hand and screamed out once more as the contraction hit.

"Where is he?" I asked in a panic.

"He'll be here soon, Marie. I checked on his flight a few minutes ago, and it is still showing on time. He should be landing any minute now."

"I need him here! He's the reason I'm in pain right now. He should experience this!" How was it that men got to have the fun part of making a baby but didn't have to go through the pain and suffering?

My mother chuckled.

"Yes, he should. He will, don't worry. Just breathe."

I wanted to smack this woman for trying to calm me in my time of pain. On the other hand, I wanted to hug her for having gone through this agony with me twenty-eight years ago. Once I finally dilated to ten centimeters, the doctor asked me to push, but I wasn't ready.

"Wait, I can't. Not until he's here!"

"Who are we waiting on?" the doctor asked impatiently.

"The father. He'll be here soon," my mother promised Satan, squeezing my hand as though she thought it would help. Truthfully, I wanted to be knocked out instead of knocked up right now. Couldn't they put me in a nice slumber while the alien creature exploded from my nether regions? I knew it was the miracle of birth and all that hogwash, but I was good with not remembering the moment.

"Well, we can't wait for him. This baby is coming now. So give me a good push."

"Augh," I screamed with each push. More cursing spewed from my lips. I couldn't believe how far I'd come in the last few years. Three years ago, my only goal in life was to take a trip around the United States. I'd never even had a serious boyfriend. My travel dreams came to life, and along the way, I found my dream of a family. I was married to the love of my life, and we were having our first child. My husband wanted four, but we'd negotiate once I got over the pain of this one ripping me apart. It was hard to believe all of this began with a bucket list dream.

"I'm here. I'm here!" Jayce panted as he burst into the room. He grasped my hand, as I gave another long push. "I'm sorry, traffic was insane. I screamed at the cabbie the entire way here."

One last push, and I crushed his hand in mine, both of us screaming at that point. The next sound in the room was a baby crying.

"Congratulations, Mr. and Mrs. Hewlett, it's a girl."

Smiling up at Jayce, he leaned down to kiss my lips, although they were sweaty and gross-looking at the moment.

"I love you," he whispered against my equally gross forehead. After shooting a watermelon out of a keyhole, I didn't really give a crap how I looked. Dr. Grainger handed the baby to me. Jayce and I gazed with love at our little pink bundle of joy.

"What are you going to name her?" Mom asked.

"Constance Hope Hewlett." Jayce and I had decided on the name the day we found out she was a girl, but it still brought a tear to his eye.

As the excitement died down, I asked to speak with Jayce alone. "How was your trip?"

"Sad, but good. Connie's parents wanted you to have a few things for the baby. They were beyond touched to hear we were naming her Constance too. They found letters for all of us in her luggage. She apparently wrote them a few days before she died. She knew it was almost over."

Questions filled my mind. *Was she scared? Was she in a lot of pain? Why didn't she tell me so we could take things slower?*

After a knock on the door, Manny's head popped in.

"Hello, gorgeous! And hello to you too, Marie." He winked and chuckled. Holding my arms out, I cried as he held me tightly. "You still have a dazzling glow, momma. I saw Constance. She is as beautiful as you are."

"When did you get into town?" I wiped the tears from my cheeks.

"A few minutes ago. Jayce called me from Canada to let me know you were in labor, and I wanted to be here. We were lucky to jump on a flight."

"I'll give you two a minute," Jayce said as he patted Manny on the back.

After the door closed, I asked, "How is Brady?"

"I'm good," said a voice entering the room.

"What are you doing here?" Seeing him again shattered

my heart once more. He looked perfect and happy. I couldn't help wondering what or who made him happy these days.

"I called him and told him I was coming, so he asked if he could come along. It's my turn to leave. I'm going to find Jayce." Manny kissed my cheek and patted Brady's back before leaving.

Brady pulled a chair over close to the bed.

"You're glowing. I saw Constance. She's beautiful. She looks like her mother."

Overwhelmed with emotions at being a mom, being married, and now possibly reestablishing a friendship with Brady, I choked back sobs. "Thank you. How have you been?"

"I'm good. I met someone. We've been together for two months. Her name is Dawn, and she's an elementary school teacher."

It stung a little to hear Brady speak about another woman, and it stung even more to see the bright smile on his face as he spoke. After the initial shock, it relieved me to know he was moving on.

"I've missed you," I admitted.

His face fell to sadness, and he cleared his throat. "Me too." It hurt for him to hear. He always had to clear his throat to hold back emotions. "The first few months without you were torture. I wanted to call. I wanted to fight for you, but I knew it was futile. You belong with Jayce. It took me a while to cope, but I get it. I won't forget the time we spent together though. It was the best year and a half of my life." He stroked my cheek with his hand and then pulled it back and cleared his throat again.

"I'm sorry, Brady. The last thing I ever wanted to do was hurt you. I really did love you."

Brady smiled sadly and said, "It's water under the bridge, Marie. Deep down, I knew there was no competition with Jayce from the moment I first watched you with him."

Cupping his cheek, the fresh stubble scratched my skin. "Trust me, there was competition. It was a close one. The hardest decision I ever made was letting you walk away from me. I hated every minute of it. It was an amazing journey with you, Brady. I'll never forget it either."

"Me too. The reason I came today is I wanted to see you, but I also wanted to clear the air between us. I want us to be friends. I think I'm at a point where we can now."

Pushing into a seated position, I covered my mouth trying to hold back tears. "Sorry, my hormones are insane right now."

"I've tried to call many times. Part of the reason I didn't was because I wasn't sure you wanted to hear from me. The other was I didn't know if I could stand hearing the happiness in your voice. As much as I want you to be happy, it still hurt it wasn't with me."

"I wish you could stay a little while."

With the back of his palm, he caressed my cheek. "I'll be around for a couple of days. It's a long drive back. Manny and I are going to get a hotel in town and maybe do some sightseeing."

"Hopefully you'll visit with us a little too. Can I ask a favor?"

Brady nodded. "Sure, anything."

"Can I have a hug?"

Brady leaned over enveloping me in his arms. Closing my eyes, I breathed in his scent; it was comfortable and familiar. Memories of our time together flooded my mind making it hard to let him go. As he pulled away, he pressed his lips against my forehead pausing momentarily.

"I'm going to find Manny and Jayce and have them come back." Brady left before I could ask him to stay longer. The pain in his eyes after our hug matched the pain in my heart. I had no idea how hard it would be to see him again. Jayce more than satisfied every one of my needs and wants, and I loved him more than anything, but part of my heart would always belong to Brady.

<hr>

BRADY

In the hallway, I ran into Manny.

"Doesn't look like it went well," Manny remarked.

"Too well. It was like old times. It was quite possibly even harder seeing her now than at the airport when we said good-bye. I think it might have been too soon for the olive branch." After Marie told me she chose Jayce, she asked for a few minutes to say good-bye to me. She wept in my arms begging me to forgive her one day.

Reluctantly I let go and promised her I would in time and then wished her and Jayce well. They left for Hawaii together, and I sat at the airport for two hours staring at the ring in my hand. My legs refused to move as I felt the crushing weight of heartbreak. In that moment, I didn't expect to ever see her again.

"Did you tell her about Dawn?"

"Yeah, I did. I made it sound like it was a little more serious than it is, though. Manny, I gave her a hug, and almost kissed her. I don't know if I can go back in there." All the pain I felt in the airport came rushing back when I wrapped my arms around her a few moments ago. Dawn had repaired my heart some, but I feared no one would ever compare to Marie in my eyes.

"We can go together," Manny offered. "And Dawn makes you happy, right?"

"She does, but it's different." Shaking my head, I laughed at the irony. "I guess I know how Marie felt when we were dating."

Manny put his arm across my shoulders. "It's rough. Be thankful for the time you had with her and knowing she is happy and well."

Palm smacked against my forehead, I said, "I'm an idiot. I'm whining about two women who are alive and well, and you lost the woman that meant everything to you."

Manny looked away for a moment. "It's cool. It wasn't a guilt trip. I just want you to look at the big picture. If I could bring Connie back, even with a promise I'd give her up, I'd do it. I feel this world would be a better place with her in it again. I miss her more than anyone could ever know. Jayce gave me this today." Manny held up an envelope with his name written on the outside. "Connie wrote it to me a few days before she died. I'm going to need you to help me read this later."

With a gentle push toward Marie's room, I followed him in.

"You're a wise man. And I'll be there for you, I promise." Manny pushed open the door, and we stood watching Marie as she held Constance in her arms. Jayce stood above her gazing down on them. Manny's words made perfect sense. Seeing the smile on Marie's face was enough to help me move forward.

Marie smiled as she spotted us standing in the doorway. "Come in, you two."

Reaching out toward Jayce I said, "Congratulations, man." Jayce gladly shook my hand.

"Look, I wanted to apologize," Jayce began.

"No need. Someone very wise gave me a new perspective on things, and I want to let bygones be bygones. Can the three of us be friends?" I asked, glancing back and forth between Marie and Jayce.

"Yes, please," Marie said immediately. Jayce seconded the sentiment. The nurse came to take the baby to the nursery, and we sat and caught up on the past year and on memories of Constance.

JOURNAL ENTRY

I felt like one more journal entry was needed to round this trip out. At the airport, I chose Jayce. My reason, it can't be explained. I closed my eyes and his face popped in my head first, and I felt it was a sign. Our first day in Hawaii wasn't the best. I spent the evening crying my eyes out over Brady while Jayce held me. Being in his arms felt perfect. My heart ached for the pain I'd caused Brady, but I couldn't help the happiness I felt trying to push through.

When Manny found out what happened, he canceled his trip to meet me. He wasn't angry, but he felt he needed to be with Brady, and I needed to be alone with Jayce.

Hawaii was amazing after the initial arrival.

Jayce and I stayed in a bungalow on the beach. The first time we made love, I thought it would be awkward and clumsy after all the years we'd been friends. Jayce set up the most romantic evening. Candles lined the room, and the door was propped open so we could hear the waves rushing against the shore.

Our first time was slow and gentle. We explored each other's bodies from head to toe before joining together. We refer to it as the night of seven times. I'm not sure what else we did on the trip. Spending time in each other's arms seemed more important than sightseeing. It never felt weird being together either; it felt very natural. No matter where we were, our bodies were touching in some way. Holding hands along the beach, curled up in bed with nothing but a sheet covering our naked bodies, Jayce's arm around me on the flight home, our bodies were magnets of different poles drawn together.

Back home, Jayce moved in with me immediately and proposed within a few months. One night, I came home from work and the house was lit by candlelight. Lining the floor from the door to the patio were trinkets. First there was a Hot Wheels car. An arrow was drawn to the next item, a stack of poker chips. After that was an arrow leading to a tiny Statue of Liberty. Drawn on the floor was a pair of lips and then another arrow. Following the line, I came upon a silhouette of Mickey Mouse with hearts decorating it. Another line to a Mardi Gras mask, and finally at the patio door was a small airplane. It was a map of the stops along the way with Jayce on my trip. On the balcony, Jayce was on one knee with a small velvet box in the palm of his hand. As I appeared, he opened the box revealing a stunning diamond ring set in a gold band with several small diamonds on either side.

"When you chose to take a trip around the U.S., we promised each other it wouldn't change our friendship. Along your journey we discovered that was easier said than done. Each day you were gone, my feelings grew stronger and harder to deny. Across the way, we found love had been staring us in the face. I'm breaking my promise now by changing our friendship." Covering my mouth with my hands, the tears fell as he choked out the words, "Will you marry me?"

Neither of us were able to speak as the moment overwhelmed us. After I said yes, he swept me up into his arms and led me to the bedroom.

Life with Jayce had been everything I dreamed

of and more. Once I let myself admit my love for him, it seemed silly at how scared I had been to take this step.

Manny and I talk at least twice a week. He didn't hold it against me for choosing Jayce. He's become my rock. He hasn't met anyone since Constance passed. He refuses to even date. I hope soon he will be able to move on.

Brady and I hadn't spoken since the day at the airport. I checked in on him through Manny though. I never asked anything personal so Manny didn't feel like he's in the middle. I'm so thankful he came to the hospital to see me.

I'm appreciative every day for Constance, my daughter. One day, I'm going to share this journal with her so she can see how her dad and I fell in love. I also want her to know the woman whose name she bears.

Everything in my life has changed in the past three years. I took a dream trip, and across the way, I found the love of my life was in front of me all the time.

For now, my writing days are over. I plan to enjoy every minute with my new family. So, in terms of this journal, this is...

The End

ACKNOWLEDGEMENTS

Thank you to Hot Tree Publishing for having faith in my writing and believing in me enough to help me make it a great story.

Many thanks to Becky and Justine—two of my favorite people in the book community. They have not only helped me for many years but have supported so many authors in the industry. There's no way to thank them enough.

I owe a debt of gratitude to my mom who has read every book I've written and supported me on this venture from the minute I confessed to writing my first book. Thank you for being my biggest spokesperson and promoter.

To the readers who have been there with me from the beginning to the new ones I've picked up along the way, your encouragement and love of my books keep me going. A shout-out to two special readers who have always supported me since my very first book: Amanda Edmunds and Leah B. These two ladies have given me more courage to keep writing than I could even thank them for! I hope they enjoyed the special cameos I put in this one for them.

Last but not least, thank you to my husband, Daniel, who puts up with me writing during every spare minute I have. For letting me bounce ideas off him and having the courage to tell me when something seems stupid, as well as for his compliment when I've hit gold with a scene. For him, I have put as many nerd-related moments as possible especially regarding Transformers, LOTR, and MOTU. He is the one who suggested I write my first book, the person who has literally been there from day one of my writing and has encouraged me every single step of the way. I love you, Daniel.

I enjoy making new friends to share my love of books with. Feel free to come join me on my Facebook pages:

www.facebook.com/AmyKMcclung is my author page on Facebook where I share information about my writing. I also pimp other authors, do lots of giveaways, and just post random thoughts at times.

WWW.FACEBOOK.COM/CascadesOfMoonlight is the book page for my first set of books, a YA paranormal romance, The Parker Harris series. I'd love for you to get to know Parker and her friends.

ABOUT THE PUBLISHER

Hot Tree Publishing opened its doors in 2015 with an aspiration to bring quality fiction to the world of readers. With the initial focus on romance and a wide spread of romance sub-genres, we envision opening up to alternative genres in the near future.

Firmly seated in the industry as a leading editing provider to independent authors and small publishing houses, Hot Tree Publishing is the sister company to Hot Tree Editing, founded in 2012. Having established in-house editing and promotions, plus having a well-respected market presence, Hot Tree Publishing endeavors to be a leader in bringing quality stories to the world of readers.

Interested in discovering more amazing reads brought to you by Hot Tree Publishing or perhaps you're interested in submitting a manuscript and joining the HTPubs family? Either way, head over to the website for information:

WWW.HOTTREEPUBLISHING.COM